MURDER IS INVISIBLE

FRIENDSHIP AND HONOR, BOOK IV

GIACOMO GIAMMATTEO

INFERNO PUBLISHING COMPANY

Print ISBN 978-1-940313-32-0

Electronic ISBN 978-1-940313-31-3

ISBN: 978-1-940313-31-3

❀ Created with Vellum

PREFACE

Warning: Spoilers for the first three books of this series are on the next page.

If you want a refresher of who some of the characters are from the first three books, read the pages that follow. If you haven't read the first three books, you may want to.

Police:

Frankie "Bugs" Donovan — Nicky Fusco's best friend from childhood. Now a Detective in Brooklyn.

Lou Mazzetti — Frankie's partner

Sherri Miller — Frankie and Lou's partner from book two and three.

Lieutenant Morreau — Frankie's boss

Carol — Admin in Homicide Department

Kate Burns — Medical Examiner and Frankie's girlfriend.

Alex — Young boy who Frankie took in after his mother abandoned him. Now his adopted son.

Keisha — Alex's friend in the apartment building.

New York Mobsters:

Dominic Mangini — Head of one of the Five Families (Also appears in Blood Flows South series)

Manny Rosso — Head of one of the Five Families. Was underboss to Tito Martelli in book one.

Tito Martelli — Was head of one of the Five Families.

Fabrizio — hit man for Dominic Mangini.

Giorgio — Works for Manny Rosso.

Wilmington, DE. Characters:

Nicky "the Rat" Fusco — former hit man trying to go straight.

Doggs Caputo — local mob boss in Wilmington, DE

Monroe — leader of a black gang in Wilmington. Served time with Nicky in prison.

Angela Fusco — Nicky's wife

Rosa Fusco — Daughter of Angela and Nicky

Sister Mary Thomas — Nun who taught Nicky and Frankie

Paulie "the Suit" Perlano — childhood friend of Nicky and Frankie

Rules of Murder

For those of you who don't know, there will be at least six books in the Friendship & Honor series—one for each of the "rules of murder," as outlined by Gianni "Johnny Muck" Mucchiato in Murder Takes Time. Each book's title is one of the rules.

1. **Murder takes time**—Never rush. Know what you are going to do

before, during, and after the job. Know your victim. Their face. Routines. Neighborhood. Family.

2. **Murder has consequences**—When doing a job you must never, ever, let it get personal. Each assignment is just a job. If it gets personal, it will have consequences.

3. **Murder takes patience**—If someone has a routine, trust it. Wait them out, and it will pay off. As for yourself, never be predictable. Don't shop at the same place. Don't eat at the same place. Don't do anything at the same place or at the same time or on the same days.

4. **Murder is invisible**—To be good at this, you must be invisible. And since you can't really be invisible, you have to practice not being noticed. There is a difference between being seen and being noticed. If you have to break rule number three, make sure you adhere to rule number four.

5. **Murder is a promise**—If you enter into a deal to murder someone, that is a promise, a secret pact. Once you take the assignment, you need to finish the job, or it could come back to haunt you.

6. **Murder is immaculate**—Don't leave any clues, and make sure you clean up loose ends.

INTRODUCTION

When is a person invisible? When they are not noticed.

Think about it. Can you describe the garbage man, the cashier at Target or the grocery store? How about the cable-TV repairman?

If you can describe them, you're rare. If you can describe them accurately, you're even rarer.

To the rest of the world, they're—invisible.

A LONG WALK HOME

It wasn't late—according to Allison—but it had been dark for hours. She thought about calling her father to pick her up, but decided to walk home—it was only four blocks, and her father would probably be pissed off as it was because she was already past her scheduled curfew. If she asked him to come get her, he'd *definitely* be pissed.

Her father was a nice man, and he loved her, but he sure needed to learn about kids—at least how kids were nowadays. He was still parenting as if it were the '80s or even earlier, when all you had to do was tell a child "no", explanation not necessary.

She pulled out her cell and called Jen, her lifelong friend. "What's up, girl?"

"Nothin'. Just chillin' wit' some tunes."

"Girl, you don't even *know* which tunes to chill with, let alone have them on your phone. I need to set you up with some real sounds."

"Shit. I got all the sounds I need. Where are you? Home?"

"Nah. On my way, though. I was over at Nate's. Just now headin' up the long walk home. I'm gonna have to probably sign out here, 'cause sure as shit, my pops is gonna be steamin', and you know how he gets when he's steamin'. No iPhone. No iPad. No nothin'. Besides, my battery is almost gone. It won't last long."

Franklin Street

Jen laughed. "As far as your dad, I know that. He's been that way all his life. Ain't no changin' him now. You'll be lucky if he lets you go to the bathroom."

The sound of Allison's laughter rolled down Fourth Street. "I doubt he'd go that far, but you never know. Anyway, see ya tomorrow."

"Later."

As Allison turned the corner, heading north on Franklin Street, headlights shone on her from behind. She thought about how tired she was as she turned to see the car; it had been a long day and track practice had been grueling.

The car looked to be a new Escalade, dark blue. She squinted, trying to adjust her eyes to the glare from the lights of the car, but then the window lowered as the car slowed. A deep voice rang out from the driver's side.

"You need a ride?"

He sounded nice enough, at least not creepy, still Allison wasn't accepting a ride from anybody at night. She knew that much, even if her father hadn't drilled it in her head. "I'm all right," Allison said, and kept walking. An uneasy feeling ran through her bones and coursed her veins. It made goosebumps on her arms.

"Smart girl," he said. "That's what I tell my sister. Don't accept a ride from anyone. It's a dumb shit who does."

Him saying that about his sister made Allison feel better. She slowed and turned to look at the car. Then she slowed her pace even more, and the car matched her. "How old is she?" Allison asked.

"Who? My sister? Fifteen going on dumbteen." The guy laughed, then said, "Probably about your age. But obviously not as sharp. Got robbed about two months ago. Happened three or four blocks from here, over by St. Anthony's, just north of Tilton Park. Fortunately, she wasn't hurt, but now, I won't let her walk home. No sense in taking chances. She calls me to come get her no matter what time it is."

Allison thought about what he said, and stopped. "I live on Franklin, just north of Monroe Street. I'll take that ride if you're still offering, and if it's not too much trouble."

"I should teach you a lesson and say 'no'," the guy said. "...but I won't." He brought the car to a halt, then opened the passenger door. "Get in," he said. "and don't mind the mess." He brushed the seat off as he said it. "Damn dog hair everywhere."

Allison laughed. "I know what you mean. We've got a boxer who sheds like crazy. Her hair gets on everything." They both laughed again, then Allison got in the front seat. She extended her hand. "I'm Allison Parker," she said.

"Josh," he said, shaking her hand. With his free hand, he zapped her with a Taser. She convulsed a bit, then fell back against the seat. She smelled something like ether as he placed a moist cloth over her mouth. A few moments later, she went unconscious without uttering a word.

Josh, or whatever his name was, smiled. *One more in the bag.*

JOSH DROVE NORTH on Franklin Street, until he hit Pennsylvania Avenue, then turned left. He took a right on Bancroft Parkway and soon disappeared.

He met up with his contact near Naamans Road.

"Busy night," the guy standing next to the truck said.

"Long night. I need some rest."

"Is she the last of 'em?"

"This is it. Unless my counting has gotten bad, she makes seven. That's what we agreed on."

The guy reached into his cab and pulled out an envelope. He handed it to the man called Josh.

Josh slid his finger along the seal and opened it. Inside was ten thousand dollars.

"Everything good?" the guy asked.

"Looks good," Josh said. "See you later."

"I hope not," the man said, and climbed into the cab.

ALLISON WOKE to the sound of rubber racing down the highway. She was in a crate of some sort. The crate had slits, and it was inside a large box or container.

She felt the roughness of the ride and thought that perhaps the crate was inside the back of a truck, a large eighteen-wheeler.

A small light was shining from the corner, perhaps a battery-controlled one.

As she looked around, she noticed there were others in the same situation—three other girls, each in separate crates. One of them was white and one looked to be Asian. The other was black, like her. Further checking showed three more girls, though they were still unconscious or asleep. *What the hell was going on?*

"How long have you been here?" she asked the girl closest to her.

"Three days," she said. "They grabbed me down by Market Street when I was goin' home." The girl pointed to the corner of the cage, where a bright orange bucket sat, the kind you get at Home Depot or Lowes. "They don't even let us use the bathroom," she said. "Empty that bucket every couple of days, and that's about it. Treat us like we're animals."

"The Printz," another chimed in. "They got me on the Printz." She was crying. "I was almost home."

"Franklin," Allison said. "I was almost home, too. Then some dude in an Escalade snatched me. Shot me with a goddamn Taser then drugged me with something."

"Same story here," the white girl said. "I was over on Baynard Boulevard when he got me. Big blue Escalade. Said his sister was robbed a few months ago. Put me at ease."

"Same here," the girl from the Printz said.

"Me too," came the comment from Market Street. "I'd do anything to get the hell out of here. What do you think they're doing? Where are they taking us and why?"

"We've gotta figure out what to do," one of the girls said. "If he snatched us off the street like that, and he got all of us, you know what he's got planned, and it ain't good. Nothin' I want any part of."

"What are you talking about?" the girl from Baynard Boulevard asked. "What has he got planned?"

"He's gonna goddamn sell us," Market Street said. "Sell us for sex. Ain't you never seen no movies, girl?"

"Forget what they have planned," Allison said, "*Monroe* is my cousin. He ain't gonna sit around and let this happen."

"It doesn't much matter who your cousin is—even if he's Barack Obama. If he doesn't know where we are, he can't do anything," the white girl said.

"We must be on an interstate," one of them said. "We haven't stopped in a while."

"Yeah, but which interstate? How long has it been? If we were on I-95 going south, we'd have hit the Maryland toll booths. Same with 295 going over the bridge. So we're either on 95 north, or he branched off onto I-76. My bet is 76."

"Does it really make a shit of a difference where we're heading?" the girl from Market Street asked. "There's nothing we can do about it. That is, unless one of you has a phone that works."

Allison quickly felt her pockets for her phone."They took my phone," Allison said. "From what I can tell, they took everything electronic, even my headset."

"Mine too," the girl from the Printz said. "And it was a brand new pair of Beats."

"Then I think we can agree that we're officially screwed. Without phones, we can't do shit." That statement came from the Baynard Boulevard girl.

They agreed, and after about another thirty minutes of talking, the truck came to a stop and the back door opened. A middle-aged man with a full head of matted brown hair entered. It looked as if he'd been sweating.

He grinned ear to ear. "How would you girls like to be in the movies?"

he asked, then he emptied the buckets and put them back where they'd been.

How would you like to be in the movies? The statement brought shivers to Allison as she imagined the repercussions. "Monroe's gonna kick your ass," she said. "In case you didn't know, he's my cousin."

The guy grinned again. "Now I know," he said, and reached to pull down on the straps hanging from the door. "And just so that you know, I don't know Monroe, and I don't care."

"You can't do this shit," the Asian girl said. Panic filled her voice.

"We can do whatever we want," the man said. "We *own* you now."

As the door slammed shut, the girl from Market Street said, "This shit ain't right."

"Right or not, it's happening, and we've got to figure out what to do about it," Allison said.

"Already figured that out," the Printz said. "Unless one of you is hiding a gun, we're screwed."

"This can't be happening," Allison said.

"Wake up, girl. It *is* happening, and it's happening despite you being Monroe's cousin."

SOMEONE'S MISSING

*A*ngie sat at the table doing bills. Rosa walked in and pecked her cheek. "Hey, Mom. How's it goin?'"

"Fine, dear. How was school?"

"About the same." Rosa grabbed a pack of peanut butter crackers from the pantry, sat in a chair next to her mother, and said, "What time will Dad be home?"

"Five-thirty, as he always is. Why?"

"Just wanted to talk to him."

"You've never 'just wanted' to talk to your father. Now, tell me what you want, and if it involves money, get a job."

Rosa laughed. "It doesn't involve money," she said. "Besides, when I tried to get a job, you wouldn't let me."

"Young lady, working at a bar for cash does not constitute a real job. Not at your age."

"What constitutes a *real* job, according to you and Dad?"

"One that pays above the table, *and* allows you to keep your clothes on."

"I would have had clothes on with *that job.*"

"That outfit they wanted you to wear did not constitute *clothes*, not in my book. And it didn't pay above the table. Remember, a *real* job has to meet all requirements. As far as I'm concerned, that job didn't meet any of them."

For the next two hours, Rosa did her homework and helped clean the house. When Nicky came home she greeted him with a glass of wine.

Nicky raised his eyebrows and stared. "Either you did something wrong, or you want something, or both," he said, then he took a sip of wine."

"How cynical, Dad. There *is* a third option, you know. I could be showing affection for my father."

"Yes, you *could* be, but for the time being, let's assume I'm right. Now, tell me what you want."

Rosa sat on the sofa. "You remember Allison Parker, the girl I played basketball with last year? She's been missing for several days."

"No, I don't remember her; you played basketball with a lot of girls. Regardless, why are you telling me about this?"

"She wouldn't just go missing. Not without telling somebody. Something must have happened."

"I'll ask my question again. Why are you telling *me* about this? If no one's done it already, they should report her being missing to the police."

"I thought maybe you could look into it."

"Despite what you may think, I'm *not* a detective."

"You could have fooled me. The way you helped Uncle Frankie bust his case down here, and then you went to New York to help again."

"Those were unusual circumstances," Nicky said. "One involved a little boy, and the other was because Bugs was in trouble. Besides, neither one was something I *wanted* to do."

"This is unusual, too," Rosa said. "Allison would never do this. And she may not be a little boy, but she's a young girl, or woman, or whatever. And besides, Jen said she was talking to her the night she disappeared and nothing was weird."

"What do you mean by *nothing was weird?*"

"I mean she Jen said she was acting normal. She didn't have a fight with her boyfriend. She wasn't pissed at her dad. *Nothing was weird.* Like I said."

"I hear you," Nicky said, "and I'm glad to know nothing was weird, but you need to take my advice—for once—and report it to the cops. I'll go with you if you want."

"Like they'll do anything," Rosa said, and her tone reflected her attitude. "They'll file it in a drawer and forget about it. When was the last time you heard of a missing person case being solved by the cops?"

"There's always a first time," Nicky said. "I'm sorry. I can't help you." He held up his glass, as if saluting. "But thanks for the wine."

"Enjoy it," Rosa said. "It will be the last glass you'll get from me." She stormed up the stairs.

"What was that about?" Angie asked, as she sat next to Nicky.

"Some friend of hers is missing," Nicky said. "Somebody named Allison Parker. Rosa said she played basketball with her last year. Anyway, she's pissed off at me because I wouldn't help her."

"Allison Parker? I remember the name," Angie said, "but that's about all. She probably ran away. That's the problem with kids nowadays."

"Probably," Nicky said, but he didn't even convince himself. Rosa had seemed too confident of the unlikelihood of a runaway scenario.

"You can't tell about kids these days. They're unpredictable," Angela said.

"You can't tell about kids *any* day," Nicky said. "Back in my day…"

"Don't start that 'back in my day' shit. Back in your day, you were hangin' on the corner, stealing cigarettes, and working poker games. And that's when you were six! I don't even want to talk about sixteen."

"Point accepted," Nicky said with a laugh. "But don't forget that later on I was also dating some foxy young thing with long, brown hair and a sweet ass."

Angie looked around quickly. "Hush up! Rosa may have heard you."

"You're right. I wouldn't want her to know you had long, brown hair. She's not old enough."

Angie smacked him. "Smart ass."

"And I wouldn't *dare* want anyone to know you *used* to have a sweet ass."

"All right, mister. That comment just earned you a night in the guest room."

"That would have more impact if we actually *had* a guest room. Dante's in there now, in case you forgot. By the way, is that little shit still napping? Shouldn't he be up to play with his father?"

"I'm just about to wake him. I'm sure he's tired, because he's been playing all afternoon with Daniella's boy. They were hilarious."

"All right. Go get him, but don't forget to whisper, or I'll tell him about your butt, too."

Angie tried smacking Nicky again, but he laughed and dodged.

Angie got Dante up for a feeding, then she and Nicky talked for a while before settling into the routine of watching a TV show, followed by a night of reading. About midnight they went to bed.

The light was still on in Rosa's room, so Angie went in. Rosa was on the bed, watching an old movie, a habit she picked up from Nicky.

"What are you watching?" Angela asked.

Rosa turned, flashed a quick smile, then said, "The George Raft Story. This guy who plays him is good. And a darn good dancer."

Angie wondered what the hell the George Raft Story was, and who George Raft was, then she smiled and said, "Who plays him?"

"Ray Danton. I don't know what other movies he's been in, but he should have been in more. I like him."

She hated to change the subject while she had Rosa talking, but she needed to. "You should apologize to your father."

"Why?"

"For talking to him the way you did. You were wrong, and I think you know it."

"I don't see him beating a path to my door," Rosa said. "Why isn't he apologizing to me?"

"Because he's your father, and besides, he's not a detective. And it's not his job to find a missing girl, even if she *is* your friend." Angie cast a quick glance down the hall. "And didn't he offer to go to the cops with you? That's what you *should* do."

"He didn't say 'I'm not a detective' when Uncle Frankie asked for help. Suppose the situation were reversed? Think what you would be like if I were missing. Wouldn't you want somebody to help? If one of my friends' father could help, wouldn't you want him to?"

Angela frowned, but then nodded. "I guess I would. Well, no guessing about it," she said. "I *know* I would."

Rosa twisted her body and sat on the edge of the bed. "I know Allison. She wouldn't do this. She's not the kind of girl who would run away, and she doesn't hang out with bad people. And Jen said she was talking to her the night she—"

"I know," Angela said, and nodded. "I'll talk to your father. Maybe there's something he can do."

The first smile of the night lit Rosa's face. "Thanks, Mom. I know he'll find her. He may say he's not a detective, but he's good."

"Don't get your hopes up," Angela said, "and don't tell anyone about this. Nothing. Do you hear me?" Then she got up and left the room.

Nicky was getting out of the shower when Angie walked into the bedroom.

"You've got one of those looks on your face," Nicky said. "What's up?"

"Rosa asked me about her friend Allison again. I have to agree that it doesn't sound like a typical runaway situation. Maybe you could ask a few questions," Angie said. "Nothing much. Just check with a couple of the guys."

"Nothing much?" Nicky said. "You don't know these guys. If they even remotely think they provided information that helped me, then I'd owe them one. And trust me, the last thing I want is to owe *them* anything." Nicky slipped on underwear and a T-shirt. "I told her I'd go with her to the cops, but that's all I'm doing."

"Rosa seemed convinced that the police wouldn't be able to do anything. There's gotta be *something* you can do. Maybe ask Frankie to look into it. He's coming down next week, isn't he?"

Nicky sat on the bed. "Bugs is a good choice, being a detective and all, but next week will be too late; the girl will either be long gone, or back home. If I'm gonna do this, it has to be now. The trouble is that I don't want to do anything."

Nicky grabbed a pair of pants from the drawer and slipped them on.

"Where are you going?" Angie asked. "It's past midnight."

"Easy, babe. I'm just talking to Rosa." He finished dressing, then went to Rosa's room.

Rosa was sitting on the edge of the bed when Nicky walked in. "Tell me everything you know," he said. "Don't leave anything out, and that includes any drugs she takes and anybody she screwed around with, and yes, I do mean *screwed* in the biblical sense. I have no time for niceties."

"Dad!" Rosa said, but it was accompanied by laughter. "That's a terrible outfit."

"I'm not going dancing," Nicky said. "Now tell me what you know."

For the next hour, Rosa told him everything, including who Allison dated, hung out with, and slept with. "She doesn't do drugs," Rosa said. "And I'm not just saying that. She really doesn't."

"Maybe she's staying with her boyfriend," Nicky said.

"There are two things wrong with that—first, she doesn't have a boyfriend she'd stay with. She's seeing a guy named Nate, but she recently started going out with him. It's not serious. And second, her father wouldn't let her." Rosa laughed. "You haven't met her father. He thinks it's still 1982."

"I'm sure he doesn't *think* it's 1982. He may *act* like it is, but he doesn't *think* it is. Either way, your point is taken," Nicky said. He then got up to leave the room. "I'll see what I can find out."

Rosa jumped up and wrapped her arms around his neck. "Thanks, Dad. I appreciate it. Oh, and one more thing. Allison is Monroe's cousin, in case that makes a difference."

Nicky sighed and cocked his head. "You know damn right well it does," he said. "It changes everything; somebody may have taken her to get back at Monroe for something he did. After all, he *is* the city's most well-known criminal."

Nicky looked at Rosa, shook his head, then turned off the light. "You have any pictures? Or should I just ask about a young black girl who *happens* to be Monroe's cousin?"

Rosa reached for her phone. "There's a pic on my phone of me with Allison and Jane."

"That'll help," Nicky said. "Text it to me."

Nicky went back to the bedroom and sat on the edge of the bed.

"What's wrong?" Angela asked.

He shook his head. "I don't know, and I think that's the problem. For the first time in my life I don't *know* what to do."

"About what? Rosa's friend?"

"Yeah. After hearing her describe things, I tend to agree with her. I don't think the girl ran away. And the girl is Monroe's cousin, which I just found out, so I should tell him. I've known Monroe since we were in prison together. He doesn't get along well with that side of the family. Still, he'd want to know."

"So tell Monroe and tell your detective friend. That's about all you can do."

Nicky nodded. "I guess so. I'll call Monroe and go see Mrozinski. At least that'll be something."

Angela sat next to him and rubbed his shoulders. "You're too hard on yourself, Nicky. This isn't your problem. It's a sin what happened, but it's *not* your problem. You can't fix the world."

He took hold of her hand and held her. "I guess so. It's just that I've never felt like this before, never wondered what to do. In the past, I've always just done it."

"And look what that got you—ten years of your life in prison."

Nicky laughed. "I guess you're right again, Angela."

She stood and smacked the back of his head playfully. "I usually am."

*R*osa rushed down the steps and into the kitchen. She leaned over to kiss me goodbye. "See ya', Dad. Thanks for helping." And then she darted through the dining room.

"Whoa! I didn't say I was helping. I *will* take all the information you gave me up to Mrozinski, Detective Borelli's old partner. Aside from that, I'm leaving this alone. And I didn't see you kiss your mother goodbye."

Rosa walked back into the kitchen, wearing a sullen face. "What do you mean? You said you'd help."

I shook my head as I swallowed the last piece of toast. "I *did not* say I'd help. I said I'll see what I can find out."

"That's the same thing."

"It's not the same thing. *Find out* means just that—ask around, and see if anybody has heard anything. I'll go that far, but I'm *not* going Sherlock Holmes on this. It's dangerous from a lot of perspectives."

"Like what?"

"Like whoever did this is more than likely associated with bad people. And it will require bad things be done." I walked over to Rosa and wiped her tears. "Forget the fact that something may happen to me. I'm not worried about that, but I don't want the law coming after me for things I would have to do."

"So, you're scared? Is that what you're telling me?"

I downed the last sip of my coffee and set the glass on the table. "Scared? Yeah. You could say that. But not in the way you think. I'm not afraid of getting hurt. I'm not even afraid of being sent back to prison—though being away from you and your mother would break my heart. What I'm scared of is turning into the kind of person I don't want to be. It takes a lot to *not* be this person. I don't want to do anything to make it easier. It's like an alcoholic refusing to drink."

"You don't have to do anything. Just find her."

"I wrapped my arms around Rosa. "I hope you're listening to yourself. It's no small task to *just find her.* That's why I'm giving this to Mrozinski. He'll get things done."

"Fine!" Rosa said, and stormed off. "If something happens, I'll blame you."

"Don't forget to kiss your mother goodbye."

She spun on her heels, stormed into the kitchen, kissed her mother, then raced through the living room and slammed the front door.

"I guess that didn't go so well," Angela said.

"Apparently not."

I cleaned the dirty plates and was rinsing them off, when I felt Angela rubbing my back. "Don't worry about that. Go to work and rest. It has to be more relaxing than here."

I turned and hugged her, planting a soft kiss on her lips. "You've got that right." I grabbed my briefcase and walked toward the door. "See you tonight, babe."

"See ya. Have a good day."

I rushed things at work that day, which wasn't good; estimating was not the kind of job you wanted to rush; it was too easy to make a mistake. But I was eager to talk to Mrozinski and try to get moving on finding Rosa's friend.

I wanted all of the information I could get for Mrozinski, so right after lunch I called Monroe and told him what I knew, and I asked if he thought it may have anything to do with him.

He assured me it didn't, then said, "But it does make me wonder about who's dumb enough to snatch girls from my turf, especially when one of them is my cousin."

"I'm sure they didn't know she was your cousin."

"I hear you, but if they didn't know it when they grabbed her, I'm bettin' Allison told them. At that point, the smart move would have been to dump her, but they didn't. That tells me the dudes aren't from around here. If they were, they'd be more cautious."

I nodded to myself. "You've got a point, Monroe. And it's a good point. I'll mention it to Mrozinski."

"Mrozinski? You're working with him? He ain't gonna do shit and you know it. Not for some black girl from Franklin Street."

"I don't see it that way. He's a good guy, and he's done nothing to make me think he's prejudiced."

"He's a goddamn Polack isn't he?"

"Yeah, but what's that got to do with anything?"

"When you figure out that they ain't gonna do anything, call me."

I listened to Monroe breathe into the phone, then said, "Listen, I've got a few people to see, but afterward—probably tomorrow—I'll stop by. If we're going to do anything, we need to get on this sooner rather than later. But I say we give Mrozinski a shot."

"What do you need in the meantime?"

"Can't think of anything yet, but I'll let you know."

I LEFT WORK EARLY, and stopped by St. Elizabeth's on my way home. I was looking for confirmation that what I was doing was right.

As I sat in the church pew, waiting for the confessional line to diminish, Sister Thomas walked by, and slowed, a concerned look on her face.

She turned her head in my direction. "Something wrong, Nicky? Do you need to confess, or are you just resting? I only ask because I know that look on your face."

I smiled, but underneath, I was grinding my teeth. *Not yet*, I wanted to say, but I held my tongue and shook my head.

"Why don't you tell me what's going on?" Sister Thomas asked. "Let me be the judge of whatever it is you're about to do. That *is* the problem isn't it? You have something in mind, and don't know if it's right?"

Sister Thomas sat next to me in the pew. "You may as well spill the beans, Niccolo. You've never been able to keep secrets from me."

"You'd have made a good poker player," I said.

"And what makes you think I'm not? You've never played Texas Hold'em against me."

I laughed. Sister Thomas always seemed to know when something was up. It was like she had a true sixth sense, especially when it came to things I hadn't done yet. "Someone did something bad, Sister. Really bad."

"And you want to punish them for it?"

I nodded. "They need to be punished," I said. "The chances are that they hurt a young girl. But I can't do this myself. It's something the cops should handle."

"The police should handle it, you're right. But it sounds as if it's something you want to take care of yourself."

"I want to, but I can't afford to. It will carve out a piece of my soul, and I'm afraid I don't have enough left."

"Then let the police do their job, Niccolo. They'll take care of it, and you won't have to get involved."

"I wish that were the case, Sister, but I can't sit around and wait to see if they do their job. This girl needs help, and the people who took her need to experience justice." I gripped the back of the pew in front of me and squeezed. "Nobody should ever mess with kids."

Sister Thomas nodded. "I understand. If it's too much, then let God do His job. It's not for you to decide."

"That's a nice thought, Sister, and I wish it would happen, but the notion of God interfering with our lives went out with Joan of Arc. I'm afraid God now uses people like me to do His job. At least, I *hope* that's the case. I hope I'm not fooling myself. At the same time, I can't risk it. If something went wrong, then Angela…"

Sister Thomas placed her hand on my shoulder. "You said they hurt a young girl." She cringed. "What kind of hurt?"

"I don't know for sure, Sister. I don't even know if anyone did *anything*. But the girl is missing, and she's not the type to go missing. Based on that, and knowing how the world works nowadays, I suspect she either has already suffered her fate or soon will. And, unless I'm wrong, it will be the worst kind. The kind the old Romans used to say was a 'fate worse than death.'"

Sister Thomas sighed, then raised her head. "Do you mean rape?"

I nodded.

She faced the altar, and seemed to be mouthing the words of a prayer, then she turned to me and said, "Do what you have to do, Niccolo. I'm not condoning violence, and I *won't* condone it, but I imagine God would believe it to be worse if anything more happened to that young girl."

I turned to look in her eyes. "So you're saying I should do something?"

"Certain actions need punishment. Look at Sodom and Gomorrah. Our laws are not infallible; they allow some people to go unpunished. I can't imagine God would want that."

"You *are* saying I should take action. I never expected that. I came here to be told the right thing to do."

"And who's to say you haven't been told the right thing? What you *want* to hear and what's right aren't always the same."

"Thank you, Sister," I said, then I blessed myself, and stood, opting to skip confession.

Sister Thomas made the sign of the cross. "Go with God, Niccolo."

I INTENDED TO GO HOME, but pulled to the curb about half a block from the station instead. Then I got out of the car and walked in.

"I'm looking for Detective Mrozinski," I said. "He in?"

The desk sergeant called his name over the intercom. "He'll be here in a minute."

A minute turned into nearly ten, but eventually Mrozinski showed up, wearing a light-gray woolen suit and a light-blue shirt.

He walked up briskly and extended his hand to shake. "Fusco. What brings you by?"

"Have you got a moment to talk?" I asked.

He waved his hand, indicating I should follow, then turned and went into his office, sat behind his desk, and gestured toward a chair on the side wall. "Have a seat and tell me what's on your mind."

I cleared my throat before starting. "My daughter says a friend of hers from school is missing."

Mrozinski's face seemed to sag, a sullen look overcoming him. "I know. I've had reports from several people in different parts of town."

I sat up straight. "Several people? Any connection?"

He shook his head. "None that I know of, but we're working on it." Then he fixed me with a glare. "But stay out of it, Fusco. I don't want the kind of shit we had with Borelli. Understand?"

I almost said something smart—like, that kind of shit is what got Borelli's kid back—but instead, I swallowed my pride. "Understand," I said.

"You have any news I can tell my daughter? She's upset."

"We've got nothing yet, but like I said, we're working on it. There are five girls and counting, and not a clue between them. Right now, we're stumped."

"If I find out anything, I'll let you know," I said.

Mrozinski stood. "I don't *want* you to find out anything, Fusco. Like I said, stay out of it. Don't get involved. Let me handle it. Is all of that clear?"

I stood and nodded. "Perfectly clear."

As I walked out of the station, two things were obvious—Mrozinski didn't want my help and Mrozinski didn't have any idea where to start on this case. I got a bad feeling that this was *not* going to be solved by the fine detectives of the Wilmington Police Department.

ON MY WAY down Union Street, I thought of St. Anthony's and of Father Vincent. He was a priest from the old country, and had been here for a looooong time. Some say he came over during the immigration wave in the 1950s. In any regard, the word on the street was that he was a stickler for the law. He was the one I should probably speak to.

St. Anthony's

I turned left on 9th Street and drove up to the church. After kneeling in the pew for a few minutes, I mustered the courage to talk, and went to see Father Vincent. Once inside the confessional, I started.

I told him the story, then explained what it seemed as if everyone wanted me to do.

"Father, I've done…immoral, unlawful…bad things before. Every time was a struggle with my conscience or my soul. But each time I did something, the next time got easier. The struggle less."

I breathed deeply and closed my eyes. "I don't *want* it to become easy."

Father Vincent made the sign of the cross. I could see through the confessional screen. "Nothing is easy, my son. God places obstacles in our path to Heaven. Perhaps this is yours. Your 'cross on Earth' so to speak."

"What are you saying?"

"I'm saying that there are times in life when you must do things you don't want to do. This may be one of those times."

"Father! I just told you I'd be as much as killing these people, and you're telling me—okay? I heard you were supposed to be tough, someone who abided by the law."

A long silence followed. For a minute, I thought he'd gone. "I do abide by the law, and I'm telling you to abide by the law. No matter how much you may want to punish these people, you have to trust in God. Allow him to get punishment. God doesn't live within the guidelines of the law. Our civic laws are not His laws, and they don't restrict Him. I'm sure that no one wants anything to happen to these young women. Not the parents, not the cops, not the young women, and certainly not God.

"If what you told me is true, and if something were to happen to the people who took these young women…I can't think of anyone who would weep for their souls. But at the same time, it's not our place to do anything. We must trust in God's will that the right thing will be done."

I was frantic, like a trapped man searching for a way out of a maze. This is what I wanted to hear—in one sense—but it wasn't what I wanted to hear in another. I knelt there, saying nothing. Finally, the father spoke again.

"The police will be searching for these men. I wouldn't worry."

Now, he had me on the defensive again. I hoped they would be looking for them, but I knew they wouldn't find them. "Yes. They will search. But they won't search for long and their hearts won't be in it. And before long they'll quit without finding the girls."

I came to confession ready to hear an admonishment from a tough-as-nails old-school priest, and he was advising me to buckle up, and let the police do their job. Something I knew wouldn't happen. I needed an unequivocal *no*, and he was waffling. It seemed as if he was telling me to let the cops handle it one minute, but that he wouldn't be pissed if something happened to them with the next breath."

I sighed. "All right. Thank you, Father."

"Go with God," he said.

I MADE up my mind on the way home. As much as I wanted to do something to these people, and as much as I wanted to help Allison, Father Vincent was correct; it wasn't my responsibility, and it wasn't my right.

Rosa was in the living room crying when I got home.

"What's the matter?" I asked.

She gestured to a DVD lying on the table. "Some kids at school had this. Oh my God, how did this happen so fast?"

"What?" I asked. "What is it?"

"You don't want to know," Rosa said. "It's disgusting. What kind of people do this?"

"Let me see it," I said, reaching toward the DVD.

"I don't want you to see it," Rosa said, snatching the DVD off the table. "It's terrible."

Rosa cried harder, then set the DVD back on the table. "If you need to look at it, go ahead, but then find her, Dad. Allison doesn't deserve this; nobody deserves this." Then Rosa left the room and ran up the stairs.

I popped the DVD into the player and began to watch. The first scene was a young black girl, who I now recognized as Allison, lying on a bed. A man entered the room, and did unspeakable things to her. He was followed by another man. This went on for half an hour, and she never said a word, but her eyes appeared to be glazed; she must have been drugged.

After those two finished abusing her, two more men entered, and she performed oral sex on them. When she finished, yet more men entered the room and did more disgusting things. It made me sick. I wanted to kill someone; in fact, I made up my mind right then, I *would* kill someone. Nobody was going to do this to that young woman if I could help it.

Angela came home near the end of the DVD. She carried a bag of groceries in her arms. I clicked off the TV before she could see what was on it. "What were you watching?" she asked.

"Something vile," I said. "Rosa brought it home from school. It's a DVD of her friend, and you *do not* want to see it. It's one of the most disgusting things I've ever seen."

"Are you going to give it to the cops?" Angela said.

"I'll make sure they get it, but based on what I heard, I doubt if they'll be able to do anything. Maybe get it listed as a crime, since she's under eighteen, but not much else. They sure as hell won't mete out the justice a crime like that deserves."

I went to Rosa's room and knocked on the door. I could hear her sobbing. She opened the door and stood with her head down. Tears stained her eyes. I hugged her. "It'll be all right. Don't worry."

She pulled back. "That's easy for you to say, Dad. It's not you, and it's not your daughter. Imagine how Allison's dad must feel."

What she said hit home. I *couldn't* imagine what her dad felt. I didn't want to imagine it. Something seemed to snap inside me. I *found* myself, and knew what I had to do. I didn't *want* to do it, but somehow I knew I had to.

I rubbed my hand across Rosa's hair. "If it's okay with you, I think we should take this to the police."

"Go ahead, for all of the good it will do. Maybe they'll all enjoy watching it in the back room."

The heavy dose of sarcasm did not go unnoticed. "I'll talk to Mrozinski myself. He'll get something done. I already spoke to him about the case, and they're working on it."

"Working on it? Do you know what that means? They're filling out forms and asking people who wouldn't know about any of it. How are *they* going to find her?"

Rosa pleaded with me. "Dad, can't you do something?"

Her plea broke my heart. I wanted to do this for her, and I wanted to do it for Allison and her family. I took Rosa by the shoulders and pulled her close. "If I do this, I'll have to do things I don't want to do. Things I *can't* do. Think thoughts I shouldn't have. It took me a long time to get those thoughts out of my mind. I don't want them bouncing around in there again."

She tore away from me and plopped on the bed. "You know what I have thoughts of, Dad—that DVD, the one I showed you. Can you imagine anything like that? Can you? Think of what I said. Suppose you were her father?"

I stood still for a few moments, not knowing what to say. Finally, I left and closed the door.

As I finished the long descent of the steps and entered the living room, Angela asked, "What are you going to do?"

When Angela asked the question, it made me think—what *was* I going to do. Rosa was right. The cops weren't going to get anything done, at least not in time to help the girls. Somebody had to help, and the way I saw it, that somebody had to be me—and maybe Monroe.

The muscles in my face tightened. "I'm going to find out who did this," I said. "Monroe thinks it's someone from out of town, and I don't disagree. We'll find them, then…well, you don't want to know what after that."

"Nicky, don't get in trouble."

"Don't worry, babe. It's not me who will be in trouble."

WE ATE DINNER—SOME gnocchi in tomato–cream sauce—and I had a few extra glasses of wine, a delicious Chianti that Angela had started buying a while ago. Then I settled down with a John Sanford novel—my favorite author—and Angela cracked the cover of a new Nora Roberts novel. In between chapters, we made small talk, and a few hours later, I got ready to leave.

"Where are you going?" Angela asked.

"To see what I can find out," I said. "Ask the guys at the smoke shop a few questions."

"At this time of night?"

"There's not going to be a better time," I said. "I should have done it last night."

Within forty minutes, I was in the back room of the smoke shop, talking with Doggs and Knuckles.

I described the situation to them. "She's a young black girl, same age as Rosa," I said. "Anybody hear anything?"

"You can ask, but nobody's going to know anything," Knuckles said. "Besides, who cares about a nigger whore?"

Instinctively, I grabbed Knuckles by the collar and slammed his head on the pool table. It was a good thing instinct had kicked in, because I'd known Knuckles a long time. I doubt I would have reacted that way if I had thought about it.

Knuckles cursed, and I let go of him, but I was still pissed off. "To answer your question, Knuckles, *I* care. And besides, she's not a nigger whore, she's a fifteen-year-old girl who happens to be black. Call her that name again and I'll crack the slate with your skull." I said that about the slate for bravado, but considering what I'd just done to him, Knuckles had to be wary.

Blood ran from the side of Knuckles' head, staining his white shirt. "What the hell? You got some kind of bug up your ass? I just said what everybody else was thinking."

"Then you should have continued thinking it and kept your mouth shut. Remember that for next time."

Doggs walked over, put his hand on my shoulder, and whispered. "Check with Johnny Smiles on 10th Street. If anyone knows anything about porn, it'll be him. Smiles does big business in under-eighteen stuff." He lit another cigarette, then said, "If you talk to him, just don't tell him it came from me."

I glared. "Don't worry, Doggs, your *honor* is safe with me." I said it, and

I didn't whisper. I assumed Doggs didn't want people to know he'd told me. Now they probably would.

"Hey, screw you, Nicky. I think Knuckles has it right—you've got a bug up your ass."

"No bug, Doggs, I just remember what it's like to be young, and, even more important, I know what it's like to have a teenage girl. No amount of money is worth what they do to those kids."

"Man's gotta make a living," Doggs said.

Doggs had carried it too far. Now everyone would definitely know. "Then Smiles better learn to make money another way," I said, "because I'm putting him out of business."

I thought about going home to get the car, then decided to walk. Smiles wasn't *that* far from the smoke shop. Besides, walking would make me think.

Johnny Smiles was a legend for his almost-permanent smile. He smiled when he lost a bet at the track. He smiled when his wife divorced him. He smiled when he had sex, and they say he even smiled when he killed his brother. No matter the situation or business transaction, Johnny wore a smile.

Despite the danger of 10th Street after dark, I enjoyed the walk to his house. It provided time to calm me down, besides, being alert for danger kept me on my toes, made me think of other things.

It took me half an hour, and when I arrived, I climbed the steps and knocked. Johnny opened the door a few seconds later. He adjusted his glasses and said, "What the hell. You know what time it is?"

"I know," I said. "But that's not important. Where's Allison?"

"Who?"

"Allison Parker. She went missing about a week ago. Fifteen-years old, black. Here's a picture." I showed Smiles the picture of Allison that Rosa had given me.

"Never saw her," Smiles said, and looked up at me. "Who the hell are you? And what business is this of yours?" Then he straightened and pushed his chest out. "And what the fuck are you doing at my house?"

"Of course, you'd say you hadn't seen her, regardless of whether you had or hadn't. As far as who I am, my name is Nicky Fusco, and I'm making finding this missing girl my business. If you're smart, you'll make finding her your business, too."

Smiles took a step back. His trademark smile disappeared. He must have heard the things people said about me. "I don't want no trouble, Fusco. I ain't got the girl, but I'll see what I can find out. Give me a few days, but my first guess is Los Angeles; all that material comes from there."

"It's Wednesday," I said. "I'll be back on Friday."

"Make it Monday," Smiles said. "I need to put some feelers out."

"Put them out faster," I said. "See you on Friday." I started down the sidewalk, then turned to Smiles. "Have the information, or you'll never smile again."

As I went down the sidewalk, I had to smile. Having a ruthless reputation had its advantages. I never expected Smiles to cave in so fast.

I took a few deep breaths, then walked to the corner and started down DuPont Street. It wasn't the safest part of town, but I walked down the street as if I belonged, as if I lived there and did this every day. When you grow up on the streets, it's something that becomes a part of some people. Perhaps it's only the ones who embrace it. I don't know why some people develop that sense and others don't. I always had it, and so did Bugs and Tony, two of the guys I grew up with. The Mick had it to a lesser extent, but Suit and Chinski never did. I was always curious about that because Suit, Chinski, and the Mick grew up with us too. Maybe it was in the genes?

The funny thing is, unless you forced it out of you, it never left. You became invisible *to* others, but everyone else was clear to you.

The other people, the ones who pay no attention, they don't hear like I do. Don't see what I see. They don't feel the changes in the air when someone is watching them. They can't tell the difference between the footsteps of someone in a hurry and someone pretending to be in a hurry. They can't distinguish between a man who steps softly and one who is *trying* to step softly. There is a mechanized...fake sound to the latter.

Once the street is in your blood, it never leaves. There were times—times like now—when I wished I never had it. When I wished I'd grown up innocent. But as Mamma Rose used to say, "A wish is nothing more than a dream while you're awake." I never thought about it much until I got older, but I think she was right.

I continued down DuPont until I passed Front Street, then cut across the playing field at Bayard School to Clayton Street.

A few blocks later, I turned the corner and headed down Beech Street, dreading what I had to tell Angie. She wasn't going to like me going to California, but, according to Smiles, California was where I had to go.

MY GIRL IS MISSING

Mr. Parker, Allison's father, finished his morning coffee and tried everything he knew to settle his nerves. He was sitting at the table, trembling when his wife walked in.

"Good morning."

Parker nodded. "It's not a good morning, and saying it is won't make it one. She's gone, Lizzie. Our baby girl is missing. And we gotta do something to find her."

"What are we gonna do that we haven't done already?" she asked. "We've reported it to the police. We've talked to everybody we know. You've put flyers out on every corner of the city. We've contacted the church and the missing persons department. There's nothing else we *can* do."

"We can raise some hell," Parker said. He pushed his coffee cup back, wiped his mouth with a napkin, and stood. "And that's what I intend to do."

"You're gonna get yourself arrested," she said. "What good is it gonna do Allison if you're sitting in jail? Suppose they find her, and you're sitting behind bars? What are we going to do then?"

"Suppose the sun don't come up tomorrow? What will we do then? There's about as much chance of that happening as there is of them finding her." He smacked the table with his hand. "Jail or no jail, I'm going."

"Why don't you call Monroe?" Lizzie asked.

"I ain't about to call that son of a bitch. Not now or ever." He slammed the front door when he left.

~

ALLISON PARKER'S father got out of the car and hurried into the police station. "I'm here to see Detective Mrozinski." His tone carried a level of impatience.

"He's not available," the desk sergeant said. "May I help you?"

Parker slammed his hand on the counter. "Not available! What the hell do you mean, not available? My daughter's not available either because she's *missing*." He stood on tiptoes and leaned as far as he could toward the sergeant. "Do you understand? She's *missing*."

"Calm down, sir. Please have a seat and keep your cool. I'll see if I can locate Detective Mrozinski."

Reluctant as he was, Parker took a seat in a chair on the outside wall. Another man about his age was sitting two seats down. "Did I hear you say your daughter was missing?" he asked.

Though Parker was annoyed by the question and hesitant to answer, he turned to the man. "Gone for almost two weeks now. She was on her way home and just disappeared from somewhere down on Franklin Street. Haven't heard a peep from her since."

"Same thing happened to my girl," the man said. "She was up by the zoo, out with a boy she shouldn't have been out with, but that's beside the point. She was walking home when it happened."

The man shook his head. "She was talking on the phone to her boyfriend, according to him. He said she was near Baynard Boulevard and Brandywine Park. Ten minutes later he called her again, and she was gone.

"I've been here every day since then trying to light a fire under somebody's ass." The man leaned closer. "Is this your first time here? I haven't seen you before."

"Hell no," Parker said. "Been here three times already, and they swear they're workin' on it. Well, this time I ain't leavin' here till they give me some answers."

Within five minutes, a tall detective with a pale complexion and a square jaw rounded the corner. He hurried to their side and knelt beside them. "Mr. Parker, Mr. Figg. I know you're looking for news. And I hate to tell you this, but I don't know anything more than I did before. We *are* working on it, though."

"Working on it? Working on it? That's what I heard the last two times I was in," Parker said. "What the hell have you done? Anything? How many people are working on this? I bet if this was some son of a bitch from Westover Hills, you'd have every damn detective in the place looking for her."

"And what about my girl?" Figg asked. "I haven't heard a single word since she disappeared. Where is she? Who took her? We're talkin' about a little girl here. A goddamn little girl."

Mrozinski wiped perspiration from his face with his hands, then dried them on his pants. "I know. Believe me, I know. I have men on this full time. Good men. Yesterday, I requested to double the team. We're going to find them. I promise." He stared into each of their eyes, and promised again. "I swear, we'll get your girls back. Don't take that lightly. I never promise people that I'll find out who did something, but this time I *am* promising, and I *will* find them. I have kids of my own, so I know how you must feel."

Parker grabbed hold of Mrozinski's lapel, not in a threatening way, more of a pleading way. "Detective, I know you don't know me from Adam, but believe me when I tell you that little girl is my life. She's *everything*! She's why I wake up in the morning. And thinking of her is what lets me sleep. I've *got* to get her back."

Mrozinski looked into Parker's eyes. "Mr. Parker, you're right saying that I don't know you from Adam, but it doesn't matter. As far as I'm concerned, your daughter is no different than my daughter. I'm treating this case as if Allison were mine. We're gonna find her, sir. I swear." Mrozinski started to stand, then said, stood. "And in case you're thinking it, it doesn't make a damn bit of difference to me that your girls are black. I'm gonna find them. Period."

Mrozinski placed an arm on each of their shoulders and spoke softly. "The best thing you can do is go home. Go back to your wives or back to work. And let us know of anything that you think might help. I'll keep you informed of developments on this end."

Parker stood and offered a hand to Figg, who had his face buried in his hands, crying. Then he turned to face Mrozinski. "All right, Detective. I'm gonna trust you one more time, but *please* do something to find Allison. Find my baby."

Parker started out the door, helping Figg. "I will, Mr. Parker. I will," Mrozinski said.

WHEN PARKER and Figg were halfway down the block, Mrozinski walked back to the front desk. "Lugullo!" he yelled, and when he didn't get a response, he yelled louder. "Lugullo!"

In a moment, Lugullo ran up from a corner office. "Yes, sir?"

"Where the hell are you on these missing girls?"

"We're canvassing the areas. We've got roadblocks set up. We've distributed flyers at the bus station, and—"

"In other words, nowhere?"

Lugullo swallowed hard. "Yes, sir. Nowhere. Not a single damn clue."

Mrozinski lowered his head and spoke clearly and slowly. "I want you to go back to all the scenes, knock on every door, and interview *every* goddamn resident for two blocks in either direction. Somebody saw something. And I want to know what."

Everybody stood watching, until Mrozinski hollered again. "What are you waiting for? Get moving. I want those girls home by Friday! Do you hear me?"

Detective Mrozinski sat at his desk, drinking cold coffee, when a knock on his open door sounded. He looked up to see Pete Murphy, a detective who Mrozinski had requested to work this case with him.

An exasperated sigh escaped Mrozinski's lips as he refocused on a pile of paperwork that demanded to be done. "What's up, Murph?"

"Kind of tough on people out there, weren't you?"

"Ask Mr. Parker or Figg if I was. I'm sure they'd have rather had me shoot a few people." Mrozinski looked up. "Do you know what it feels like? Do you have kids?"

Murphy turned a twisted smile. "Yeah. I have two boys—six and eight."

"Ever lose them at the beach or at a carnival—for just one minute? Take that feeling and imagine it's two weeks! It's a wonder Parker and Figg haven't killed somebody." Mrozinski shook his head as he lowered it. "I won't say it to them, but I might have."

"Okay. I see your point. What do you want me to do?"

"I want you to find these kids. I don't care what you have to do. These aren't corpses lying in a ditch—not that we know of—so let's not wait until they are. However, that's all presuming you are assigned to the case. Paperwork's not in yet."

"Yes, sir," Pete said. "Assuming that paperwork goes through, I'll get Franklin to help. We'll start with a re-canvass. In fact, I could get started now on the re-canvass. We can worry about the paperwork later. We need to find these girls."

"Good," Mrozinski said. "Keep me posted. And I mean daily."

"Will do," Murphy said, and headed out.

A FINE DAY

"Get up, Frankie. It's a beautiful day."

Frankie pulled the covers over his shoulders and shivered. "Beautiful? If you want to call freezing your ass off 'beautiful,' then yeah, it might be a beautiful day."

Kate walked in with a cup of coffee, the steam rising from the hot liquid, and the aroma wafting through the apartment. "Ready to drink," she said.

"And I'm ready to drink it," Frankie said, "though I hoped you'd have woken me with a kiss, or something more."

"A kiss? What the hell have you done to deserve a kiss?" Kate asked. "And you can forget about 'something more.' I cooked dinner, cleaned the always-messy house, and went to the grocery store. And the entire time, you and Alex sat on the couch and watched TV."

"Always-messy? I'm insulted. My place is clean. Besides, I'm still injured," Frankie said, and then held up his hands, ready to fend off the pillow attack he knew was coming.

"Your kitchen and bathrooms are clean, and your closet is impeccable, but forget the rest."

She began fluffing the pillow and heading closer. "As to the other, all I can say is—injured my ass," Kate said. "You've been itching to go back to work for two weeks. You're incorrigible. And you're teaching Alex the wrong things. Before you know it, he'll be faking and lying like you. You're lucky I don't spill coffee on you." Then she swung the pillow at Frankie.

Frankie dodged, laughed, and said, "Just for that, you're going to have to give me a kiss, *and* something more."

Kate lay next to him. "Be careful, or I'll spend the night and make your wish come true. Who knows, it may even be fun?"

Frankie grabbed hold of her ass cheeks and squeezed. "Am I still dreaming?"

Kate smacked him. "You're a dirty old man, and you're not even old yet."

"You could have fooled me," Frankie said. "I feel ancient."

"That's the first sign," Kate said. "And remember, I did qualify that statement by saying, *yet.*"

Frankie reached to grab her, but she easily moved away. He groaned.

"Side still hurt?"

"Side, kidneys, stomach, all of it. When the hell is it going to stop hurting?"

"It's going to take a while," Kate said. "Besides, you're lucky to be alive, so stop complaining about a few aches and pains. You're the one who's been crying about being bored and wanting to go back to work. You sound like a whiner, and you know what I think about whiners."

"Do you give whiners special treatment?" Frankie asked, trying to hold in the laughter.

"They're not eligible for *something other*, if that's what you mean."

"You're brutal," Frankie said. "And what do you mean by 'lucky to be alive'? I guess that's one way to look at it but there are other ways."

"What other ways are there?"

"That I should have shot the son of a bitch first—that's one way."

"That's not like you, Frankie. You're a good person."

"I used to be, but that may change. Getting stabbed will do that to you. It changes your frame of mind."

"It won't happen," Kate said. "You won't change because you still need to set an example for Alex."

Frankie grunted. "Speaking of which, I might take him with me down to Wilmington. That is, if he wants to go."

"You know he wants to go," Kate said. "He'd go anywhere with you—even to the ninth circle of hell. Plus, for some reason, he looks up to your friend Nicky."

"A lot to look up to," Frankie said. "Remember how much he helped us."

"I'm not ungrateful," Kate said. "Just cautious."

"He's a different man than he used to be."

"I've seen what that 'different man' can do," Kate said. "Those murders were some of the worst I've seen, and I've worked some doozies."

"They were gruesome for a good reason," Frankie said.

"Depends on who you talk to," Kate moved to the mirror and began brushing her hair to get ready for the day. "When *are* you going back to work? You're starting to get on my nerves and I don't even live here." She set the brush down and moved back beside him, wrapping her arms around him as she did.

"I should be healed within two weeks, by the time I get back from Wilmington. I hope."

Kate sighed. "They may be the longest two weeks of my life."

Frankie wrapped his arms around her and pulled her closer. "They could also be the most sensual," he said. "All you have to do is come with me."

"You can forget that," she said. "In the first place, you can't even throw a pillow at me without whining. In the second place, I'm not going with you."

"Why? We could make this a vacation. I leave in two days. Pack a few things and come with us. A few skimpy things."

"How did I know you'd want me to pack skimpy things? Ordinarily I'd say *yes*, but Wilmington, Delaware is *not* my idea of a fun vacation."

"Think of it more like a visit with friends."

"That would be fine, but Nicky is *not* my idea of 'friends'"

"Give the guy a break," Frankie said. "He never did anything to you."

"The same kind of break he gave Renzo, Johnny Muck, and Nino Tortella?"

Frankie sat on the edge of the bed. "How did you remember their names?"

"How can I forget? I still wake up at night, remembering what he did to them."

"Those guys deserved it. You know that."

"*Nobody* deserves what he did to them," Kate said. "It takes a special kind of sickness to do what he did to someone. I can't believe you're defending him. I find that amazing."

"Are you forgetting what they did to him?"

"That's what the *law* is for," Kate said.

"There are some people who don't subscribe to that theory," Frankie said. "And while—being a detective—I'd never say it in public, I can't say that I blame those people. Some criminals deserve more than the justice system dishes out."

Kate sighed again. "Okay, here's the plan. You go down to Wilmington and visit. Take Alex with you. I'll stay here and work—somebody's got to work."

Frankie sighed. "Since it doesn't look like I'm going to come out ahead on this argument, all of that sounds good. Enjoy work while I'm having fun." He smiled. "I wish you were coming with me, but Alex should have fun—somebody will."

"Alex will have fun *if* your family doesn't ruin it," Kate said.

"You've got a point. What are they gonna say when they find out I have a son who is black?"

"Let's *hope* they say 'congratulations.'"

Frankie winced. "I know *that* won't happen, so I'm hoping for the best —like no nasty remarks."

He shot a sideways glance to Kate. "Speaking of nasty remarks reminds me that I've got to call Nicky and let him know I'm coming down."

Frankie pulled out his phone and pushed Nicky's number. "What's up, Rat?" he said when Nicky answered.

"Bugs! What the hell are you doing?"

"Thinking of coming down for a visit."

"No shit! I was hoping you'd keep to your word and come down. Well, you know you've got a place to stay. We'll just move Dante, and you can have his room. He's always ready to share the bed with me and Angela, and if that strategy fails, he'll settle for Rosa."

"Thanks for the invite, but I'm bringing Alex with me. We're going to stay with my mom. She's got two bedrooms open, so it will work great—I hope."

"Glad to hear it, and good luck with it. If it doesn't work out, use my place as a back-up. Anyway, this is great timing. You can help me with something."

"Anything, Nicky. Just name it."

"It's probably nothing, but one of Rosa's friends is missing. Been gone for more than a few days. Probably ran away, but I told Rosa I'd ask around. Maybe you can help?"

"I'll do what I can, but I don't know how much that'll be. Locals don't usually like to share, but I could check with that guy, Mrozinski. You remember him—Borelli's old partner?"

"I'm not thinking of asking the cops for any more help; I already tried that route, but it's something you might check into." There was a pause, then Nicky said, "Call when you get here."

"You know I will. Tell Angie I said hi. Rosa, too."

KATE GOT HOME EARLY the next day, planning to surprise Frankie with one of his favorite meals. Frankie was outside with Alex and Keisha, pitching quarters against the stoop. She stood behind them and shook her head. It never ceased to amaze her what he got these kids involved with.

After a few minutes, she said, "Is this what you teach them when I'm not here?"

Alex yanked the cigarette out of his mouth and handed it to F.D., hoping Kate hadn't seen.

Frankie knew before he turned around that he was in trouble. "I was helping them brush up on their math."

Kate's hands rested on her hips, and her eyes held a disbelieving look. "Math?"

"You know, geometry, proper angles, all that stuff."

"Well if you can break away from *homework* long enough to help with dinner, I'd appreciate it." She opened the door and went inside.

"I'll help," Keisha said, and scooped up the last round of quarters then followed Kate.

Alex shook his head and grabbed his smoke back from Frankie now that the coast was clear. He took a long drag, causing the ash on the end to glow red. "Damn, Keisha always quits when she's winning."

"That's because she's always winning," Frankie said.

"I guess so," Alex said.

Frankie snatched the smoke from Alex and put it in his mouth. "What the hell do you think you're doing? You're not allowed to smoke. And quit cursing, too."

"I know I shouldn't smoke, but you aren't allowed to either. You told Kate you were quitting."

Frankie thought for a moment, then tossed the smoke in the gutter. "All right, shit, let's get ready to eat."

"And now you're cursing," Alex said. "How do you expect me to learn from such a bad example?"

Frankie shook his head as he opened the door. "Let's get ready for dinner, you little shit."

A NIGHT AT THE MET

rankie came out of the shower to a ringing phone. Instinctively, he picked it up, but glanced at the caller ID when he did. It was Lou.

"Donovan."

"When the hell are you comin' back to work? Ain't you been milkin' this long enough?"

"I'll be back when you finish grammar school. And from the sound of it, you've got a long way to go."

"Screw you, you potato-picking prick."

Frankie laughed. "Mazzetti, I thought you'd be retired by now. Or dead. What's up?"

"They won't let me retire, so I'm workin' on the dead part. Climbed four flights of stairs yesterday and started gettin' pains in my chest. If I didn't have Miller's ass to stare at, I would have died." Lou paused. "Come to think of it, staring at her ass might have been what caused the pains in the chest. Got too much blood pumping to the wrong place."

Frankie laughed. "Now I know you're full of shit. Miller's got a nice ass, but nothing would get your heart pumping blood to that part of your body."

"What's that about Miller's ass?" Kate hollered from the other room.

"Nothing," Frankie said. "Just talking about one of Lou's many obsessions."

"Anyway, we've got a body," Mazzetti said.

"What are you telling me for? I'm about to go on vacation."

"Don't do that shit to me, Donovan. I can't work this case alone."

"Nobody's asking you to work it alone. Take Sherri on the case. Isn't that what you've been doing while I've been gone? Besides, as you've already told me, her ass is better than mine, though I find that difficult to believe."

"I know what I said, Donovan. But look at the facts—the first case we worked with Miller, she got shot. Then you got stabbed on the next case. I figure it's my turn now."

"Nobody's going to waste potential prison time on killing you, Mazzetti. One look at you and they'll know you're going to die soon anyway. No sense in shooting a dead man."

"Screw you, too, Donovan. When are you coming back? And don't tell me you're going on vacation. Vacations are for pussies, and while *I* know you're a pussy, I don't think you'll admit it to the world."

"I *am* going on vacation, and I'll be back in a couple of weeks. By the way, where's the body?"

"It's not hiding. It's right in front of the Met. Can you believe it? Somebody wanted this guy found and quick. If not, they'd have dumped him in the goddamn East River."

"Look on the bright side, Mazzetti. At least you'll get a dose of class.

You can tell everyone you went to the Met and mingled with the elite today."

"Screw you again, Donovan. Bye. Have fun in the jungle."

"That was Lou?" Kate asked as she entered.

"Yeah," Frankie said. "And by the way, your hair looks nice that way."

"Thanks for noticing. So what's Lou's problem with Miller's ass?"

"He doesn't have a problem. At least nothing that a few napkins wouldn't cure so he could wipe the drool from his chin. His problem is that her ass is firmly attached to *her* body and not *his*."

"And how is that wrong?" Kate asked.

"Because it conflicts with his ultimate wish list. Or at least the list he's brave enough to talk openly about."

Kate laughed. "I hope that wish is restricted to Lou."

Frankie grabbed her waist and pulled her close, then kissed her. "You know it is. I don't look at anybody's ass but yours."

"You better not," Kate said. "But I know you're lying."

"Maybe I look," Frankie said. "But I don't do anything. Of course, if she offered *something more*...who knows?"

Kate smacked the back of his head. "No looking, either."

LOU PULLED up to the crime scene and got out of the car. Miller was already there, as was a crowd of onlookers. Everyone was staring at the body on the sidewalk.

"What have we got?" Lou asked.

"Three GSWs to the back," Sherri said. "Two of them exited the chest. "And it doesn't look like robbery; his wallet is still in his pants pocket

—with a few hundred dollars and a host of credit cards still inside, not to mention a ring with a diamond the size of…well, a damn big ring."

"How big?" Lou asked.

"Never mind. It was a big ring."

"The size of what?"

"Leave it alone, Lou. It was a big ring, all right?"

Lou scowled. "So they didn't even want it to look like robbery?"

"Apparently not. And the ME says it looks like a dump job. Not enough blood for it to have happened here."

"Makes you wonder why they dumped it here," Lou said. "They must have wanted to make some kind of statement. But what? Who did they want to find this and why?"

"Could be anything," Sherri said. "This *is* high society. They're different, so maybe their killers are, too."

"Name?" Lou asked.

"You're gonna love this," a uniformed cop at the scene said as he stepped forward. "License claims his name is Manual Ramirez."

"Manual Ramirez? What the hell? What kind of name is that?"

"Maybe it was supposed to be *Manuel*," Sherri said. "You know, with an 'e' not an 'a.'"

"Somebody should have looked at the birth certificate longer," Lou said.

"Does make you wonder why he didn't change the name," Miller said. "It looks as if he had the means to do so."

"Yeah, put back the 'e' and his name goes from a joke to semi-normal."

"You're ridiculous," Miller said. "It's times like this when I wonder why I agreed to partner with you."

"Me? I'm not the one who named him."

"Turns out there was a benefit here last night," the uniform said. "And from the reports, Manual was in attendance."

"Was he with anyone?" Lou asked.

"Not formally, but he was seen talking to a young man, and for a long time. They were last seen going into the men's room."

"Good place for a couple who didn't want to be seen meeting to meet," Lou said.

She shook her head. "We don't know if that's why they met," Sherri said. "Let's just solve this case, so I can enjoy normal conversation again. Or at least so I can appreciate conversation again."

"That's not going to happen," Lou said. "I mean the 'enjoy the conversation' part. Nobody enjoys talking to you; you're too crude. On the other hand, I fully intend to solve the case, so let's go. We can at least talk to the people who were here and determine what they didn't know."

Fortunately, most of the attendees of the previous night's event were attending another event. By the end of the day, Lou and Sherri had questioned most of them, and gotten decent cooperation—even from the so-called elite.

It seems as if Manual had been generous with his money *and* his time, especially when it came to nice-looking, young men in the fifteen to twenty-five age bracket. He seemed to have a penchant for that age group.

"Aside from age, was there anybody in particular?" Lou asked the lady he was talking to.

"The gentleman he was chatting up last night was not someone new," she said. "There were others, if gossip is to be believed, but that young gentleman was ahead of the pack. I've seen him around a few times, and he always accompanied Manual."

"Were they living together?" Sherri asked.

"I doubt that, as the 'arm candy' he called a wife would have no part of it, despite knowing it went on. She didn't want anything to potentially interfere with her money. I guess it won't now."

"So he had a wife?" Sherri asked. "Is she here?"

The lady gestured to the left, with a nod. "The one in the pearls—oh, yes, and the green dress. She's surrounded by the three men with drool on their chins and dollar signs in their eyes.

"If I'm not mistaken, she's probably busy picking out her next victim, though now it shouldn't be as difficult with her newfound money— freshly inherited. Not like that stopped her before, but now…"

"Are you saying she should be a suspect?" Lou asked, thinking there was no love lost between these two.

"Everyone should be a suspect," she said. "But that determination is up to New York's finest, isn't it?"

"I guess it is," Sherri said. "Is there a reason why you don't care for Mrs. Ramirez?"

"You mean other than her general demeanor?"

Sherri flashed a fake smile. "If you'll excuse us, we have work to do."

Once they were out of earshot, Lou said, "Good call. We'd gotten about all we could from her, despite her weak attempt at smearing the newly created widow."

"That's what I thought," Sherri said. "I figured it was time to get our gossip from another source, one not so biased if possible."

"Let's try a direct approach and talk to the new widow herself," Lou said, and pointed to her.

Sherri smiled. "Does wanting to talk with her have anything to do with her shapely curves?"

"It might," Lou said. "But it's probably more the pearls. Either way, it'll give me something to dream about. I'm not too old for dreaming."

Sherri and Lou inched themselves forward, into the crowd that had gathered about Mrs. Ramirez. "Excuse me," Lou said. "I'm Detective Lou Mazzetti and this is Detective Sherri Miller. We're investigating the death of your husband. Do you have a few minutes to answer some questions?"

"That depends on how many questions there are, and how few the minutes are." She turned to her all-male audience and smiled, as if awaiting applause, then focused her attention on Lou and Sherri.

"What would you like to know about Manual?" she asked. "I don't know if I can tell you more than you could read in any gossip column worth its salt." She looked around again, and once again was greeted with laughter that sounded as if it had been manufactured in a plant in El Paso. "But with the proper cues, I can try."

"I want to know a lot," Lou said. "But that depends on what you can tell me."

"I can tell you he wasn't much of a man," she said.

"Because he was gay?" Lou asked. "Or is there a real reason you brought that up?"

She cocked her head backward. "You seem offended. Did I strike a chord, Detective?"

"Just a sour note. And yes, I was offended. I am anytime that a person is judged on anything but merit."

"Well, if you must know the reason for the statement, it was because he didn't enjoy spending time with me," she said.

"From what I've seen so far, I'd say that placed him at the top of the perceptive pile." Lou sneered.

Sherri kicked his leg, but Lou ignored her.

"I beg your pardon." Mrs. Ramirez shot Lou a look that would have cowed most people, but Lou wasn't most people.

"You can beg all you like, but you're not getting my pardon." Lou excused himself. "Forgive me, ma'am, I have to leave. But you've been helpful. At least now I know why your husband was killed; he must have begged for someone to shoot him, just so he could get away from you."

"Well, I never!—"

"And you never will," Lou said, then Sherri grabbed his arm and they left.

"Lou, you can't talk like that. That lady's got muscle, or she soon will. It will cause you trouble."

"I can talk any damn way I please. If she doesn't like it, she can file a complaint. But she won't file a complaint because she's too damn lazy to, and if she does, that's fine. I'll retire a few days early."

"So, what do you think?" Sherri shook her head. "Scratch that. From the tone of the interrogation, I *know* what *you* think, but what do you think as a detective?" Sherri said.

"I'll tell you what I think. That woman's got her head up her ass. I've got a neighbor who's gay. He's been living next to me for twelve years. Every week he comes to visit and to eat dinner with me and my wife. You couldn't find a nicer guy. It pisses me off when an ignorant woman like that says such things about her husband, especially after she's sucked him dry under the guise of marriage."

"I know what you mean, but I'm surprised to hear you say that," Sherri said. She rested her arm on Lou's shoulder. "But now that you've got that out of your system, tell me what you think of her as a suspect."

"You mean do I think she had one of her boy toys take him out? Maybe. She stood to gain a lot of money."

"Let's go home," Sherri said. "We'll look at this tomorrow with a fresh set of eyes."

JOHNNY SMILES

I was hard at work estimating a new addition to an elementary school when Bugs called. The connection was piss-poor, and I found myself yelling so he could hear me. "Bugs, where are you?"

"I had to take the Commodore Barry Bridge," Bugs said. "Bad accident on the turnpike. Traffic was backed up for miles."

"Good, you'll be in time for lunch. Want to meet at Casapulla's?"

"Of course I do. And I have Alex with me. He's never had a sub, at least, not a good one, so he's in for a treat. See you around 1:00. How's that?"

"Perfect," I said. "See you then."

In total, it took Frankie almost three hours to get to Wilmington. He exited the freeway on Delaware Avenue, and drove west, until he turned onto Union Street. At 6th Street, he stopped and picked up some baked goods.

"What are you doing?" Alex asked. "I sure as hell hope you're getting some food, because I'm hungry."

Union Street Market

"We're meeting Nicky in a few minutes and having subs. But right now, I'm getting something to take to Nicky's house. No way I'm showing up empty-handed. And no, you can't pig out before we get there."

Once inside, Alex scanned the pastry shelves. "I thought the Rat liked sfogliatelle. I don't see any."

"That's his preference," Frankie said, "but his favorite bakery burnt down, so he'll have to be happy with a few cannoli."

I met Bugs and Alex at 1:00, and we all got subs for lunch. Bugs and Alex got smalls and I went for the large, as always.

Five minutes later we had two small Italian subs and one large, which we took outside to eat on the bench across the street.

We unwrapped the subs and spread the paper on the bench. I placed a few extra hot peppers on mine, and we settled in to eat.

Alex was only on his second bite when he said, "Damn, this is good!"

Bugs reacted by lightly smacking the back of Alex's head. "No cursing," he said. "Remember what we said?"

"You said it, not me. Besides, I think Nicky has heard 'damn' before."

I laughed. "He's got a point, Bugs. Leave the kid alone. He's gonna say it if you're not here, so what's the difference? As long as he sticks to innocent curses, you shouldn't mind. Besides, what red-blooded American ten-year-old isn't going to say damn—at the least?"

Frankie looked at me, then Alex. "I guess you're right. But don't tell Kate."

Alex was busy munching away on the rest of his sub. I nudged his shoulder. "It looks like you're hooked already. I don't know why it's taken Bugs so long to let you have subs, but now that you've had them, I bet you want more."

"Heard enough about 'em," he said. "And I have to say, they're as good as F.D. said they'd be."

"So what's up?" Bugs asked. "You said you needed something."

"How long are you here for?"

"Two weeks," Bugs said. "Why? What do you want me to do? You still want me to talk to Mrozinski?"

"Like I said on the phone, I need your help. One of Rosa's friends has gone missing, and we think she was grabbed by a sex slave operation; in fact, we're sure of it." I waited for Bugs to show interest, then said, "At first, I thought maybe she was a runaway, but from a DVD Rosa showed me, it's obvious that it's a child porn ring."

Bugs put his sandwich down and stared. I knew that this would hit a soft spot in his heart. "I'll see Mrozinski right away, but what else do you want me to do?"

"I don't want the usual bullshit the cops spit out to the public. Last time you were here you did a favor for Mrozinski and Borelli. As you know, Borelli's not here anymore, but Mrozinski may be inclined to return the favor and maybe share what he's got. I figured you're the best guy for that, so I thought you could ask him what he knows and maybe get the real scoop."

"Is Mrozinski the one handling it?"

"One and the same," I said. "I already spoke to him, and he confirmed that he thinks it's a kidnapping also; in fact, when I talked to him, he said he had five girls missing. The problem is, he doesn't seem to be anywhere on the case. I know it's early, but a kidnapping is like a murder, isn't it? If you don't get a lead quickly, the less likely it is to be solved."

"It's close to the truth, although not an absolute," Frankie said. "But a good lead would definitely help. I'll see what I can do. What else?"

I took another bite of sub. "As far as Mrozinski goes, any real information you can get is good. As far as 'what else', *anything* you can think of. You know how this works."

"All right, I'll see what I can do."

"And for you to give Mrozinski, tell him Johnny Smiles may know something," I said. "He should know Smiles, but in case he doesn't, Smiles does business out of his house on 10th Street, by DuPont. And he's into porn big time—soft and hard."

"Good," Bugs said. "Mrozinski will be more willing to dish out information if I have something to give him."

I shrugged. "You can't lose by giving him the lead. He may have information on Smiles already—I don't know. If he doesn't, it's a solid lead. If he does, at least he'll know you're serious."

"Good deal," Bugs said. "How about if you and Angela and Rosa come for dinner on Friday? I'm staying at my mom's house, so it's only a couple of blocks. Hell, you could walk there."

I dabbed more hot peppers onto my sub and said, "Love to, but I can't. I'm leaving for California with Monroe and one of his guys."

I noticed the questioning look on Bugs' face. "The missing girl is Monroe's cousin. I thought I told you that."

"Poor fuckers," Bugs said.

"He's not that close to her, but she's still his cousin."

"I meant poor fuckers who did this. Between you and Monroe, I wouldn't want to be caught drinkin' coffee with them."

I half-smiled. "Yeah. You got that right. Gonna be some sorry sons of bitches when we catch them, and we *will* catch them."

"When are you comin' back?" Bugs asked.

"Whenever I'm done," I said. "And not before."

"See ya then. In the meantime, I'll stop by Mrozinski's office, and call you afterward."

I slapped Bugs' hand. "You got it," I said. "See ya when I get back. And don't make yourself a stranger at the house. You know Rosa will have a fit if you don't bring Alex to dinner so he can taste her cooking."

"You know I will," Frankie said. "I'll see you later. Besides, you know I wouldn't pass up Rosa's meatballs or Angela's ravioli."

"Don't forget. Call me if you get anything," I said. "I mean *anything*."

After lunch, Frankie and Alex went to Frankie's mother's house. I went back to work to finish out the day.

Frankie stopped by to see Mrozinski. After exchanging pleasantries, he said, "I hear you've got a possible kidnapping."

"Whoever's filling you in isn't up-to-date," Mrozinski said. "It's up to seven possibles, and the possible part is all but gone."

"What are you doing about it?"

"Not that it's any of your business, but I'm gonna put three of my best guys on it." Mrozinski shot a suspicious look at Frankie. "And we're doing it by the book, no vigilante stuff."

"Why did you mention vigilante stuff? What's that all about?"

"It's about the last time you were here—when those guys took Borelli's kid. Don't get me wrong, I appreciate what your friend did for Jimmy, but I didn't like the way he went about it. I was cleaning up the mess for several months."

Frankie nodded. "I've been there before, but it's not gonna happen this time."

"If you're telling me it's not gonna happen, I'll believe you, and I'm willing to share information as long as it's a two-way street, *and* as long as you stay out of my way."

"You know I can work with that," Frankie said.

"No. I *don't* know, so I need your word on it." He stared at Frankie until he got an answer.

"Deal," Frankie said, extending his hand.

Mrozinski looked at Frankie. "So what have you got for me? You wouldn't have come here empty handed."

"Ever hear of Johnny Smiles?" Frankie asked.

"I've heard the name, and I know what he does, but what's that got to do with the case?"

"Word is it's got everything to do with it. Word on the street is that Smiles probably knows who's involved and may even be a part of it."

Mrozinski made some notes and pulled up a file on the computer. "Is he still on 10th Street?"

"That's the one," Frankie said.

"Okay. Thanks, Frankie. I owe you for this."

"Good," Frankie said. "I was counting on that."

Mrozinski stood and shook Frankie's hand. "Keep me posted. I'll do the same."

Frankie smiled. "Sounds like a deal. Between the two of us we'll get these pricks."

"Guaranteed," Mrozinski said. "See ya around."

Frankie drove home, parked on St. Elizabeth Street, and he and Alex walked the rest of the way. It had been a long time since he'd been to his childhood home. Not since his father died.

"Why'd you park so far away?" Alex asked. "It doesn't look that crowded."

"I needed some time to think," Frankie said. "And to prepare you for the greeting we're about to receive."

Alex cocked his head and looked up at Frankie.

"What do you mean by that?"

Frankie hesitated, slowing while he did. "Alex, you know some people are prejudiced. They don't like a person because they're Irish or Polish or Italian—"

"Or black?" Alex said.

Frankie nodded, then he picked up the pace. "Yeah," he said. "Or black. Not everybody's like that, but unfortunately, my family is."

Alex grabbed hold of Frankie's hand and squeezed. "Don't worry about it, F.D. I can handle a little prejudice. Not like I haven't dealt with it before."

"That's the spirit," Frankie said. He had forgotten for a moment that Alex was a lot older than his years. "And remember what I said. Not everybody is like that."

In another minute or so, Frankie walked up the steps leading to the house. His mother answered after the second knock. She smiled, then looked down at Alex.

"Who is *this* young man?"

Frankie stepped into the living room, letting go of Alex's hand so that he could hug his mother. "This is my son, Alex." He patted him on the shoulder. "Alex, this is Grandma Donovan."

The smile disappeared from Mrs. Donovan's face. She replaced it with a fake one. "Your son? I didn't know you had a son."

"If we talked more, perhaps you would know. I adopted Alex almost two years ago. His mother had left him alone and he had nowhere to go."

Alex beamed when Frankie called him his "son." He looked up at Frankie and smiled, then reached to hug his new grandma. "Nice to meet you," he said. "Dad's told me so much about you."

She winced when Alex said "Dad" but she recovered quickly. "Do your sisters know? I mean that you have a son?"

"Or did you mean, do they know that I have a *black* son?"

Alex stepped in place, glancing first at Frankie, then his grandmother.

"I don't see what being black has to do with anything," she said.

"That's good. Neither do I," Frankie said. "Now that we've got that settled, should we stay here, or at Nicky's house. He offered."

Mrs. Donovan blushed, perhaps embarrassed. "Here, of course. Why would you stay at Nicky's?

"Get your things," Mrs. Donovan said, then she looked around. "Where are your bags, Frankie? You and Alex can take the front room. There are two beds there."

"Bags are in the car," Frankie said. "I didn't know what kind of reception we'd get."

"Nonsense," his mother said. "Get your bags and take them up to the front bedroom as I said. You can sleep there. Alex can stay with you or take the back bedroom. We've got plenty of space."

"Okay, Mom," Frankie said. He hugged her one more time, then grabbed Alex by the arm. "Come on, Ace. Let's get our stuff."

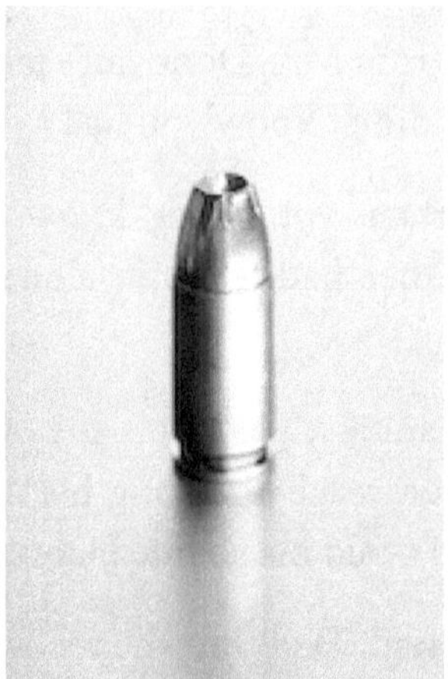

After work, I drove to the hospital to see the boss. He'd been sick for a few months—the result of a stroke—and I felt sure he was worried about the business. Besides, it was too early to see Smiles.

Joe was lying in bed, looking like shit when I arrived. Tubes were up his nose, and another one was in his stomach, since he couldn't eat without help. An IV was in his right arm and monitors were hooked up to his chest, wired to electrodes.

"What's up, Joe?"

"Nicky!" He struggled to sit but finally resorted to raising the head of the bed electronically.

"Keep still," I said. "I just dropped by to check on you. No need to disturb yourself."

"Nicky, it doesn't look good for me getting back to work any time soon. We may have to call it quits if I can't."

"Bullshit," I said. "Business is better than ever; in fact, we had to hire two new crews to handle the load."

Joe's eyes widened, and a light shone in them. "What? How?"

"I paid some visits to a few people. We got lucky and it resulted in a couple of jobs. Now we're swamped."

Joe smiled, and this time he did manage to sit up some. "Are you shitting me? For real?"

I smiled back. "For real, Joe. We got the new warehouse by the waterfront, the condos on North Market, and the new elementary school near the Brandywine. And all at good prices. The condos are at a great price."

He tried to sit up higher, but slipped. "Nicky, you're a genius. I owe you big-time for this."

"You don't owe me a thing, but I may have to take off for a week to help somebody with a problem. I'll have Alphonse cover for me."

"Take as much time as you need; in fact, when you get back, I'm giving you part of the business. I've been thinking about this for a long time, and my stay in the hospital has convinced me. You'll eventually have an opportunity to earn it all."

What he said was beyond my wildest dreams, but I shrugged it off. "Don't worry about it, Joe."

"I'm not worried about it. I had my doubts when I hired you. Those doubts disappeared a long time ago. Besides, I've got no son. A couple of no-good nephews and a sweet niece, but no one to take over the business. It seems tailor-made for you. And after this, I'm ready to retire."

I leaned down and kissed his forehead. "Thanks, Joe. You're the best."

I stayed for another hour, shooting the bull, before I said goodbye and left for Johnny Smiles' house.

The traffic was so bad it took me almost half an hour to drive to

Smiles' house. I assumed he was expecting me and had the information I needed. *That better be the case.*

Johnny wore a smile when he answered the door, but when he saw who it was, the smile vanished. "What do you want?" he asked.

"It's Friday," I said.

"I know it is," Smiles said, "and I hope this is what you need, Nicky. The guy who sells these things to me didn't know much, and there's no address or company name on the video." Johnny handed me a DVD. "Here, see for yourself."

It disgusted me just knowing something had already been done; these people obviously wasted no time. I said that before looking at it, but I presumed it was the same DVD that Rosa gave me. Now, I really wanted their asses.

"Where are they?"

"I don't know," Smiles said.

"Who sold you this?" I asked.

"I don't—"

I bundled his shirt and dragged him into the kitchen. Once there, I grabbed a frying pan and smashed his knee.

The pain registered immediately. "Jesus Christ! Mother fucker! What did you do that for?"

"You gave the wrong answer," I said. "You know who sold this to you. You're going to tell me or you're going to die, and it won't be a quick death."

"Merk sold it. A guy named Merk. His real name is Reggie Grimm. Hangs out by the YMCA near Washington Avenue."

"And where are the DVDs made?" I asked.

"I don't have any idea. You gotta believe me."

"Where?"

"I have no idea," Johnny said, so I smacked him with the pan again, this time on the other knee.

"Fuck me!" Johnny said, and fell to the floor. "I can't walk."

"I'm gonna make that prediction come true permanently if you don't tell me where the girl is, and where those films are made."

"Los Angeles. It's Los Angeles."

"I need a name."

"I got no name, Nicky. I swear, but I got a company name. I don't know if it's real or not, but it's a name. And I know they got more girls than Allison. Got five or six from what I heard. Maybe more."

"What's the name?"

"Mezzanotte Productions. Mezzanotte means midnight."

I sneered. "I know what it means, and they'll pay extra for using a pretty name for such a vile business."

Johnny's swallow was noticeable. "I don't know if the name's real. I checked it out, but nothing came up."

I grabbed him by the collar. "Stay out of it, Smiles. If I hear you said anything to even one person, I'll cut your tongue off and feed it to you. And you know I'll do it, so don't try."

Smiles gulped. "You got it, Nicky. *Nothing*. My lips are sealed."

"Make sure they stay that way," I said. "When I get there, if I get a hint that anyone knew I was coming, you'll *wish* for a slow death."

"You got it, Nicky. Nobody will know you're coming. No problem."

Smiles was still lying on the floor when I turned to leave. I looked back as I was going out the door, then I pointed at him. "If this doesn't pan out, I'll be back, and I'll bring things with me. If you're still alive by the time I leave, you'll wish I hit you with the frying pan again." I stared. "*Capisci?*"

"I understand," Johnny said.

~

I STOPPED by the house and got Allison's address, then left to see her parents. They lived in a row house on Franklin Street, not far from Smiles. It was a nice-looking house, at least from the outside.

I knocked on the door and a man who appeared a little older than me answered.

He wore a grim look on a haggard face. "Can I help you?" he asked.

"My name's Nicky Fusco. I'm here about your daughter, Allison."

His eyes went wide and his mouth agape. "Is she all right? Are you with the police?"

"As far as I know she's all right," I said, not brave enough to tell him the truth, not about his daughter. "And no, I'm not with the police."

I noted the questioning look on his face, so I explained further. "My daughter is friends with Allison. She told me that Allison was missing."

He opened the door wider and stepped aside to let me in. "Come in and sit."

I sat on the sofa and mustered enough courage to say, "I've been asking around about this, and I have reason to believe Allison is in California."

He sat erect. "California? What the hell is she doing in California? She wouldn't—"

"No," I said. "I didn't mean she went there on her own. I think she was kidnapped, along with several other girls."

I was hoping he'd make the connection between the porn capital of the world and his daughter—and others—being missing, but he didn't; those thoughts seemed to exist on different planets to him.

"I don't know what she's doing in California, but I'm here to get information. Anything you can tell me about Allison might help. I'm also going to ask her cousin Monroe to help."

"Monroe! He's a low-life, drug-dealing, son of a bitch. Why would you ask him?

"Does your daughter have anything to do with him?" Parker asked. The grim look returned. "And besides, what's a white boy doin' helpin' my daughter?" The angrier he became, the more his enunciation slipped into street talk.

And the guy's attitude pissed me off. "In the first place, the color of my skin has nothing to do with helping your daughter, and you shouldn't be worried about that. As for the other, no, my daughter has nothing to do with Monroe, but I understand he *is* Allison's cousin, and he has a lot of resources. I thought he could help."

Mr. Parker thought for a second, then nodded. "I guess you're right. Can't be choosy where you get help. And you're right about Monroe having resources. He has plenty of resources. Maybe he *can* help."

"I *know* he can help, and I'm sure he will. Monroe is a lot of things, but he *is* a good person deep down. Trust him."

Parker nodded, then stood. "Wait here," he said, and left the room. He returned in about ten minutes and gave me a few pictures, contact information for her friends, and even phone numbers of her best friends, including a list of the guys she dated before. It coincided with the list Rosa had given me.

I stood and thanked him. "Mr. Parker, no matter what you think of Monroe, he's a good guy, who's true to his word. I'm sure he'll help find Allison. As far as what you think of white people, put that aside and let someone help."

Tears formed in his eyes. "I never thought I'd say this to a white man, but thank you. I'm grateful."

I swallowed hard. "We'll get her, Mr. Parker. I promise. We'll get her. And trust me, no matter what you thought of doing to the people who took your daughter, what Monroe and I will do is going to be worse."

Mr. Parker wiped tears from his eyes and hugged me. "Thank you. From the bottom of my heart, thank you."

THE PLAN

I received a phone message from Johnny Smiles. He confirmed Allison was in L.A., which sounded right, but whether they were in Los Angeles or Hong Kong didn't matter. There would be no hiding for the bastards that had taken Allison and the others.

I drank my wine and cracked open another new mystery from John Sanford, and at the end of a riveting chapter, I placed the book on the table and looked over at Angela.

"I need to go to California," I said.

"California? What the hell for?"

"I told Rosa I'd look into this missing girl situation. Remember?"

"I remember the missing girl, but I thought that was restricted to a few questions for the guys at the smoke shop."

"Yeah, well it got a little more complicated. Now we've gotta go to Los Angeles."

"We've? Who is we've? And why do you *have* to go?"

"*We've* is me and Monroe. Remember, I told you he was Allison's cousin. And we have to go because that's where the girl is."

Angela slammed her book on the table. "Son of a bitch. I *knew* it would come to something like this." She glared at me. "I don't like it, Nicky. I don't like it one bit."

"I don't like it either, but sooner or later, you'll realize it's the right thing to do—a girl is in trouble. She needs our help. Besides, you're the one who convinced me to help."

"And what about if you get locked up? Or killed? Who's going to be there for us?"

"If either one of those things happen, it means I screwed up. That's on me, not Rosa or you or anyone else."

"It doesn't matter who it's *on*. It won't be any relief for me on those lonely nights when you're away, not one way or the other, in prison *or* dead."

"It won't come to that, but if it does, we'll worry about it then. If I'm in prison, we can both worry. If I'm dead, you can worry. No matter what, I'm not leaving some girl to suffer. You saw that DVD." I got up and refilled my wine glass. "Would you want that happening to Rosa?"

Angie picked up her book and stormed off to bed, her bare feet slamming the hardwood floors.

I opened my book and started reading again. There was no sense in going to bed when she was in this kind of mood.

I waited about an hour, then climbed the steps to the gallows, or at least that's what it seemed like. The light was still on in the bedroom. I opened the door, walked in and quietly slid under the covers.

"I'm not trying to be a nag," she said.

"You're doing a good job of it," I said, and laughed. She laughed, too.

"I'm sorry."

I rolled over and kissed her. "I know you worry. And I'm not going to lie, you have a right to; these are probably bad people. I take that back. These are *definitely* bad people, and they're probably dangerous people. But Allison needs our help, and I'm not letting her down."

I kissed her again. "The cops will be too late. They won't get anything done soon enough. It's up to me and Monroe. We've got to do it, or nobody will. And we've got to do it my way. These aren't folks who will listen to a plea for mercy."

I wiped tears from her cheek, then kissed her goodnight.

In the morning, I was greeted by the smell of fresh-brewed coffee, and a warm kiss, something I hadn't expected.

"You're awful perky today," I said.

She sighed. "I couldn't sleep last night, so I got up to read and saw Rosa's light on. I sat and talked with her for a long time."

Angie gave another sigh and poured a second cup of coffee. "I don't have the strength to fight both of you." She reached over and twisted the timer on the toast. "Go on. Go get the girl. But don't call me if you need to get bailed out."

I kissed her and went upstairs to grab a bag of clothes. "I won't call you if I'm dead, either."

She laughed at that. "Make sure Monroe has the instructions. I want to be the last to know if something goes wrong."

I kissed her on the cheek. "Nothing will go wrong," I said. "I'll be back in no time. Now, I've got to pack."

"Is Joe going to be angry? You just took time off to go to New York and help Bugs?"

"That was months ago; besides, Joe owes me for all the business I've brought in. And I already told him I'd be taking off. He offered me a part of the business. How's that for success?"

"What?" Angela said. "And now you're going to risk it all? After we've waited so long."

I grabbed her cheeks and kissed her. "Put yourself in Allison's parents' position. If your child were missing, would you care about a job?"

Angela teared up. "Nicky, you're one of a kind. Just remember, we can't afford to lose this job. And we can't afford to have you killed, either."

"Nobody's losing a job and nobody's dying. Now, let me get ready so I can leave."

I finished dressing, packed lightly, and started to go. As I was walking out the door, Angela said, "And bring her back safe." She paused for just a second. "No matter what you have to do."

I smiled. No words could have been sweeter. This was far better than a blessing from Sister Thomas. Even though the blessing from Sister Thomas was nice, an "okay" from Angela was nicer.

I tucked the bag of clothes under my arm as I walked out the door. *It was going to be a good trip.* These sons of bitches were going to pay. One way or another, they *would* pay for what they did.

I reconfirmed with Joe that I'd be gone for two weeks or so, all the while praying that would be enough time. Ordinarily, I'd say yeah, but I planned on driving, not flying, so the extra time was needed. I figured it would take three days to drive out if we switched drivers. Even so, I planned on four to be safe, and figured on the same amount of time driving back. We could shorten that if necessary, but four days was already mildly aggressive as we'd have a carload or two filled with teenagers. That left us six days to get things done—not a lot, but hopefully enough. *First, though, I had business with a scumbag named Merck.*

~

EARLY IN THE MORNING, I picked up Monroe, then parked near the corner of Washington Avenue and Pennsylvania Avenue and watched the newspaper kid across the street. I had arrived early and paid him good money to point out Merk the moment he saw him.

Twenty minutes had gone by and still no sign of Merk, which made me start to worry. I was in the middle of an Usher song when I saw the kid take out a cigarette and light it—our pre-arranged signal.

I squinted to get a better look at Merk. He was about my height and weight but was somewhat unkempt, with greasy hair that hung down over his eyes and a face that looked as if it hadn't seen a razor in days. He bought a paper from the kid, then took a seat on the bench, opening the paper to read.

It was perfect. I opened the car door, got out, and moved slowly across the street. I bought a paper from the kid also, gave him an extra ten spot, then took a seat on the bench next to Merk.

I opened my paper the same way Merk had, but I pulled out my gun when I did. It had a silencer on it and had never been registered, so nothing could be traced. Even the bullets had been wiped clean of prints. Beyond that, not much more than a loud popping sound would be heard, not enough to draw attention.

"Hey, Merk," I said.

Surprised, he put down the paper and looked over at me. "Do I know you?" he asked.

"Probably not," I said. "But you do nasty things, like dealing in movies that feature young women. Now tell me who you work for."

He sneered and went back to reading his paper. "I don't know what you're talking about."

"I figured you'd be too smart to talk, so I followed you home last night. I saw your kids playing out front and I saw your wife hanging the clothes out to dry. It's nice that she does that. Not many people do anymore."

He set his paper on his lap and looked at me. "If you think of touching my family, I'll—"

"Don't worry. I would never hurt your family. I just want to know where the girls are, and who has them."

"I have no idea."

"That's a shame," I said, then handed him a piece of paper with seven names on it.

He looked at the paper, then turned to me again. "What the hell is this? I don't know these people."

"You should," I said. "Those names are the fathers of the girls you took." I stared, focusing on his eyes. "I said I wouldn't hurt your family, and I meant it. I wouldn't do such things. But I can't guarantee what these fathers will do. In the heat of the moment, they may do anything to anybody. And if they figure out what you people are using the girls for…Let's just say I wouldn't put it past them to cut your dick off and feed it to you. They may even do it in front of your family."

Fear showed in Merck's eyes. "Whoa! There's no need for any of that."

"I think there is," I said. "See, I promised a relative of one of the girls that I'd get information from you." I pointed toward my car. "See that guy in the car over there? That's Monroe. I'm sure you've heard of him. One of the girls you took was his cousin. He's taken a personal interest in finding her. Now, you can give me the information on where they are, and who has them, or I give you to Monroe first, then turn you over to the girls' fathers."

Merck held up his hands. "Okay. Okay. They took them to California, down by Los Angeles. Company's name is Mezzanotte Productions. That's all I know. I swear."

"That's a shame," I said, "because if you don't tell me more, I'm going to kill you."

He didn't even glance my way, just said, "Do your worst, but that's all I know."

"I will," I said, and shot him three times in the side of the chest, just below the heart. At least one of the shots was sure to have punctured his lung. Assuming it did, he'd be dead before long. Merk let out a gasp and started to slump, but I caught him and propped him upright, making it appear as if he were still reading the paper.

I sat next to him, and read for another minute, then stood to leave, taking my paper with me. Merk wouldn't be dealing in porn any longer; in fact, he wouldn't be dealing in anything.

TIME TO GO

 spent the rest of the day preparing to leave, and making sure Alphonse had everything he needed. After work, I drove to Monroe Street and parked near the corner of 7th. Two guys were standing near the corner, leaning against a brick wall. They were trying to look inconspicuous, and to most people, probably did. I knew they were guards for Monroe, and both likely had .45s tucked in their waistbands.

"What's up, boys?" I asked, as I started up the block. "Monroe in?"

"He's in," one of them said. "Who are you?" His hand was already moving toward the back of his waistband.

"That's the 'Rat'," the other one said to his buddy, then looked at me. "S'up, Nicky?"

"Not much on my end, but I know you need to be thanking someone that it's a cool evening for standing guard. Last week was a bitch."

The second guy walked over and knocked on the door. "Comin' in," he said, then turned the knob and opened it. He stepped aside to give me room.

7th and Monroe

I started up the steps, thinking of how far things had come. Last year I would have been searched three times before being allowed in, and the year before that, I may have been shot. *Times change.*

Monroe sat in a chair near the far corner. I say far, but it was only fifteen feet away. DuPree, his lieutenant and another one of his cousins from the other side of his family, rested on the couch next to him. Monroe sat up when I came in.

"My man. What brings you here?" Monroe said.

"Nothing good."

He flashed a gold crown. "Tell Papa Monroe what 'nothing good' is."

"It's about Allison. You were there when we got confirmation she's in California. We're gonna have to go out and get her."

Monroe stood. "California? And you think we gotta go? No chance of any help from your boys?"

I shook my head. "It's not my people, Monroe. If it *was* them, we may have been able to do something. So you know what has to be done. It's up to us."

Monroe popped the top on another beer, then sat down and gulped it. "Any other good news?" he asked and tossed me a beer from a cooler at his feet.

I caught the beer and sat in the chair opposite Monroe. "No good news at all. I talked to Allison's father, too. He doesn't think much of you, which you probably know, so whatever the cops may have told him, he's keeping to himself."

"You got that part right," Monroe said. "That man wouldn't piss on me if I was on fire."

DuPree leaned forward. "What's this got to do with you, Nicky? Why are you involved—if you are?"

"My daughter asked me to look into it. She's Allison's friend."

"Allison's black," DuPree said.

I laughed. "Tell me something I don't know. So are you. And she's also Monroe's cousin, who's also black." I shot DuPree a look. "And for the record, DuPree, I don't hold it against you that you tried to rob my daughter. I'll make the assumption that you didn't know who she was. Now you do, so if you try again, I'll shoot you."

"What?" Monroe said.

"Shit!" DuPree said, and looked at Monroe. "I stopped as soon as I saw she carried your coin. And I gave her everything back."

Monroe smacked DuPree on the side of the head. "What the hell, DuPree? When did this happen?"

DuPree cowered. "Man, this was ages ago. Maybe six months."

Monroe turned to Nicky. "Why didn't you tell me? I'd have straightened his ass out."

"No harm done," I said. "I think he learned his lesson."

Monroe smacked DuPree again. "You don't need to rob little girls. If you want to rob somebody, go over to the Printz or pick out a couple of PR dudes down on Harrison Street. Grow some balls! Robbing girls is for pussies. Are you a pussy, DuPree? Well, are you?"

"I ain't no pussy," DuPree said, and lowered his head. "And I'm sorry. It won't happen again."

"Sorry don't cut it. I got half a mind to let Nicky cap you."

I pulled the DVD out of my jacket and handed it to Monroe. "I never showed you this because it's so disgusting. My daughter gave it to me, and it's why we've got to get Allison back. People that do this shit to young girls shouldn't live."

Monroe watched the DVD, clenching his fists the whole time. When we finished, he stood, pacing. "These pricks are dead. You hear me? Dead. Forget little girls. People who do this shit to *anyone* shouldn't live."

"You won't get an argument from me," I said, "But we've got to find them first."

"How do we do that?" DuPree asked.

"I've got a lead from a guy up on 10th Street," I said. "It should pan out."

"With or without trouble?" DuPree asked.

"It doesn't matter. If we can't get the information we need the easy way, then I'll smash his dick with a hammer."

"Jesus Christ!" DuPree said, and grabbed hold of his crotch. "It makes me hurt just thinking of it."

"Yeah," I said. "Imagine what he'll feel like after the hammer hits his dick the first time?"

"Motherfucker, you're cold," DuPree said.

"Remember that if Nicky ever asks you a question," Monroe said. "He doesn't ask twice."

"Don't worry," DuPree said. "I ain't pissin' blood for nobody."

"We should talk to her parents," Monroe said, but they don't like me much, as you've already noted."

"Already talked to them. I've got everything we need. Friends, boyfriends, pictures, all of it."

Monroe looked surprised. "Talked to them? You? They don't like white people. Like 'em even less than me. A white cop shot his oldest son."

"For whatever reason, he cooperated. Maybe he was willing to swallow pride to get Allison back."

"What the hell?" Monroe said. "Shit never stops surprising me. That man barely talks to me, let alone a white dude."

"When are we leaving?" DuPree asked. I need some time to get ready.

"Tomorrow morning," I said. "And we need to leave early. You don't have time to get ready. Besides, all you need is a gun, a knife, and a couple of changes of clothes."

DuPree looked at Monroe. "You hear that? Better get your ass in gear so you can get plane tickets."

'We're not flying," I said. "A set of wheels will do fine. And it doesn't even have to be a good set. We're not going far before we rent one."

"A set of wheels? Are you crazy? I'm not *driving* to California."

"Plane tickets are too easy to trace," I said, "and we don't want to be traced. That means no credit cards, no real licenses, nothing that could trace to us if things go wrong." I looked to Monroe again. "That means cash and probably plenty of it."

"Why not fly?" DuPree asked. "We haven't done anything."

"Not *yet*," I said, "but these people are not just gonna give the girls up, so I imagine it will take a little convincing. By the time we leave California, we *will* have done something. I don't want records of three guys and a group of girls flying back to the east coast after what we'll have to do."

"You mean—"

"Better if you don't know," Monroe said.

I smiled. I didn't want to do anything wrong, but I knew I'd have to. People like the ones who made this movie didn't give up meal tickets without a fight, and if it was a fight they wanted, Monroe and I would give it to them. "Like Monroe said, 'Better if you don't know.'"

DuPree said, "Okay, count me in. Who else is going?"

"Just the three of us," I said. "We shouldn't need more than that. Meet here at 5:00 a.m. And we'll need someone to drive us to Baltimore."

"I'll get Dixon," Monroe said. "He's reliable."

"Baltimore? What the hell for?" DuPree asked.

"I'll explain on the way."

A KNOCK on the door sent DuPree to answer it. Razz, one of Monroe's men, showed a row of white teeth. "What's up, DuPree?"

DuPree went outside to talk to Razz.

"Headin' off to California, that's what."

"California? What for?"

DuPree looked over his shoulder. "Don't know if I should say. It has to do with one of Monroe's cousins. Leave it to say we're gonna kick some ass."

"So who's going with you to California?"

"Monroe and Nicky the Rat."

"Who's that?"

"What? What the hell, man? You don't know who the Rat is? Where the hell you been livin' for the past few years?"

DuPree took a long sip from his can of Pabst Blue Ribbon. "Rat is one of the meanest motherfuckers I've ever seen. I'd put him up there with the best—Invincible Factor of nine."

"Nine! Get the hell outta here. If he's a nine, who's a ten?"

"I don't know, maybe Batman or Daredevil."

"What about Superman?"

"Get outta here; Superman's a pussy. Throw a green rock at him and he cries."

"What about—"

"Don't give me no what abouts. Thor ain't shit without his goddamn hammer. Green Lantern can't even beat a girl if she's wearin' a yellow dress, and Iron Man is a straight out pussy, no questions asked. No, it's either Batman or Daredevil, maybe Flash."

Razz nodded. "Okay, you convinced me. When you leavin'?"

Monroe stepped outside and stared. "If you two are through playin' Superhero, we'll be leavin' tomorrow, Razz."

"Tomorrow! Why so early? I'm not ready," DuPree said.

"Then you better get ready. You heard Nicky inside, so stop trying to be the martyr and get your ass ready. The people who have Allison aren't waiting. If you're not ready to go, I'll have to invite that pussy, Iron Man."

DuPree scowled, but then he nodded. "I'll be ready." He then turned to his buddy and said, "Gotta go. Gonna go kick some ass."

WE DROVE to the Baltimore airport rental-car site and got a car using a fake ID. We even went so far as to have one of Monroe's buddies rent the car so our picture wasn't on the camera. Assuming we cleaned the car, there'd be no way to trace us.

From Baltimore, it didn't take long to get on Route 81, then follow it to Route 40, heading west. We'd be on 40 for a long time. We planned on staying in sleaze-bag motels along the way, paying cash so there'd be no record. There was also close to zero chance there would be any photo records of our stay—hell, most of those motels probably had no cameras.

On the third night, I found Monroe drinking beer by himself poolside. I pulled up a chair.

"What's goin' on, Monroe?"

"Just thinkin'."

"About what?" I asked.

"I think you know about what. I'm thinkin' about what I'm gonna do to the pricks that took Allison. Damn shame what that girl's goin' through."

"We're gettin' all of them," I said.

"What? All of who?"

"There are more girls than just Allison. And I'm not leaving any of them for cocksuckers like this. Not even if I have to kill them all."

Monroe nodded. "I'm with you on that, Rat. I don't care what color they are; nobody deserves to go through this."

I held my glass of beer up and tapped his bottle. "We'll get 'em, Monroe. Don't worry about that. We'll get 'em."

CLARIFICATION

Nicky finished his beer, then called it a night. DuPree was arriving when Nicky was leaving. He furrowed his brows and looked to Monroe. "What did the Rat mean by 'We'll get 'em?'"

"He isn't going to kiss them," Monroe said. "And he ain't going to California for the scenery. If Nicky has his mind set to *persuade* a man to do something, believe me, they're either going to do it, or die—probably both. And the dying won't be peaceful."

"And how do you know this?"

"Because I saw what he could do when we were in prison, and I've heard of what he did in New York, which was worse."

"I didn't sign up for no killin'," DuPree said.

"What did you think you signed up for?"

"I don't know, but I ain't plannin' to kill no one."

Monroe walked over to where DuPree was sitting and leaned in close. "Make up your mind, DuPree, because once we get to Los Angeles, you're either with us or you're not. And if you're not, you'll likely suffer the same fate as the ones we're after. You may be my cousin, but that don't mean shit."

DuPree stood and paced. "What do you mean by that?"

"I mean that if you tell Nicky you'll have his back and don't deliver, he'll soon have your ass. So, if you're going with us, make up your mind. There can be no hesitation. If you have to pull a gun and shoot somebody, it has to be done. And if Nicky doesn't kill you for not doing it, I will."

"Goddamn! I mean goddamn. This ain't right."

"Right or not, it's the way it is. So make up your mind."

"I didn't come with you so I could kill people."

"Nobody wants to kill people, but some people need killing. It's as simple as that."

"Ain't nothin' simple about it; this is killing!" DuPree said. "They hang your ass for that."

"They don't hang people anymore, DuPree; they shoot chemicals into you. Besides, they have to catch you first, and we don't plan on getting caught."

"Oh, you don't plan on getting caught? Damn. Stupid me. I guess all those people in prison planned on it?"

"If you don't want to go, don't. I don't need you. I'll have Dixon fly out to meet us. I know Dixon won't have a problem with pulling the trigger. Problem is, if I have to call Dixon, that means I have to leave you in the desert or the bushes on the side of the road."

DuPree took a swig of beer and grunted. "I came this far, might as well go the rest of the way."

"That's not how you look at things," Monroe said. "Like I said, you're in or you're out. There is *no* halfway. Either say you're leaving, or go along, but don't bring the subject up again."

DuPree thought for a moment, then said, "I'm in. Don't worry. I'll do what I have to do."

"Okay. That's what I thought," Monroe said. "One piece of advice—when the shootin' starts—and it *will* start, swallow your balls and squeeze the trigger. As long as you do that, it won't be a bullet from me or Nicky that takes you out."

"Not a lot of comfort," DuPree said.

"It's the best I've got," Monroe said. "And it's the best you're gonna get, so you should take it."

Nicky's phone rang. "Hello."

"Rat, it's Bugs."

"What's up? Everything okay?"

"Yeah. I just wanted to see if you found out anything?"

"Not yet. Not even close to L.A. We're still in New Mexico."

"I figured as much. It's a long drive from here, but I thought I'd check." Frankie paused. "Anyway, I saw Patti."

"McDermott?"

"The one and only. She's still the hottest thing I've seen, and she's pointing the finger at the Campisis. Not that I blame her, with them killing one of her brothers and being responsible for the other's death, but she may have a point."

"Are you thinking with your head or your dick?"

"I hope both, but that's why I want to bounce it off you. To make sure I'm looking at this right."

"Okay, what have you got?"

"She says that two of the Campisi brothers are into porn. Says everyone knows that. I'm inclined to believe her; the Campisis are into anything that generates money, and there's a lot of money in porn."

"Porn's a big business, there's no doubt about it, but this kind of porn I'm not sure about. Most of it is instant cash, although I'm wondering how big the market is. Soft porn I can see. This…"

"I don't know what they're into, at least not all of it. Don't know that *yet*, but I'll find out. In any case, just being in the business makes them worth looking into."

"I've got no argument with that," I said. "You know there's no love lost on the Campisis from my end—not ever since the gang fight—but at the same time, I don't want to put them away just because I don't like them."

"I've got you covered," Frankie said. "Let me tell you what I have so far."

"Go on."

"Patti said that anyone renting films knows if you want any kind of porn, you go to Johnny Smiles—like you said—and anybody who's anybody knows the Campisis supply Smiles. He makes sure the movies get in all the right places."

"How does Patti know this?"

Frankie hesitated. "I don't know. I guess she's got connections."

"But are Campisis' movies the kind of porn we're looking at, or are they soft porn? And if I were you, I'd ask about Patti's connections. We don't want to be working off a grudge accusationn."

"I got that, Nicky. And as far as what type of movies, from what I've heard so far, they deal in soft porn, but I haven't seen any of it."

"There's a hell of a difference, Bugs. It's like going from mugging someone to murder. It's a different league. If you see someone whose rap sheet shows only muggings and you're looking for a serial killer, you're not going to immediately drag him in."

"I know that Nicky. I'm not an ass. But Patti said the Campisis have been seen with Smiles at the coffee shop and even at the Columbus Inn."

"The coffee shop may be a coincidence," Nicky said. "Anybody can run into someone at the coffee shop. But the Inn is a different story. I'd put more weight on that. In all the years I've lived here, I can count on one hand the number of times I've 'run into' someone at the Inn."

"That's what I was thinking," Frankie said. "Regardless, maybe I need to see Mrozinski again. He might be able to steer me in the right direction."

"I would. Tell him what you've got and see what he says. Just leave out my involvement. I don't want him knowing I'm in California."

"I'm not stupid, Nicky. I wouldn't say anything."

"Okay, call me when you get something. And don't stare too long at Patti—or her ass. You've always had a weak spot for her, especially her ass."

"Like you didn't."

I laughed. "Not as bad as you, and the trouble is, she knew it then and she knows it now."

"Screw you, Nicky. I'm not falling for any traps."

"Keep thinking that, Bugs, and in the meantime, say hi to Kate."

"You're a prick."

"And you're a slave to your urges."

Frankie laughed. "Okay. I got it. I'll talk to Mrozinski, then call."

"I'll be waiting," I said. "See ya.'"

ANOTHER BODY

*L*ou was at his desk, reading the paper, when Sherri walked in.

"Hoping *The Times* will solve your crime, Mazzetti?"

"I wish they would," Mazzetti said. "Then I could retire in peace. Besides, how did you know it wasn't the Wall Street Journal I was reading?"

"Two reasons: first, the name is on the front page, which is facing me, and the other reason is you're not smart enough to read the WSJ."

"Damn, that's low."

"Sometimes the truth hurts."

"Anything new?" Mazzetti asked.

"Nothing on anybody from the BCI. How about your end? Any connections look suspicious?"

"We're not that lucky. Seems like all the guy's friends were gay, and that's a tight-lipped community. Damn near as bad as the groups down on Mulberry Street or Canal Street."

"Gays aren't bad if you know who to talk to," Sherri said.

"And who would that be?"

"In my experience, no matter who you're dealing with, it's the same. Find someone who needs a deal and then negotiate. It really doesn't matter what nationality or group they're with."

"Then let's find a scumbag who needs a deal," Lou said. "Based on your vast experience, that is."

Sherri handed Lou a file. "No sooner said, than done. Meet 'Stevie Boy,' the wonder hustler of Tribeca. It took me half the morning to find him—while you were sleeping, I may add."

"Hey, I was here at 8:00. I can't help it if you sacrifice sleep for work. I don't know why anyone who maintains the least bit of sanity would."

"And you'll never understand," Sherri said.

"And what kind of favors might 'Stevie Boy' need?" Lou asked.

"He was caught with an ounce of heroin, so a 'C' felony. If we offer to make it go away, I guarantee he'll deal."

"If we're going to make it go away, he'd probably say the pope killed Manual, and he might have, considering the situation, but..." Lou breathed and sipped again on his coffee. "In either case, our boy Stevie better have something good."

"If he doesn't, we don't deal," Sherri said.

'STEVIE BOY' sat across the table from Lou, his stare fixed on the blank wall behind Mazzetti.

Lou snapped his fingers in front of Stevie's face to draw his attention. "Hey, wacko. You had an ounce on your possession when they arrested you. According to New York State law, that's a 'C' felony."

Lou grinned. "I think you know what happens to your type in Attica. Let's say, you'll receive a *warm* reception and be introduced to a lot of new friends, some of whom may not be friends."

"So how does this go away?" Stevie Boy asked, and he said it with a half-smirk planted on his face.

"Who said anything about it going away?"

Stevie Boy flashed that half-smirk again. "I wouldn't be here if you didn't want something. And you're smart enough to know I'm not giving you anything unless I get something in return. At least, I think you're smart enough to know that." He glanced back and forth between Lou and Sherri, and said, "But now that I look again, maybe you're not."

Lou rested his hands on the back of the chair. "What can you tell me about Manual Ramirez? And I don't want any smart-ass comments about his name. Heard enough of them already."

"What do you want to know?" Stevie asked.

"To start with—everything you know. After that, you can tell the rest."

"I don't know what the hell you're talking about. If you expect cooperation, you need to speak more plainly. I'm not here to solve riddles."

"See, that attitude will get you ten years—and the aforementioned 'lots of friends.' Tell me what you know, and that term might come down to five. Tell me *everything* and it might turn into a walk."

"Ah. Now, you're talking plain English. I assume what you mean is, like who Manual was sleeping with, and who he *wanted* to sleep with?"

"A list of who he was sleeping with might get you ten," Sherri said. "Who his wife was sleeping with might drop it to five. But who he *wanted* to sleep with should make everything go away."

"I can handle that," Stevie said. "As they say, the devil is in the details."

"Let's get started," Lou said, and turned the recorder on. "Start talking."

"Stewart Patrick is the first name that comes to mind, though he isn't the only one. Paul Raymond is another choice as is Morgan Alou.

"For the good wife—if you're in a generous mood, and that's what you want to call her—try Radcliffe Sutherland, Morris Tantril, Carlo Fiore, or any number of the many doormen who have worked at the building. She's not that selective."

"You think one of them might have done Manual in?" Sherri asked.

"I doubt it. There was no jealousy involved; in fact, Manual introduced her to Radcliffe, and I heard Manual even participated now and then with *select* partners; his hinges swung both ways."

"How about who he *wanted* to do?" Sherri asked.

"You keep pressing that angle," Stevie said. "It's interesting but is there a reason you ask?"

"Not that it's any of your business, but I'm thinking maybe he pushed too hard, or decided to use some sort of blackmail. Tell us what you think, because either way, it could be motive."

Stevie pursed his lips. "Hmm. I hadn't thought of that, but it's a good point. Considering that, you might try Ricky Santiago or Foster Wentworth. Both of them live in the city, but have studios in Williamsburg. You can try them, but I doubt if it will pan out. Manual wasn't the pushy type. He was more of a 'do what you want, live and let live' type."

Lou pushed a pen and a yellow pad of paper in front of Stevie. "Write the names and addresses. If this plays out, you'll walk. But there's a bright side; if it doesn't pan out, you'll make a lot of new friends."

Santiago Scenery and Wentworth of Williamsburg weren't more than four blocks apart, and both were crowded when Lou and Sherri arrived, if five or six people constitutes a crowd.

The crowd consisted mostly of middle-aged men wearing $500 Hermes scarves and $1,500 Tom Ford shoes, mixed with young girls wearing Levi's jeans with holes in them that exposed just enough skin, and beat-up Nike tennis shoes. Also with holes that exposed too much skin.

Ricky was trying to interest two people in a new artist's painting for the paltry sum of $25,000, a drop in the bucket for these folks, though all Lou could think about was how much espresso he could buy—or how many cannoli—or both.

Lou watched Ricky work his magic on the unsuspecting customers, then stood in amazement as both of the shoppers wrote checks for twenty-five grand for different paintings by the same artist. Once they had left, Lou approached him.

"May I help you?" Ricky asked.

"Not in the way you think. In fact, not in any way you think," Lou said. He flashed his badge, then, "I'm Mazzetti, and this is Detective Miller. We're here about Manual Ramirez." Lou waited for recognition to light the man's eyes, then he said, "What can you tell me about him? And don't leave anything out."

Ricky smiled. "Since you didn't ask if I knew him, I'll presume you know I did. I'll confirm that presumption."

Ricky fiddled with a few receipts in the drawer, then turned to Lou. "Manual was a client. He purchased several paintings from us, and they were valuable ones—maybe $400,000 or $500,00 each. I don't know what your thoughts are, but there is certainly no reason on earth why I'd want him dead. Keeping him alive should have been my primary directive, as Captain Kirk's directive was not to interfere in another planet's evolution."

Sherri furrowed her brows, as if to say, 'What the hell are you talking about?' but Lou nodded as if he understood.

"What else can you tell me about him?" Miller asked, eager to get off the subject.

"He supported the arts. He supported the community and the area, donating a huge amount of money to building a park here. And he truly loved art. Overall, a nice man. Certainly not a man I would want to kill. Not a man *anyone* would want to kill, at least in my opinion."

"And you had no relationship with him?" Lou asked.

"You mean physical?"

When Lou nodded, Ricky shook his head. "Detective, you have the wrong idea about me. I'm married, with three kids. The only relationship I had with Manual was a business relationship. I sold paintings and he purchased them. It was lucrative for me, but all above board. If I display mannerisms or traits that suggest otherwise, they were probably learned through osmosis."

Lou didn't know what the hell osmosis was, but a quick glance to Sherri confirmed that she was satisfied with the answer, so Lou let it go.

Ricky stopped to give an employee instructions. "See if you can help Mrs. Marshall. She's been here for five minutes already, and you know she doesn't like to be kept waiting."

Ricky turned back to Lou, the smile returning to his face. "Detective, if you're looking for a more sordid arrangement, you might talk to Foster Wentworth. Some people will tell you there's animosity between Foster and me, and they wouldn't be wrong, but that's not why I'm suggesting it. Foster is not to be trusted; that's why I'm mentioning it."

"Sordid in what way?" Lou asked, his curiosity now piqued.

"I can't swear to it, but I've heard that Foster throws parties where things happen that normal society would not readily accept. Things sexual and drug related."

"And Ramirez attended these events?" Sherri asked.

Ricky laughed. "From what I understand, Manual 'hosted' and paid for the events—which wouldn't surprise me—but you didn't hear that from me. I think he hosted them so that he could recruit new talent, if you catch my drift. Don't get me wrong, though, Manual was a nice guy. And a generous one."

Lou and Sherri left Santiago's and walked to Wentworth's gallery, using the time to discuss their visit. "I don't think he's a suspect," Lou said. "He was too open. He didn't try to hide anything."

"I have to agree," Sherri said. "I didn't pick up any negative vibes, and I usually do when they're dirty."

It took less than ten minutes to reach the gallery, and once there, they talked to Foster. The studio wasn't as nice as Ricky's and neither was the decor. The clientele seemed the same. Lou walked up to the register. "What can you tell me about Manual Ramirez?"

"I don't believe I know him," Foster said. "Should I?"

"Since he 'hosted' your sordid parties, yes, you should," Sherri said. "You want to rethink that answer, or should I ask the question again?"

Foster Wentworth tilted his head skyward and appeared to be thinking. "Manual Ramirez. Manual Ramirez. Now that you mention it, I may know him."

"Now that I mention it, think harder. We have solid evidence that you not only knew him, but frequently associated with him." Lou leaned against the counter. "Think, Foster. Time started ticking a minute ago, and you only have five minutes."

After being pressed, Foster checked his books, and "discovered" that Manual had purchased two paintings from WOW Studios, both valued at more than a million dollars.

"That's something I wouldn't think you'd forget," Sherri said. "I remember if someone bought a used car from me."

"Slipped my mind," Foster said. "But now I recall him."

"How convenient," Sherri said. "Once you realize we know that you knew Manual, you suddenly recall being familiar with him."

"Now, tell us what you know," Lou said. "Or you can tell us while your ass warms a chair at the station."

Foster sat on a chair behind the counter. He cupped his hands over his right knee. "You have to understand, Manual liked to *associate* with the 'cool' crowd. In order to do that, he was not opposed to spending money and a lot of it. He spent a couple of million here on artwork, and hundreds of thousands more financing parties for the young, hip crowd."

"Why didn't you say that when we asked the first time?" Sherri asked.

"For the same reasons you're pressing me now. I figured you'd think I had something to do with his murder. The fact is, that couldn't be further from the truth. I had no reason to kill Manual, and no reason to want him dead. He spent a small fortune at my gallery, and he funded my—shall we say—extracurricular activities."

"So who *did* want him dead?" Lou asked.

"I have no idea. I'd love to say it was Ricky Santiago, but he had no more reason than I do. Manual spent money at both of our shops."

"What about his wife?" Sherri asked.

"I don't know her," Foster said. "And that's the truth. Manual never brought her to our events. He thought she'd interfere with his *interests.*"

"And what do you think? Would she have interfered?"

Foster smiled. "I only met her twice, and both times it was brief, but if I were forced to answer, I'd say, probably."

"Anything else?" Lou asked.

"Nothing I can think of," Foster said.

Sherri handed him a card with her number on it. "If you do think of anything else, give us a ring. And I'm positive you *will* 'recall' something."

"I certainly will think on it," Foster said. "And I *will* call."

Lou and Sherri walked out of the studio, but they were both carrying a load of suspicion.

"He knows something," Lou said. "Nobody 'forgets' two sales of more than a million dollars each."

"You're right," Sherri said. "He's hiding something; the question is, what—and why. We've got the same situation as we have with Santiago—motive. Why kill a guy who spends millions with you?"

"You've got me pondering," Lou said. "I like Wentworth for being dirty, but I don't know why."

On the drive back to the station, Lou got a call. Another body had been found, and the events were similar to the scene where Manual's body had been dumped.

When Lou and Sherri arrived, a crowd had already gathered. Jacques Monfrer lay face down in the gutter out front of the opera house, blood staining what appeared to be a newly pressed tux.

"What have we got?" Sherri asked.

"Not much," a uniformed officer said. "Two GSWs to the back. Wallet intact, complete with cash, and a fistful of jewelry on his arm. Obviously robbery was not the motive."

"Or they were interrupted," Lou said.

"Keep believing that," the uniform said. "As for me, I've gotta get home for the Easter Bunny."

Lou laughed. "Okay, I'll eat chocolate at your house. In the meantime, have you got anything on the dear deceased—Mr. Jacques Monfrer?"

The uniform straightened. "Not much. Wealthy socialite. Big patron of the arts. Rumor is, he was gay, but I only heard that from some onlookers. I've got nothing else to support that."

"And you think Monfrer knew the first victim, Manual Ramirez?"

"The people I've spoken to say they were seen at the same events and hung out with the same crowd."

"In other words, these guys didn't meet at the local 5&10 cent store or share a nickel bag of popcorn at a Saturday matinée movie?"

The uniform laughed. "I don't think so."

"And they weren't stick-ball buddies," Lou said. "They were chasing each other around at the Met, or playing hide-and-seek at the Guggenheim. Something like that."

The uniform said, "And I forgot to mention, other than the gossip, this guy had Ramirez's name and number in his phone contacts."

"Interesting," Lou said. "Might have been more than just casual acquaintances. Did you overhear anything about motive?" Lou asked. "Any reason why someone would want either one of them gone?"

"Not a damn thing."

"All right. Keep everybody away until the M.E is done, then oversee the clean-up. We need to canvass the crowd."

"Got it, Lou. Good luck."

A TWIST IN THE CASE

We were less than a day from California, cruising along on Interstate 10 and making good time, when a call came in from Frankie. "What's up, Bugs?"

"Where are you?"

"Not far outside of Phoenix, Arizona. In case you're not up on your geography, that's one state over from California, about six hours. Why? What's up?"

"I've been up on my geography since grade school, but the important thing is I saw Patti again."

"Patti McDermott? Again? How did she look this time?"

"As good as the first time."

"That doesn't tell me anything," I said. "You've always had a soft spot for her, so I don't trust whatever information you get from that source."

"You're jealous. I know you're dying to know about her."

"I haven't been jealous of anyone since I've been thirteen. You'd do well to take a cue from that. It might help with Kate. You *do* remember Kate, don't you? Medium height, pale complexion, vibrant personality. Someday to be mother of your children."

"You know, Rat, you can be a real ass when you want to be?"

"Yeah. I know. Angela tells me that all of the time, but that doesn't take away from your problem. You need to get those blinders off."

"I hate to say it, but you could be right, I *might* be wearing blinders, but that doesn't take away from what she looks like."

"Okay, now that the bullshit is over, tell me why you really called. It certainly wasn't to tell me how Patti looked, and, if it was, then I'm calling Kate. I'm sure she'll be more interested than I am."

"You're a prick, Nicky."

"Now I'm a prick? Well, I've been called worse, and by better people. So don't waste your breath telling me."

"Okay, forget Patti, but in case I forgot to tell you, Mrozinski said he has reports of seven missing girls in the past three weeks, all of them under eighteen. That's two more than he told us before."

"Sounds like we've got an epidemic on our hands."

"Yeah, and at every abduction site, there has been a black or blue car spotted within an hour or so beforehand. This is according to witnesses who were interviewed at the locations."

"That's good info. Any idea who owns the car? Or is that too much to ask?"

"The cops have their eyes on Patti's little brother, Raff. He's into movies, and he owns a similar car, but I doubt it's him. The closest Mrozinski can come to a match is a dark-blue SUV."

"You're making a distinction between a car and an SUV, but remember, on that part of Franklin Street the residents are probably older, and to them there might not be a distinction—a car is a car. Hell, one of Rosa's friends has a grandmother who calls *everything* a car, including trucks. To her, anything that has four wheels is a car."

"Yeah, I hear you," Bugs said, "But guess who else owns a blue SUV—the Campisis."

"Son of a bitch!"

"Yeah, that's wha*t I* thought. Porn would fit their style, those scumbag sons of bitches."

"Keep checking on this, Bugs. Don't let on that you know anything, and don't suspect the Campisis just because you hate them, but keep on it."

"Hey, Nicky. I've been doing this a while. I think I know how to handle an investigation."

"I know you know *how* to conduct an investigation, Bugs, and I'm not trying to bust your balls. I'm just helping out in case you're still thinking with other parts of your anatomy."

"You know, Nicky, sometimes you can be a—"

"Yeah, yeah. Just get on the case, and call me when you get something real. I don't want to hear about Patti's ass anymore or any other part of her body. And by the way, stop by and tell Angela to give you the DVD that Rosa got at school. It's something Mrozinski should have. I forgot to give it to him before I left."

"You want him to know where it came from?"

"Definitely not. Make him think it came from your investigation. Maybe you'll earn another star."

Frankie got the DVD from Angela, and could tell by the cover it was not something he'd want to watch. He decided to take Nicky's advice and pay Mrozinski another visit. The first time he met with the detective, neither of them had anything other than the Smiles' lead. Now, at least, Frankie had *something*.

Donovan waited outside the station until the detective pulled up. "What's up, Mrozinski? Got anything for me?"

"What would I have for you? I told you I'd call when I had something new. I don't know how you do things in Brooklyn, but down here when you tell someone you'll keep them up to date, you stick to your word and do it."

Frankie nodded. "I know, I grew up here, remember? But if you've got a minute—and you can pull your head out of your ass—I'd like to go over what you *do* have." Then Frankie reached out his hand and offered the DVD to Mrozinski. "And by the way, you might want to take a look at this. I'm assuming you haven't seen it."

Mrozinski glanced at the cover. "Ah, shit. I figured as much but I didn't want it to be so." He looked at Frankie. "Where'd you get this?"

"Can't say," Frankie said. "And I mean, can't say, as in I don't know where it came from originally, though an educated guess would be the West Coast."

Mrozinski nodded. "Figured that much too." The detective sighed. "Anyway, you've got a deal on the few minutes. Meet me at my desk. You can read a magazine, stare at nothing on TV, or beat off, while I get coffee."

Mrozinski turned his head as he walked in the door of the station. "You want any coffee? It's probably cold and definitely terrible, but it's free."

"None for me," Frankie said. "But thanks."

"Less than five minutes later, Mrozinski returned, coffee in hand, and took a seat. He pulled out a case file and opened it. "Like I said last time, we've got reports of seven missing girls, and at every locale there was a dark-colored car spotted."

"Did the witnesses say *car* or *SUV*?"

"I don't know," Mrozinski said. "Let me check." He rifled through the file until he found the paper he wanted, then he leaned back in his chair and read. *Car*," he said. "They said a dark-blue car." He grabbed a pen with green ink in it from his holder and made marks on the paper. "Good point, Donovan. Thanks."

"How do we know where the girls were abducted?" Frankie asked.

"We don't know exactly, but in every case, the car was spotted in the vicinity of where the girls were last seen."

"What? You're shitting me."

"No kidding." Mrozinski took on a more serious tone. "But this has *got* to stay between us. The last thing I need—like I said before—is some vigilante asshole messing this thing up."

Obviously, he doesn't know Nicky went to California. Good. "I got it," Frankie said. "No need to worry here. I know where you're coming from."

"I'm counting on that, Donovan. Let's keep this investigation clean."

"Anything in common between the girls? Friends? Places they frequented? Schools?"

"Nothing," Mrozinski said. "We've dug deep. Churches, movie rentals, video games, social media connections. Nothing fits. I can't figure out how they tie together, unless they don't. Maybe they're random kidnappings, though I don't believe much in that."

"Even *random* can have a pattern," Frankie said. "Time of day, location, description, nationality…"

Mrozinski shook his head. "I've been through all that. Time of day is 'dark', which might translate into opportunity.

"Location seems random—stretching from the Governor Printz to Franklin Street. Description is blonde hair, black hair, brown hair, different color eyes, you name it. And nationality is all over the board, too, from black to white, to Middle Eastern, even Asian. The only thing that seems to fit a pattern is age. They've all been teenagers—thirteen to fifteen."

"That's not much, but it's something," Frankie said. "We focus on the people who distribute porn dealing with young girls. That's a separate part of the business. And no, I don't say this from 'viewing' experience. I busted a few porn cases in New York."

"Which brings something to mind. I asked about the *car/SUV* distinction for a reason. The Campisi brothers, who are known dealers in movies of questionable quality, own a dark-blue SUV."

"Interesting," Mrozinski said. "I've had a few run-ins with our friends the Campisis in the past. Let's just say I'm not fond of them. And if memory serves me right, neither are you."

Frankie shook his head. "Not even a little bit. Bobby, one of the brothers who died, was married to my sister. He was a real prick. A lowlife if I ever saw one."

Mrozinski nodded, then he sipped his coffee and thought. "Imagine for a minute that you're the one charged with grabbing these girls up. How do you do it? How do you target them?"

Frankie leaned back in the chair. "Good point, Mrozinski. If we figure it out from that angle, we might have something. Hard to get inside the head of someone like that, though. It makes me sick just trying."

"Me too," Mrozinski said. "Every time the subject comes up, I think of my little girls. It makes me want to do things to these guys I shouldn't even be thinking of."

"Exactly," Frankie said. "These are the kind of people I'd like to let Nicky have a go at."

Mrozinski laughed. "I don't want any parts of that, but it would be justice, wouldn't it?"

Frankie sighed. "Anyway, what have we got on locations?"

Mrozinski shuffled through the papers again. "Governor Printz, Franklin Street, 4th and Market, 28th and Market, Front Street by the Waterfront, Delaware Avenue by Orchard Street, and Baynard Boulevard by the zoo."

Frankie placed thumbtacks in a map hanging on the wall while Mrozinski read out the locations. When they were done, Frankie looked at the map and said, "No pattern that I can see. Seems to be random as hell."

"You know, Donovan, if you had told me what you were planning, I'd have taken you to another office where we *already* have a map pinned out. We left the stone age last year, and now we're trying to keep up with modern investigative techniques." Mrozinski finished his coffee. "But you're right it does look random. That's what I thought, too."

"Let's look at the nationalities again," Frankie said. "What have we got? I ask because to some people—Italian, Greek, Jew, Middle Eastern—they're all the same. All Mediterranean. To some of these porn people it's the look that matters, not the actual nationality. And until they open their mouth, it's often difficult to tell one from the other. Once I have their name, or once they start talking, I can usually tell, but until then it's tough."

Mrozinski shook his head, and he mumbled while he dug through the papers until he found what he needed. "You're worse than my brother said. Were all of you people this prejudiced?"

"Prejudiced? This isn't prejudiced. Prejudiced would be when I tell you a Polack's head was only good for driving nails because it was round as a basketball and hard as the face of a hammer."

Mrozinski laughed. "You're an asshole, Donovan." He looked down to the file again. "There were two white girls, two blacks, one from Iran, one from Vietnam, and one from China."

Frankie hit the wall. "No goddamn pattern there. What the hell? How are they deciding who to take?"

"If we could figure that out, we might have something," Mrozinski said. "But don't worry, we'll get it. I've got three other detectives working on this."

"What else?" Frankie asked.

Mrozinski looked at his file. "As far as religion goes, two were Catholic, two Baptist, two Methodist, and one Muslim. Age—three were thirteen, two were fourteen, and two were fifteen. Again, no pattern, other than the short age spread."

"And two were wealthy, the rest were middle-class or poor. Nothing to go by."

Frankie paced. "Okay, forget how they're targeted for a minute. Let's take a look at the car. I told you who owns one."

Mrozinski squinted his eyes. "Yeah, I know, Donovan, but we've got nothing on them, and no reason to suspect them. And don't forget, Raff McDermott owns one too. He's far from cleared. I've got people who say he's a known distributor of porn."

"The Campisis distribute pornography!" Frankie said, his frustration showing. "I *know* that."

"Pornography? I've seen what they sell. It's barely worse than what you get on regular TV, and it's not as bad as some of the cable stuff. I'd have a hard time calling it pornography. You were closer earlier when you called them movies of questionable quality, though that description might cover a much broader spectrum."

"Still," Frankie said. "It's worth a look. It can't hurt to see what the Campisis have been up to."

"Donovan, just because you've got a hard-on for the Campisis doesn't mean they did anything wrong. We're playing this by the numbers, and that means no 'off the books' investigations, and no harassing people for no reason."

Frankie slammed his fist on the desk. "Yeah, and in the meantime, girls lives are in danger. Or did you forget that?"

"I didn't forget, but if you go on a wild goose chase after the Campisis and turn up nothing, those girls' lives are in just as much danger. We're doing this *my* way. We're investigating. We're following leads. Let us do our job. I told you before that you could tag along, but don't get in the way."

Frankie nodded. It was a line he had delivered many times to grieving family members and friends. He took a deep breath and reached his hand out to Mrozinski. "Okay, you've got a deal. When I see you coming, I'll step aside."

"Good. You can start by stepping aside right now. Get off the Campisis. If there's something there, I'll find it."

As Frankie walked out the door and onto the street, he knew one thing—he was getting to the bottom of this with, or without, Mrozinski.

As he was getting back into the car, Mrozinski called him. "Hey, Donovan."

Frankie looked up, surprised by the visit. "What's up?"

Mrozinski handed him a folder bulging with papers. "Here's a copy of the interview reports from the initial canvass. I had made it for you earlier and forgot to give it to you." Mrozinski shrugged. "It's not that I don't trust my people, but it wouldn't hurt to have an objective eye— even if it's not that objective."

Surprised as shit, Frankie nodded. "Got it, Mrozinski. I'll let you know. And don't worry, I know your ass is on the line."

"Donovan, try to read it with both eyes open."

Frankie started to close the door, when Mrozinski said, "And thanks."

As Mrozinski walked to the front door, Murphy passed by and grabbed his arm. Murphy's face was all smiles. "Did you hear? Transfer came through. Or at least, a temporary transfer. I'm reporting to your squad in two days."

Mrozinski smiled back. "Sounds great. I could use the help. You'll be teaming up with Franklin, like we planned."

"Got it," Murphy said. "See you in two days."

Mrozinski hustled back into the station, thinking that, for once, things were going right.

∼

FRANKIE TOSSED the file onto the passenger seat and put the key in the ignition. *This was going to be a long night.*

We made damn good time, and, on the fourth day—after driving through deserts and mountains—we hit Los Angeles, sprawled out before us not long after we crested the rise out of Palm Springs. Everybody used to talk about Palm Springs as if it were a destination, when it wasn't much more than a hot, dry town in the desert where the wealthy went to play.

Once we got to the city, it didn't take long to locate a motel close to where we needed to be, and we settled in for a rest. Everyone was tired, despite having had taken turns driving. Even riding makes you tired, especially if you can't sleep, and more so when you need the air conditioner running at close to maximum just to make the temperature tolerable.

After a few cups of coffee, we pulled out notes, and a map we had picked up in a gas station just east of Palm Springs, where the outside thermometer read 112 degrees. It was so damn hot, the parking lot blacktop burnt my feet—right through my shoes. I know people talk about humidity and say, 'yeah, but it's dry heat' and shit like that, but let me tell you, when it's 112 degrees, it's *hot*. No matter how you put it—dry, humid, or some combination of both—it's *damn hot*.

In a couple of minutes—after a brief orientation—we located where we had to be. I had gotten the name from Johnny Smiles before we left, and, once we knew that, it wasn't difficult to find the company, especially knowing what business they were in.

Mezzanotte Productions occupied several buildings northwest of the city in the heart of the porn capital of the world.

"Shouldn't be tough to find," Monroe said, looking at the map.

I shook my head. "Nah. Not even with DuPree driving."

"Screw you," DuPree said.

"Be careful, DuPree. This might be a tough job. I mean you might have to make two turns."

"Screw you again."

"*DuPree,* that kind of language might offend me."

"Fuck you three times."

I laughed, joined by Monroe. "Hey, if you can't take the ribbing, you shouldn't have gotten lost in Arizona," he said. "I mean, come on, who gets lost in Arizona?"

"Fuck you too," DuPree said to Monroe. "I got us here, didn't I?"

DuPree slugged on his beer, and after a few minutes, he relaxed. "I do have a question, though. How are we gonna do all this Superman shit, then get outta here without being caught? Ain't they gonna have a description of us? Or are we wearing masks or something like that? I mean somebody's gonna see us breakin' these girls outta here."

I laughed. "Good question, DuPree. And the answer is we turn invisible."

"What the hell are you talking about?"

I set my can of beer down and turned toward DuPree. "The guy who taught me told me he had six rules, and he said that the fourth rule of murder was to learn to be invisible. Obviously, you can't be truly invisible, but what he meant was not being seen or not being noticed."

DuPree furrowed his brow and leaned backward. "I still don't know what the hell you're talking about."

I leaned back also. "There are a lot of meanings to invisible, there is the real invisible—which no one is or can be; there is the camouflaged kind, like a sniper; the stealthy kind—almost like a ninja—where you are stealthy and no one sees you; and there is the kind I like the most. The kind where you're not *noticed*—in other words, you become a different kind of invisible. You're there. You're present, right in front of people, but no one pays attention, and if they're asked afterward, they have no idea what you looked like because you weren't important enough to notice."

DuPree smiled. "So, when you're invisible, you're like the garbage man. No one knows what their garbage man looks like."

I joined DuPree in the smile. "Exactly. The garbage man, the person who waits on you at a fast-food place, a cashier at the store—any of them," I said, then got back to the business at hand.

I had tried before to get details on the company—corporate officers and such—but Mezzanotte Productions was a private company and it had no listing. Getting the address was a different matter. I got the street address an hour after Smiles told me who they were. They made it easy to get the address. I guess they didn't want to miss out on prospective customers. But they must not have wanted those customers to know who ran the company.

"I'm getting itchy," Monroe said. "I'm ready to do something."

"Take it easy," Monroe. "We'll get there."

We spent the rest of the day relaxing and planning our strategy. The biggest question was how to get inside, and how to be invisible. We still hadn't resolved that, but I was working on a plan.

The next morning, with our problem still looming ahead of us, we took a long swim and then ate breakfast. After a rest, we headed out toward Mezzanotte Productions, stopping to steal a license plate on the way.

"What are we stealing a plate for?" DuPree asked.

"In case anyone reports the car, it won't have our plates on it. Just a precaution."

"We ready to go now?" DuPree asked.

"All set. Get your ass moving."

It wasn't much of a drive, even with DuPree driving.

Once there, we sat outside and watched the cars exit the lot. It amazed me that so many people worked at a place that made these kind of movies; they *had* to know what was going on, which meant they were guilty. No matter what job you did, you were guilty of something. Working there meant that the people were either cowards or incorrigible bastards, or both. No matter the case, they should be killed, and I was happy to volunteer for the job.

After a few minutes, a dark-blue Infinity with lightly tinted windows rolled out the gate. The man driving looked to be a professional—suit, tie and requisite cap.

"Tail that one," I said.

"Why that one?" DuPree asked.

"Because it's a bigwig. There's a guy in the back seat and nobody in the passenger side. Nobody rides that way unless they are a passenger and have a driver. That man will know what we want, or who we want to talk to. Either way, we need to follow him."

"You don't think he's gonna talk, do you?" DuPree asked. "He ain't just gonna tell you what you need to know."

"I'm sure he'll be cooperative," I said. "It might take some *persuasion*, but he'll eventually see things our way."

"Fuck me!" DuPree said.

"No thanks," Monroe said. "Got enough pussy from my bitches at home."

DuPree mumbled something, then pulled away from the curb and fell a few spots behind the car.

"Not too close," I said.

"I know how to follow someone," DuPree said. "Don't need instructions from some Nazi torturer."

Monroe rolled down the window and spat. "Do what Nicky says or I'll show you what a Nazi torturer does, asshole."

"What we need to do is find out who is responsible for making these DVDs and take care of them," I said.

Take care of them how? Monroe asked.

"I think you know," I said.

"Let's presume I don't," Monroe said. "What's your solution?"

"Easy. Find out who is producing the stuff, and force the guy into giving us his customers. Then we have a talk with them if need be."

"This guy's not going to do that just because we ask," Monroe said.

"No, but if you have him lay his dick on a concrete ramp and tell him you're gonna smash it with a hammer, he sure as hell will."

DuPree winced and Monroe smiled. "Suppose he doesn't believe you?"

"If you smash a knee or an ankle beforehand, he'll believe you. Trust me. If that doesn't work, we'll try the elbows and wrists."

"You're some sick fucks," DuPree said. "Remind me never to get on your evil side."

Monroe laughed. "Nicky ain't got no evil side; he's evil through and through."

DuPree chuckled, but he cast a sideways glance at me and shuddered.

FOR A LONG TIME—MAYBE twenty miles—we tailed the guy, staying two or three cars back. We positioned ourselves so we didn't lose sight of him, but far enough back so that he would have a difficult time spotting a tail, even if he was looking for one.

After about two more miles, he slowed down. I could tell as we got closer that he was looking in his rearview mirror.

"Don't slow down," I told DuPree. "Get in the right lane and get off at the next exit."

"What for?" DuPree asked.

"Because he spotted us. Now do what I said."

DuPree kept the pace, then exited to the right. We had lost our chance on tailing him, so we called it a night.

"Son of a bitch," Monroe said. "Now what are we going to do?"

"Doesn't matter," I said. "We needed a new car anyway. We'll have to rent one tonight and use that tomorrow. He won't be expecting a new car. We'll make sure to get heavily tinted windows, too."

I rented a van using my fake ID, and I made sure it had dark tint so that our target couldn't see inside. At least from the other lane he couldn't. Monroe drove the new car and followed DuPree back to the motel. The next day, we lounged around until afternoon, then set out to intercept him along the freeway. There was no way he'd be expecting that.

We waited, with Monroe driving, and picked him up as he passed us on the freeway. We followed him for a few more miles, until he turned into a nice subdivision, where it seemed as if all the houses had hilltop views and every room had a balcony for enjoying the scenery. The driver parked the car and let the bigwig out, then he entered the house through a side door. The driver turned around and departed. I made note of the address and told DuPree to leave. "We'll come back," I said.

"Come back when?" DuPree asked.

"When we need to," I said. "Now that we have more information, I want to figure this out."

"You ain't got shit," DuPree said. "All you got is a man's address, and you don't even know who the man is."

"This is a backup plan. Not the main one," I said. "I like to have a backup plan in case the first one doesn't work. And it's good to have it in place before you start. That way, you don't rush to decisions. If the first plan doesn't work, we use this one. Besides, I don't want to kill a man if we don't have to."

DuPree gulped. "What do you mean, kill a man? Who said anything about killing a man? What the hell are we gonna kill a man for?"

Monroe laughed. "Don't start any shit, DuPree. I already told you about this. What do you think we're gonna do with him—invite him to dinner? Offer him mashed potatoes and gravy?"

"He *might* listen to reason. Or maybe we could threaten him?" DuPree said. "If he thinks we're serious, maybe he'll listen."

I looked at DuPree and shook my head. "He *won't* listen to reason, and if we threaten him, he'll tell the cops or his people at Mezzanotte. Either way, we're screwed. The bottom line is, if we question him, we have to kill him, regardless of the answers."

We spent the rest of the night cruising and talking about how we'd get into the facility. The company sat behind guarded gates, so we knew it would be difficult to get in—they didn't have guards at the gates for nothing. In the end, I decided an up-front, direct approach might be best.

~

As I sat in the room that night, I thought about what all of this meant. I was here to rescue some girls—a good thing. But to do that I knew I'd have to resort to violence—more than violence, I'd have to kill people.

I didn't *want* to kill people. I didn't *like* killing people, but some people needed killing, and nobody else was willing to do it. I wondered once again if this was God's plan for me, if He *wanted* me to kill people so He didn't have to. It was stupid to think that way, but I wondered. Even Sister Thomas seemed okay with what I was going to do. I as much as told her, and she gave her approval. Hell, even Angela said okay. That should have been enough for me.

I pondered some more, sipping on a glass of cheap Chianti, when Monroe walked in.

"What's up, Rat?"

"Just thinking, Monroe. Wondering if we're doing the right thing. Or should we turn this over to the cops? I know it's a hell of a time to be wondering this, but I'm wondering."

"Wonder all you want. I *know* I'm doing the right thing. If we turn this over to the cops the chances are they'll investigate and nothing will happen. Even if something happens, the bigwigs at Mezzanotte Productions will spend the money they're making off these girls and spring themselves.

"How's that fair? Where I grew up, if you did wrong and got caught, you were punished—by someone. It might be your mom or it might be a neighbor. It really didn't matter, what mattered was the imme-diate consequence." Monroe laughed. "Don't tell me it was any different in your neighborhood. I know better."

I took another sip of wine. "You're right. There's no doubt that these pricks need killing, I'm just wondering what gives me the right to pull the trigger, so to speak."

Monroe sat next to me and put his hand on my shoulder. "Don't matter. You might not have the *legal* right, but you sure as hell got the *moral* right. Think back to the old days of the Crusades." Monroe cocked his head back at my expression.

"What? You don't think I learned that shit? Just because I didn't go to no school with soldier queens don't mean I didn't learn nothing."

"I guess so," I said. "Although from listening to your grammar I might debate the 'don't mean I didn't learn nothing' statement."

"Eat shit," Monroe said. "Anyway, back then God had whole armies do His shit for him. Maybe now, He's just using you. So think like that. Pretend you're on a Crusade and you're as righteous as hell."

I smiled. "Monroe, I like that line of reasoning, good grammar or not."

"I'm glad," Monroe said. "Now don't ask me to tell you a lullaby or tuck you in, 'cause I ain't gonna do it. How's that for good grammar?"

I laughed. "You're a character, Monroe."

"Character or not, Rat. I'm scared. This ain't gonna be easy."

I sighed. "I know that, Monroe. Been thinkin' about it all the way out here. Not that I'm scared for myself, but I don't want to leave Angie and Rosa alone. For better or worse, they need me."

Monroe sipped on his beer. "How do you do it, Rat? How do you bury the feelings that have to be there?"

"What are you talking about?"

"The killing. I know I've got a nasty rep, but that's mostly what it is—a rep. A bad rep helps in my business. But I know you, and I've heard of the things you've done, and I've seen things you've done. How do you live with that? It's one thing to shoot somebody in self-defense, like we had to do with the drug gang, but you've killed a lot of men who never saw it comin. Don't ever tell anybody this, but I've never killed anyone except that time I was with you."

I grabbed hold of a cigarette Monroe was smoking and took a drag for the first time in years. "I just do what I have to do, Monroe. Sometimes it's hard to see what has to be done, but once I make up my mind, I do it. Simple as that."

Monroe shook his head. "Ain't nothin' simple about it, Rat."

I looked Monroe in the eyes and held his gaze. "But you're ready if need be?"

He nodded. "Don't worry about that. I'm ready. I saw that video, and what they did to Allison. Somebody's gotta pay for that. I'll catch up on sleep another time."

I smiled. "That's what I like to hear, Monroe, because I'm pretty sure you'll need to be ready."

I'M BEING FOLLOWED

*A*ngela walked out of the shop and headed south on Market Street. She only had an hour before Rosa would be home, so she had to get moving. Besides, it was a snowy day in hell when she went downtown anyway.

As she walked down the street, she noticed a guy who looked to be in his thirties staring at her from the corner of 6th and Market. When she looked his way, he shifted his gaze to something he was holding in his hand—a picture maybe.

Angela kept walking down the street, but continually glanced over her shoulder as surreptitiously as she possibly could. As far as she could tell, the guy was following her but trying his best not to make it seem that way. He stopped to look in a store window midway between 5th and 6th, where he lit a smoke before casually walking along, but all the while he kept staring at Angela. She could *feel* his presence as much as *see* him. Maybe that was something she'd picked up from Nicky, if that was possible. She'd often heard him talk about things like that.

She didn't know what to do, and since Nicky wasn't home, she couldn't get him to help. As a last resort, she got in her car and headed north to Pennsylvania Avenue then west to Union Street.

She had only gone about six blocks when she noticed the guy was still following her. She could see him in her rearview mirror each time she looked. Not knowing what else to do, she picked up the cell phone and called Nicky's burner cell number. She knew she wasn't supposed to call him, but this was one of those exceptions Nicky always talked about.

"Hello? What's up, babe? Anything wrong?"

"Someone's following me," Angela said. Her voice was controlled, but she wasn't.

"Take it easy," Nicky said, probably sensing her fear.

He tried to calm her. "Are you sure someone's following you? It might be—"

"Nicky, you taught me to be suspicious and how to tell if I was being followed. I'm telling you. *I'm being followed.*"

"Okay. I believe you. Stay calm. Slowly look around and tell me what's going on."

Angela told him everything, up to the minute. "I'm passing 6th Street now," she said. "Let me back up. I'm on Union, passing 6th. The man who has been following me—since Market Street, I might add—is about three cars back. He's wearing sunglasses and a blue collared shirt. I remember that from Market Street. I don't remember anything else."

Mrs. Robino's restaurant on Union Street

I THOUGHT FOR A MOMENT. Angie had provided a calm report of what was going on. And for someone to be following her from Market all the way to Union was more than a coincidence. Regardless, I had to find out. "Okay, listen close. Keep driving down Union and park as close as you can to the smoke shop. It's at—"

"I know where the smoke shop is."

"Good. I'll call Doggs. Somebody will be waiting for you. Park the car and go inside. They'll do the rest."

"What's going to happen? What are they going to do?"

"Don't worry about little things. Just do what I say."

"All right," Angela said. "I'll call you later."

"Great, but unless it's important, remember the deal we agreed to regarding the phones."

"I will," Angela said. "I love you."

"I love you, too. And don't worry, things will be fine."

I hung up from Angie and dialed Dogg's number. He answered right away. "What do you want, Fusco?"

I didn't like asking Doggs for anything. Despised it. But right now I had no choice. Angie might be in trouble.

"I need a favor, Doggs. I'm out of town and Angela called. She said someone is following her. I told her to go to your shop. She should be there any minute."

"My shop! What the hell for?"

"Take care of this for me, Doggs. Do it, and I'll owe you one."

A long pause followed, then Doggs said, "You already owe me more than one, but don't worry, I'll take care of it."

"Thanks," I said.

"And don't think I won't collect," Doggs said.

His last statement hit hard. I had no doubt Doggs would collect, and it would probably be something I didn't want to do, something nasty. I hated owing Doggs, but I had no choice; I *had* to protect Angie.

DOGGS HUNG UP THE PHONE, and before long Angela walked into the smoke shop. Jimmy the Gem was in front talking to Bobby Belts, so named due to his love of belts.

Somebody once said Bobby wouldn't wear the same belt more than once a month, and Knuckles and Doggs laid bets on it and kept track. Sure enough, every day for thirty-four days Bobby wore a different belt. Knuckles lost $200, Doggs won $200, and Bobby…well, Bobby had his belts, lots of belts.

Angela started to say something, but Doggs stopped her. "I just hung up from Nicky. Don't worry, Angela. We've got this covered."

Doggs nodded to Belts, who walked toward the door. "Is the guy outside?" Doggs asked.

"Parked a few spots behind me," Angela said. "He followed me from downtown. He's in a blue minivan. Chrysler, I think."

Belts returned about five minutes later, a guy about five foot ten being shoved in front of him. He wore a blue collared shirt and sunglasses, as Angela had described to Nicky.

Belts had one hand on the guy's collar. "Where you want him, Doggs?"

"This way," Doggs said, and he pushed a button, which opened a secret door on the side wall. It was a narrow door, and one that Patsy the Whale—who frequently guarded the front—often had a difficult time squeezing through, but he eventually could make it by turning sideways.

Belts followed Doggs into the room, but Doggs told Angela to wait for him out front. "In fact, you might as well go home," he said. "We'll take care of things from here. And tell Nicky we have him covered."

Angela nodded and reluctantly left to get her car. She looked all around before getting in, then started the engine and hurried off, down Union to Sycamore Street.

Doggs walked through the back room and into another with Belts following him. He stopped in front of a large wooden table. "Right here," he said.

Belts pushed the guy into an oversized wooden chair and stepped back about three feet.

Doggs approached the table, wiping steam from his glasses. "So, why were you following the girl?"

"Girl? Wasn't no girl. She's a woman, and I was just casing her joint."

Doggs laughed. "When you're as old as me, they're all girls. But really?" Doggs said. "Casing a joint on Beech Street when you've got all those mansions in Montchanin and Greenville."

The guy gave Doggs a sideways glance. "Yeah. I guess so."

"And you're not going to tell me what you were really doing following her?"

"That's it. I swear."

"I'm wondering, who do you swear to?" Doggs asked. "I bet it'll be somebody different before I'm done."

Doggs nodded then stretched his hand to the side. "Hammer, please," he said to Belts.

Belts handed Doggs a hammer.

"Nails," Doggs said.

Belts handed him about eight of the sixteen-penny nails.

"Hold him down," Doggs said, and when Belts held the guy's hands to the table, Doggs hammered nails through his palms—two in each.

The guy screamed and screamed, but no one said a word, except the guy screaming.

Doggs turned to the side, stared at Elbows and said, "Send someone to Alapocas. It needs to be ready in a couple of hours."

"You got it," Elbows said.

Bobby "Elbows" Ciccione was named for his penchant to always lean on his elbows, no matter where he sat. He'd been doing it all his life, so long, in fact, that both elbows had developed thick calluses on them, much like a dog who lies around too much.

"Hey, you gonna let me go?" the guy nailed to the bar asked. He was crying. "I didn't do nothin' but follow her."

"I'll set you free in a minute," Doggs said. "But first, *stay* there."

The comment drew a chuckle from the Gem, who had come in and was playing solitaire at one of the tables. He and Belts were the only ones around, since Elbows had left. "You need me to watch him, Doggs?"

Doggs was leaving the room. He turned to look at 'The Gem'. "Nah, but if he tries anything, you or Belts need to put another nail or two in him.

Doggs put the hammer on the ledge by the window. "And this time, try his legs. Right above the shins should do fine."

"You got it," Gem said, and moved a red nine to a row displaying a black ten.

The guy waited until Doggs left the room, then tried lifting his head to get Gem's attention. "Hey! Get me out of here before that maniac comes back. Come on, man. I'll make it worth your while."

"I'm sure you will," Gem said. "But that maniac you're referring to would kill me, so I'm not gonna do it. I'd rather be alive than rich." Gem placed a black queen on a red king. "Sit tight, though. You won't have long to wait. Doggs has a dinner meeting, and he has always been a punctual man."

Doggs returned about twenty minutes later, and he had a few guys with him. He grabbed the hammer from the sill and handed it to one of them. "Yank those nails out and load him up. Don't take long, though, I'm meeting my wife for dinner."

Gem turned to the guy and smiled. "Told ya."

In ten minutes, they were driving past the old Wanamaker's store. At the top of the hill, Doggs said, "Take a left up here and go through the woods."

About halfway through the woods, the driver pulled over. "This good?"

Doggs opened the back door. "You know it is." Then he signaled to the others. "Bring him with you. Bring the tools too."

Half a mile into the woods, Doggs stopped before a freshly dug grave. He nodded, and the men with him threw the guy in. He landed with a thud, followed by a scream and then moaning.

Doggs and the others began covering him with dirt. The guy started begging. Doggs stopped and said, "If you tell us why you were really following the girl, I might let you live. But if I don't like what you say, we'll continue filling in the hole."

The guy said "Okay, okay," while nodding. "I was told to scare her. That's all. Just scare her. I wasn't gonna touch her ever."

"Why were you following her?"

"They said they wanted her husband, Nicky, distracted. They didn't want him going to California."

"Who is *they*?" Doggs asked.

"I don't know," he said. "If I did, I'd tell you. Trust me. It was two young guys, about thirty, and some bitch."

"Why did they want Nicky distracted?"

"I don't know. I wasn't asking any fuckin' questions. Just get me out of here."

"Do you know who you were following? Do you know that she is Nicky Fusco's wife?"

The guy nodded. "That's what they said."

"Just wondered what stupidity money could buy nowadays," Doggs said. "By the way, you won't like what I'm going to do, but be thankful it's me and not Nicky. You *really* wouldn't like what he would do."

Fear covered the man's face. "Are you gonna let me out of here?"

"Sure," Doggs said, and threw a shovel of dirt into the grave. Soon, he was joined by the others. The muffled screams of the guy faded into the night.

"Clean everything up. Don't leave any traces," Doggs said. "I don't want him found. I don't even want the fuckin' worms to find him."

"You got it," Elbows said.

∾

ON THE WAY TO pick up his wife, Doggs called Nicky. "You owe me one," he said, when Nicky answered.

"Everything okay?" Nicky asked.

"For now," Doggs said. "But somebody wanted you distracted, and I don't know why. Oh, yeah. And they knew you'd be in California."

"Is that so?" Nicky said. "Very interesting. That bit of information just might help."

Nicky hung up the phone, then called Angela, despite not wanting to use the phone. He reassured her things would be all right, spoke to Rosa, then said goodnight.

Somebody had come after his family, and family was off limits. The rules had been broken. *Now, somebody is going to pay, and I have a good idea who.*

MEZZANOTTE PRODUCTIONS

*M*ezzanotte Productions sat at the top of a long, not-so-steep incline that led through hundreds of houses that had been built during the 1950s suburbia rush. A short, much-steeper hill rose to a pair of wrought-iron gates behind a typical corporate guard house manned by two guys wearing uniforms. The gates appeared to have been built for the sole purpose of keeping people out.

"Drive past slowly," I said. "I want to get a look."

I looked at the guards again and made a judgment. The uniforms they wore were a gray-brown material that resembled those worn by security guards at malls. They lacked the rich texture and luster of the county sheriff or LAPD uniforms, and they gave the appearance of being in a constant state of dirty, unwashed and wrinkled.

We slowed and drove past the facility while I scoped it out, then we parked about a block away, so as not to be conspicuous while I figured out what to do. It wasn't going to be easy to get into the building, and, as the guard house showed, Mezzanotte meant to keep it private. I suspected the inside would be as difficult, if not worse.

Finally, I hit on a plan. It wasn't much of one, but if nothing else, it would tell us how serious Mezzanotte Productions was about keeping people from entering their property. I explained the plan to Monroe and DuPree, then we circled the block.

A steady stream of high-priced cars waited patiently to get through the gates. From what I could see, once inside the gates a person had full access to at least several buildings. The problem was going to be gaining access to the area inside the gates.

We entered the back of the line and waited our turn. When we reached the gate, a guard asked to see our IDs. I pretended to look for mine, then said, "Damn, I can't find mine. I'll bring you back a copy in a minute."

"Sorry, buddy," the guard said, "but that's not how it works, and I don't know you."

I put on my best smile. "Sure you do. I started working for Bob last week, over in engineering. I've got a card but I must have left it at Janice's house." I laughed. "Good Lord, though, don't tell Bob. He'll have a shit-fit." I turned to Monroe and laughed again. "That's all I need." Then I turned back to the guard. "Of course, considering the way Janice looks, I'm lucky that's all I left."

The guard poked his head inside the car window and peeked around. He looked like one of those emus at a drive-through animal park.

After a moment, he gestured with his head to Monroe. "Who are you?"

"Morgan," Monroe said. "I work with Bob too, but unfortunately, I ain't fucking Janice."

The guard laughed at that. I think it was the statement that got us in. "Okay," he said. "But you better have your card tomorrow."

"Don't worry. I'll have it," I said, and drove through the gate.

When we got in, I looked around to familiarize myself with the area.

The landscaping was what I expected, indigenous flora surrounded by rocks of all sizes, thick green grass, and hidden cameras that were not so hidden, accompanied by obtrusive floodlights that undoubtedly disrupted the area's nighttime peace.

It was everything you'd expect of a flourishing young business in Los Angeles, which translated to *fake*. Everything I'd seen since I arrived had looked the epitome of new and successful. The trouble was, it was all *fake*.

I'd rather see a new business made up of a couple of old offices decorated with used furniture and set in a ramshackle building built in the early twentieth century. That kind of setting might inspire confidence. At least I wouldn't wonder about who controlled the finances.

We parked in front of the first building and worked our way inside. It was crowded, and even though there were more guards, no one questioned us. I guess the gate access was the most controlled. Sort of a "once you were in, you were in" kind of mentality.

After we were inside, I began looking for the production department. If anyone knew where the girls were being kept, it would be them.

We navigated two halls and passed a dozen people. About halfway down a long hallway, a guy wearing a dark-blue suit with an open-collar white shirt approached. He had a gun on his hip and it was unholstered. It looked to be a .38. Might have been an ex-cop, used to the feel of the piece.

Most amateurs went for the big items—.44s or .45s—not realizing that they were so big it was like trying to shoot a cannon. The ones who carried .38s, though, they usually knew what they were doing and how to handle them.

"Looking for something?" the guy asked.

I needed to bluff our way out of this if possible. "Maybe," I said. "If you can point me to engineering that would help."

He looked at me suspiciously, then brushed his hand against a device on his belt. It was about the size of a pager, but it was something else.

When he removed his hand, there was a red light glowing on the left side that hadn't been glowing before. He then moved his hand to the hilt of the gun he carried.

"I *could* point you to engineering, but I won't. I'm afraid that's exactly what you want me to do."

Just then, three more suits came around the corner, guns drawn.

The guy in front of me drew his gun. "Okay," he said. "Hands up and no funny moves. Don't make this worse than it needs to be."

The next thing I knew, we were sitting in a holding cell in the county jail. We hadn't been printed, which was good, as it hinted at the possibility that this was simply a scare tactic, and we'd be released soon.

"What the hell are we gonna do now?" DuPree said.

"I know a guy who might help," Monroe said.

"That guy won't do us any good if he's back in Wilmington," I said.

"He's here," Monroe whispered. "And he has a lot of connections. He might be able to get us out of here and—even better—into Mezzan-otte Productions."

"That would be sweet if he could," I said. "But how's he gonna manage that? And why the hell didn't you say anything before this?"

"He's filthy rich and into porn, but it's soft porn, not the hard-core stuff. And I didn't say anything because we didn't need anyone else knowing our business. But now…"

"How rich, and how do you know him?" I asked. "And, more impor-tantly, can you trust him?"

"Filthy rich—like more than $100 million—and I know him 'cause we did a nickel together a long time ago, so yeah, we can trust him."

"What was he in for?"

"Statutory rape," Monroe said. "But it ain't like it sounds. He was twenty and she was seventeen. Unfortunately, he happened to be in a state where the age of consent was eighteen—and her father had friends—hence, the nickel."

"Bad judgment or bad luck or both," I said. "It doesn't matter. How's that going to help us?"

"I'm sure he's got enough legal juice to spring us from here, and as far as getting into Mezzanotte, we could send him in and have him pretend to want to 'buy' a special production, one featuring fifteen-year-olds, and maybe even a particular nationality.

"If he says he's willing to pay big money for it, I can't see them refusing. And if they check him out—which I'm sure they'll do—they'll see more than enough money combined with a prior sex-crime history. If they just look at the record on the surface, I think all it shows is 'sexual predator' designation—pedophile stuff."

I thought for a moment, then laughed. "I knew there was a reason why I liked you, Monroe. Let's give your friend a call. The only question I've got is why you didn't think of this *before* we got tossed in jail."

"Maybe because I'm a little slow," Monroe said, "but I kick it into high gear under pressure. Or maybe it's because I didn't want to broadcast what we were doing, as I said earlier."

Monroe got the guard to let him make a call. He waited for privacy, then dialed Farouk's number that he had in his cell phone contacts.

The phone rang several times before anyone answered. "Hello?"

"Farouk Mazullah?" Monroe said.

A deep, baritone voice said, "This is he."

"Farouk, you old dog. This is Monroe."

There was a slight pause, then recognition. "Monroe! Where are you? Are you here? In California?"

"Damn near outside your door. Want to meet for a cup of coffee?"

"Name the place and time. I'll be there."

"We're over in the San Fernando Valley now, so anything close by here would be great. There's only one catch: I'm in jail with a couple of my friends. Anything you can do to help?"

"Which jail?" Farouk asked.

Monroe filled him in, and Farouk said, "No problem. Sit tight, and I'll send someone over. It won't be long. And I'll send over a different legal team so they don't know it's from me."

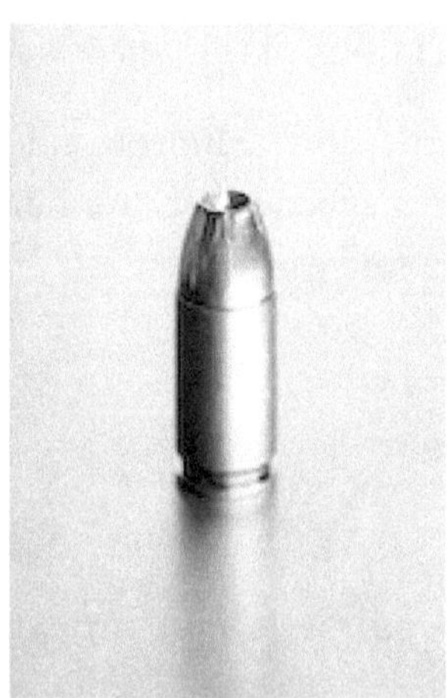

True to his word, Farouk's high-priced legal counsel had us walking in a few hours. We went back to the hotel to regroup, and the next morning, we met at a coffee shop at the southern end of the Valley.

The coffee shop was crowded, at least twenty people inside, and another dozen or so at tables enjoying the breezy day. It would have been easy to eavesdrop on someone, but then you wouldn't be able to tell who was eavesdropping on you.

Already-read newspapers were scattered about, littering tables as if someone still occupied the chairs, and sitting under benches as if they'd just been dropped. The new-copy rack was long since emptied, so if you wanted to read, a used paper would have to suffice.

Rows of pastry sat on the shelves, a telltale sign of it being stale. If the pastry had been fresh it would have sold long ago.

"I'll have a raspberry scone," I said.

"Fat chance," the young girl said. The scones and cinnamon twists sold out early, even the stale ones. All that's left are nondescript pastries that no one wants or even knows what they are. Oh, and there are a few sandwiches that either were fed to the homeless or given to the airlines."

"Are you like this with all of your customers?" I asked.

She smiled. "It's my last day."

I placed an order for drinks and left it at that. Then we carried them to a table and took seats. The coffee was burnt, which I could tell from the orders being placed by the people ahead of me. Hardly anyone ordered plain coffee—most opting for lattes or cappuccinos, or something that would hide the burnt taste of a regular brew.

It was a sad statement of American life that the well-established coffee bar of Italy had given way to the gathering place of American cities. Regardless, that's where millions of people decided to stop for their pick-me-ups.

When Farouk arrived, Monroe introduced us, and over a few cups of espresso, I told Farouk what we wanted.

"We need to find out where they're keeping these girls," I said. "If not where, then we need to know *who* knows where."

"That shouldn't be too difficult," Farouk said. "But it *is* going to cost me some face. These are powerful people you're messing with."

I took a sip of possibly the worst espresso I'd ever had and looked over the rim of the cup. "I can't pay you, and since this isn't my town, my 'owe you one' won't count for much, but I'll owe you one all the same."

Farouk smiled. "That's all I need. Monroe has told me many stories of 'The Rat.' Consider that we have a deal."

I smiled. "Thanks, Farouk. I owe you one." I laughed. "Had to say it to make the deal formal."

We finished our espresso, suffered through another, then filled Farouk in on what we wanted him to do. His part would be critical, but he seemed to think it wouldn't be a problem.

"I've done this before. Not with Mezzanotte, and not with such hardcore stuff, but that all might play into our hands."

I nodded and stared at Farouk. "Just do the part you rehearsed and everything will be fine. They're not turning you in for asking them to do what they do. At worst, we'll get a 'no,' and at best, we'll get a location for the girls. Even a 'no' will tell us something. At this level, the 'no' will have to come from someone with juice, and when it does, we'll have him."

"I like that," Monroe said. "Slicker than cat shit."

I said, "I don't know how slick cat shit is, but thanks—I guess."

Farouk left to meet someone, and we stayed for yet another round of shitty coffee.

"So, what's the plan now?" DuPree asked. "Do we sit and wait for Farouk, or do we try something else. 'Cause sure as shit, the last try didn't work."

"We wait for Farouk," I said.

Farouk was presenting us with the perfect opportunity to become invisible, even if he didn't realize it, and I was not going to let it slip through my fingers.

All the way out from Delaware, I had thought of how to be invisible, and now Farouk was handing that to us on a golden platter. If we went in as his "production supervisors" then for all intents and purposes, we were invisible. No one would look twice at us. And, we would have full access to the girls, and the rest of the facilities. What more could we ask for.

I climbed back into the car, taking the passenger seat across from Monroe. DuPree was in the back today. I turned to him and said, "To get back to your question, DuPree. Our initial foray didn't work, yes, but part of the 'why' might have been because they were expecting us. Smiles must have told them we were coming, which is why Angela was followed. *Somebody* alerted Mezzanotte, and Smiles is the only one who knew, other than people I trust completely."

Monroe shook his head slowly. "Fuckin' Smiles. We should have done something about that."

"We're going to," I said. "Call Dixon. Have him get in touch with me."

"You sure about this?" Monroe asked.

"Sure as shit," I said. "Make the call."

Monroe made the first call on his burner and two hours later, my phone rang. I didn't like making a connection via the phone, but it had to be done. "Hello?"

"It's Dixon."

"Where are you?" I asked.

"Down on Madison, hangin' out."

"Get over to Johnny Smiles' place, up by 10th Street at DuPont. You know where it is?"

"I can find it."

"Good. Call me when you get there."

"You got it. I'll call soon."

A half hour later, Dixon called back. "Are you there?" I asked.

"Sittin' in the kitchen," Dixon said.

Dixon was efficient. "Give Smiles the phone" I said.

"What?" Johnny Smiles said. "Who's this?"

"This is Nicky. Why did you let them know we were coming?"

"I didn't let them know," Smiles said.

"Then who did you tell, because they *knew* we were coming? Which means *somebody* told them."

"I didn't tell no one. I swear."

"You shouldn't swear, Johnny, especially when it isn't true."

"I didn't tell anybody," Smiles said.

"Look at it this way," I said. "Nobody but Monroe, DuPree, and me knew the name of the place we were going—oh, and you. And Monroe and DuPree are with me, so I'm sure it wasn't them. That only leaves you, so tell me *why* you told them."

A long hesitation, then, "I didn't think you'd mind. What difference does it make? You were going anyway."

"You're probably right. It doesn't make much difference to me, but you shouldn't have involved my family. For that you're going to pay."

Then, I said, "Give the phone back to Dixon."

"What do you mean? I'm sorry, Nicky. I didn't mean anything."

"Give the phone to Dixon," I said.

"What?" Dixon said.

"Give Smiles a message for me," I said.

"What kind of message?" Dixon asked.

"The kind that says he shouldn't have talked. The kind of message that makes sure he will *never* talk again."

"Got it," Dixon said. "See ya when you get back."

DuPree sat on the other side of the room, listening. "That was cold. You could've just kicked his ass."

"That's true," I said, "but then he could have done the same thing to me or someone else some other time, and he would have. Now, he'll never do that again."

DuPree nodded. *Fuckin' cold. That's what it is.*

I NEED A FEW FILMS

"How do we work this?" Farouk asked. "I know what you need, but what do you want me to do? I won't go back to prison for you, but anything short of that, just ask."

"Do you know anyone who can vouch for you?" I asked. "They're going to check you out; I'm sure of it."

"I know Chuck Paluska. He's a good friend. He has plenty of connections and, he knows everyone in this business."

"How well do you know him? Can you trust him? Do you know his family?"

"I can trust him. I had dinner at his house a week ago."

"All right, see if he's okay with you using his name, but ask him to be ready to cover for you in case they check. And don't forget we're gonna need the names of who to deal with. See if your buddy Chuck can get those."

Two hours later, and with no more than a few calls, Farouk had the name and number he needed. He went to the living room to place the call to Mezzanotte Productions. Meanwhile, we sat in the kitchen drinking coffee.

"You think it will work?" DuPree asked.

"It better work," Monroe said. "It's the only plan we've got."

"It'll work," I said. "Don't worry."

Farouk dialed the number his contact had given him. A man answered within a few rings.

"Hello?"

"Calvin Finestro, please," Farouk said. His voice was silky smooth with just a hint of a Middle Eastern accent.

"Who is this?"

"Farouk Mazullah. Chuck Paluska gave me your name and number."

"Chuck Paluska. How is he? How's his wife, Margie?"

"I don't know about Margie. I never met her, but his wife Susanna is fine."

There was a pause at the end of the line, followed by a chuckle. "Can't blame me for testing. What can I do for you?"

"Nothing," Farouk said. "But thank you anyway."

"What's the matter?" Finestro's tone held a taunt. "Upset that I challenged you?"

"On the contrary, I expected nothing less. But you should keep up with things; Chuck's wife, Susanna, or should I say *former* wife, left him two weeks ago," Farouk said. "But as I mentioned, she *is* doing fine."

"Shit. I didn't know. If you'll consider that a temporary error, I'll see what I can do for you."

"I'll call you tomorrow," Farouk said. "This might take more checking. But give me a different number. I don't like to call the same phone more than once."

Calvin gave him a new cell phone number and suggested he call around 2:00 p.m.

Farouk walked into the kitchen with a smile on his face. "Consider us in the movie business. I'm supposed to call tomorrow at 2:00."

Nicky jumped up and high-fived him. "Way to go, Farouk. I knew you could do it."

"I told you he was good," Monroe said. "Do a nickel with me and *somethin'* is gonna wear off."

Nicky laughed. "Monroe, give the man credit. He did his job."

"Now that we've gotten this far, what do you want me to do?" Farouk asked. "At this point, I think I can get anything. He was embarrassed."

"Then let's go for the gold," Nicky said. "Negotiate a financial deal for the movies, then insist on two of your people being present during shooting. That'll be me and Monroe. And tell them you don't want any blacks in the first movie. Tell them your people are prejudiced against blacks and only want Asians."

Nicky looked sideways to Monroe, who was staring at him. "We don't want them torturing Allison again. Not if we can help it. I hate to do it to the Asians or whoever, but if we're gonna bust the girls out of here, somebody's got to pay."

Monroe nodded. "You don't hear no complaints from me. Do what you have to do, Rat."

"What else?" Farouk asked.

"If you can, I also need some pipe bombs," Monroe said. "Maybe ten. And they need to be loud and powerful."

"I don't know if—"

"Don't give me that shit," Monroe said. "You're a fuckin' Arab. Your people know bombs like my people know watermelons. Just get the goddamn bombs."

Farouk sighed and turned his head. "Okay. Will ten be enough? Because I'm not going back for more."

"It better be," Monroe said. "Or there will be a lot of bodies out there."

"We need something else to convince them of who they're dealing with," Nicky said. "Get Calvin over here for discussions. I've got a plan." He then told Farouk, Monroe, and DuPree what he had in mind.

When he was finished explaining, Farouk said, "I can get everything. Have no worries. Be here tomorrow by 5:00. I'll tell them to arrive at 7:00."

"Sounds good," Monroe said, and they left.

THE NEXT DAY at precisely 2:00, Farouk called the number Calvin had given him.

"Hello?"

"Calvin, this is Farouk Mazullah. We spoke yesterday."

"Yes?"

"I've decided to move forward with our planned partnership. Perhaps we should meet to discuss it."

"And where do you have in mind?"

"My house is fine. I'm alone, so we won't be bothered."

Calvin said, "I'll be bringing an associate if that's all right."

"I don't care who you bring. Just tell me how many so I can advise the chef." He provided Calvin an address, then said, "Be here at 7:00 sharp, if you don't mind; Carlos despises it when his food is served cold."

"We'll be there."

Farouk called Monroe and told him everything was set. "Don't forget to be here early," he said.

DuPree pulled into the driveway about forty-five minutes early.

"Park in the garage," Monroe said. "Farouk doesn't want them to see the car."

DuPree pulled into the garage. They entered the house through the back door.

It took about half an hour to prepare, then they waited around, drinking wine and chatting until the guests arrived—about 6:50.

"Welcome to my home," Farouk said, as he opened the door. "Or if either of you speak Arabic, "*Ahlaan wasahlaan bik fi manzali.*" He bowed his head.

Calvin bowed his head slightly, then lumbered in, trailed by a muscular man who appeared to be in his twenties. Calvin stretched out his meaty hand. "I'm Calvin Finestro," he said, "and this is George

Shank. I don't know any Arabic, but I'm pleased to meet you. And thank you for having us over."

"As I am pleased to meet you," Farouk said, and bowed.

They followed him to the kitchen, where Nicky, Monroe, and DuPree were sitting around the table.

"I thought this was a private dinner," Calvin said, with a hint of suspicion.

"It *is* private," Farouk said. "Since you mentioned you were bringing an associate, I decided to invite a few of mine."

Calvin showed a quick smile and nodded to the men seated at the table.

"Let's get on with business," he said. "I'm assuming we can discuss business in front of them."

Farouk laughed. "By all means. They are well aware of my proclivities and have even participated on occasion."

"Good, then why don't you spell out what you want while you pour a glass of red," Calvin said.

Farouk laughed. "Red it will be," he said, and reached for an open bottle that was sitting on the island.

"As to what I want, it's fairly simple. I need a total of three films. The first starring Asians, the second Latinos, and the third Anglos or Middle Easterners. And all of the girls must be under the age of sixteen."

Calvin took a long slow sip. "That's a pretty strong request, my friend. And as I'm sure you realize, it's illegal."

"If it's too strong, let me know. We can enjoy the dinner and the wine and go separate ways. I can do business elsewhere. This is not an inexpensive operation, and I'm sure I can find others who are willing to participate."

"When you say 'not inexpensive,' what figure did you have in mind?"

"For all three films, I expect it will be about six million. Of course, that's with no locks. We will assure the films won't be copied more than three times."

Calvin sighed. "That's a lot of money, but it's also a lot of risk. Even if I could grant you what you want, how do I know I can trust you?"

Farouk laughed. "Trust? Is that all that is separating us?" He walked across the kitchen to the table, pulled a gun and shot DuPree in the side of the head.

Blood splattered everywhere. The chef ran in from the other room.

"Is everything all right, Mr. Mazullah?"

"Fine, Carlos. Go back to work. You saw nothing."

Nicky and Monroe stood against the wall, hands by their chests.

"What the hell did you do?" Calvin asked. "What *the hell* did you do?"

Farouk stepped over to DuPree's body, lying on the floor. He pulled out his license, a California driver's license that claimed him to be Charles Jackson. He handed the license to Calvin. "Now you have something on me," he said. "You witnessed me commit murder."

Calvin handed the license back to Farouk. "I don't need this."

George stood wide-eyed behind Calvin, but then Calvin slowly regained his composure. Finally he cracked a smile. "I like the way you do business, Farouk. I think we'll do fine together. It's a shame about Mr. Jackson, though."

"No matter," Farouk said. "He had gotten sloppy of late anyway."

"Sloppiness cannot be tolerated."

"Good, it seems as if we understand each other. Based on this, I'll assume we have a deal. But remember, even though you have something on me, it also means I have a reason to want you to disappear;

you saw me commit a gruesome murder so don't get any ideas of crossing me."

"No fear of that," Calvin said, then he patted George on the head. "And George here is as tight-lipped as a mute."

"Good to know," Farouk said. "I've always been fond of mutes."

"One more thing. I would like my two associates to be present during production. And I want it soon. Asians first."

"Fine, presuming a twenty-five percent down payment can be arranged."

"You'll have it by week's end," Farouk said. "Just tell me how to address the check and to whom. It will be there on Friday by special messenger. Then we can agree on twenty-five percent at the completion of each…shall we say…project?"

Calvin smiled. "Agreed. I like doing business this way."

"As do I," said Farouk. Then he spread his hands wide. "Shall we eat?" He gestured to Nicky. "Please clean up this mess and tell Carlos we're ready. And tell him I apologize for keeping him waiting."

"Yes, sir," Nicky said, and he and Monroe grabbed hold of DuPree and dragged him across the kitchen.

Half an hour later, Calvin stood. "It's time for me to go," he said. "Tell Carlos that dinner was magnificent, and the wine selection was superb."

"I'm glad you enjoyed it," Farouk said. "And don't forget to call tomorrow with the details. Presuming everything is all right, the messenger will be there on Friday."

"I'm sure it will be fine," Calvin said. "I simply have to get approval from the board. We'll meet tomorrow, and I'll call by 1:00."

"Talk to you then," Farouk said. They shook hands and he escorted Calvin to the door. George followed him out.

Ten minutes later, when they were sure Calvin was gone, Nicky, Monroe, and DuPree came back into the kitchen.

"Farouk, you were perfect," Monroe said.

"Thank you. I tried."

"You looking to get in the movies?" Monroe asked.

Farouk smiled. "One does not spend this much time in Hollywood without *some* aspiration of acting."

"You'd get my vote," DuPree said. "For a minute there, I thought the gun might really be loaded."

"He didn't suspect a thing," Nicky said. "Did you see his face when you supposedly shot DuPree?"

"Shit, it even scared me," DuPree said. "He had me convinced."

"The gentleman I used for this does special effects for a few of the Hollywood studios. He knows what he's doing. I've been to a few of his rehearsals, and I was convinced that things happened when they never did."

"Some amazing shit," Monroe said.

"Yes, it is," Farouk said. "But that's enough of this congratulatory talk. Let's get ready for the next phase."

Monroe grabbed another bottle of wine and plopped in his chair. "Fill up this glass. I'm ready."

A PHONE CALL FROM ANGELA

espite Monroe's pessimistic attitude, I was celebrating, internally at least. Farouk had done a good job and it looked like we were going to have a way to get "in" with Mezzanotte Productions. Not an easy thing to do. That didn't guarantee anything, but at least it got us a foot in the door.

I was sitting on the edge of the bed, sucking on a beer and feeling generally upbeat, when the phone rang. I jumped, startled, as I wasn't expecting any calls.

I looked at the caller ID. It was Angela. *What the hell was she doing calling again?*

I picked up the phone. "Everything all right?" I said.

"Fine. Fine. I just wanted to call. See what you were doing."

"I'm not doing anything. Monroe and I are trying to figure out how to get these girls out of here."

"Girls? How many? I thought you just went to get Rosa's friend."

"Angela, I told you there were several of them, and you knew I wasn't coming for Allison and leaving the others."

"What are you going to do? How long will you be? When are you coming back?"

"Angela, that's a lot of questions, and I have no intentions of answering them all. As to how long we'll be, I don't know. And those three words are the best answer I can give for all of your questions. I don't know what I'm going to do, so I don't know how long I'll be, and since I don't know how long I'll be, I don't know when I'll be coming back. There. I said I wasn't going to answer all of your questions and I did anyway."

I breathed deeply. "When we get the girls, we'll come home, but I don't know when we'll get them." *Or how.*

"Nicky, I might have been hasty in telling you to go to California. I've been hearing more about this case, and it sounds dangerous. Maybe you should come home."

"I can't do that, Angela. And you know it."

"What do you mean, can't? Of course you can. Just pack up and leave."

"Angie, do you remember a few weeks ago when you were doing dishes, and you dropped the wine glass on the floor?"

"Of course, I do. How can I forget? You threw a fit."

"I didn't throw a fit. I told you to be more careful, that's all. Anyway, that's beside the point. If you remember, you dropped the glass and tried to catch it. You missed, and it fell anyway."

"I remember. So what?"

"The point is that once that glass fell, it was gone. It's no different than you telling me to get Allison. From the minute you told me to go, it was a done deal. You can't call me back. You can't ask me to do something, then tell me not to. It doesn't work that way. I told you I'd do it, and I'm doing it."

I let silence fall for a moment, then said, "Besides, these girls are counting on me. They might not know it yet, but they are, and I'm not about to let them down. I came here to do something. Now, I'm going to get it done."

"Nicky, I'm scared. I don't want anything to happen. If you know where the girls are, tell the cops. Let them handle it. The Los Angeles police are supposed to be good. I'm sure they'll do a wonderful job."

"There is no 'handling it.' These movie people have money and lots of it. In L.A., money is everything. If I let the cops handle it, the movie people will probably get away with a fine, which means Mezzanotte Productions will be a little poorer, and the cops—or somebody—will be a little richer, and the girls will still be locked up and used in ways that nobody should be. Nothing will have changed."

"And what do you think you can do? You're not an avenging angel, you know."

"I don't know what I'm going to do yet, but I'll do something. I promise, I'm gonna do *something*."

~

I HUNG up and sat down, thinking. Then, I dialed Monroe's room and had him come over.

Ten minutes later, he knocked on my door. I shoved a cold beer into Monroe's hand and asked him to sit.

"We're gonna need a few silencers," I said. "I didn't think we would, figuring the noise might work better in L.A., but now I'm not so sure. We might want to try a different approach. Besides, if we need noise, we'll have the bombs."

"What about hand-made silencers?"

"I want professional ones. If I don't want noise, then I don't want noise. The pop is too loud on the hand-made ones—at least the ones I've seen. Maybe somebody can do it, but why risk it if we can get real ones? See if Farouk can get a few."

"I'm sure he can get them," Monroe said, "Farouk can get anything. But why do you think we'll need them?"

"Because we're going into buildings where *work* might have to be done in stages, in different parts of the building. I don't want the other guards to know we're there, or what we're doing. If we use silencers, they probably won't. Not necessarily, but probably."

"Good enough for me," Monroe said. "I'll call Farouk. How many? Three?"

"Might as well, and call him now," I said. "We don't have time to waste."

"How many guards do you think they'll have?" Monroe asked.

"I don't know," I said, "but we'll find out before we go. I'm sure Calvin will tell us. In fact, I know he will."

"And you think he'll just tell us?"

"No, but using a little 'blunt persuasion' might help."

Monroe smiled. He knew what I was referring to, because we had DuPree buy an extra hammer at the Home Depot today. He bought it along with a few other tools so that it wouldn't be flagged for an individual purchase, still, it was a risk I didn't like taking.

Regardless, the hammer would be gotten rid of when we were finished with it. Nobody would find it. I'd make sure of that.

"How are we going in?" Monroe asked.

I thought for only a moment. "I figured you and I would go in first, leaving DuPree to watch the outside. It's not that I don't trust DuPree, but I don't want to rely on him."

"I'm with you on that," Monroe said. "He's a good guy, and I don't think he'd ever betray me, but I don't want to be counting on him for anything serious."

I smiled. "We're on the same page then."

"Same fuckin' paragraph," Monroe said.

"So, we go in the first target building, take out the guards—no matter what it requires—and then move on to the girls. I figure we'll have to use a little force to extricate the girls, but again, we'll do what it takes. I figure they can't have more than five or six guards. A lot, but not too many, especially with the bombs from Farouk—if we need them."

"Between the silencers and the bombs, they don't stand a chance," Monroe said. "What about after we get the girls?"

"Take them to a motel, let them wash up, then move them to the bus station and send them home. Allison and the other Wilmington girls will be with us."

Monroe grinned. "Sounds like a plan I can live with. We're gonna have to do something about them keepin their mouths shut, but I'm ready."

I thought for another moment, then said, "We'll have to figure out what we want them to tell the cops. In the meantime, let's go over the details one more time. If anything happens to me, you need to be able to get these girls out and get home safely."

"Ain't nothin' happenin' to you, Rat. If it does, I'll blow up the whole compound. Down to the last bush."

I laughed about it, but I was afraid he was serious. He'd do it.

Either way you looked at it, we had it mapped out. Farouk had a job to do, Monroe and I had ours, and DuPree had his. Unless something went drastically wrong, we were set.

DuPree joined us, already drinking a beer. "We got a plan yet?"

"Mapped it out already, DuPree. We'll take care of Calvin, spring the girls, take care of the board, then go home." I turned and looked at Monroe. "Ain't that right, Monroe?"

"You got that shit," he said.

"We might reverse that and kill the board first, but either way will work."

I felt good now that I had it mapped out. I picked up the phone and called Angela. "Okay, Babe. I'm set. I should be on my way home early in the week."

"Really? That's great, Nicky. I can't wait. I'll make ravioli and have it ready for you."

"Make enough for Monroe and DuPree also. They'll be joining us."

"Okay, see you then."

"And don't forget to use my phone."

"I won't."

"Using your phone at home is all well and good," Monroe said, "but if anyone checks, they're gonna be wondering who she was talkin' to in California. And when they see it's a burner, they're gonna get damn suspicious. Of course, it's a far cry from proving anything, but no sense in leading them to a scent if you don't have to."

"I got that covered, Monroe. I only talk to her once in a blue moon, and then not for long. She could explain it any way she wants. She's even got a friend out here who would vouch for her. I had her cover that before we left."

Monroe nodded. "Okay. Just checking. But that makes me think that I should have Farouk vouch for me if I need it."

"Wouldn't be a bad idea," I said.

Whenever a situation like this arose, I bought burners and left my phone at home.

Angela would occasionally browse the mobile sites I normally do and call the people I typically talked to just to have it on file.

She would dial her own number, too, and just sit for ten or fifteen minutes so that it appeared as if we were talking. And she'd call Frankie and Doggs and a few others that I knew I could count on. It was a good plan that hadn't failed me yet. I didn't plan on having it fail anytime soon.

THE CONNECTION

*A*fter they got back to the station, Sherri said, "What do you think, Lou?"

"I think you should have taken a left and cut through the park. You would have avoided the ever-present traffic jam at the expressway if you did."

"I didn't mean that, and you know it."

"What were you talking about? Did you mean what did I think of the fruits at the gallery?"

"Lou, you can't talk like that."

"Why not? That's what they were."

"Santiago wasn't gay, besides, if they were black, would you have called them 'spades' or 'spooks'?"

"Probably. Maybe not with you here, but that's not the point. I didn't mean anything by it. No hard feelings. It's just what they are, like an Irishman is a mick, an Italian a dago, a German a kraut, or a Puerto

Rican a spic. It's just that you young people take things the wrong way.

"And I didn't say Santiago was a fruit, I was talking about Wentworth and the other fruits at his gallery."

Sherri shook her head. "Mazzetti, you're a mess."

"Hey, I don't mean anything by it. My best friend is a potato-picking mick, and that's what I call him. And he calls me a dirty wop, dago. We don't take offense, just laugh it off."

"Lou, I know you don't mean anything by it, but I don't want to see your last few months go sour because of something you said. It could ruin thirty years of good work."

Mazzetti lowered his head. "Okay. Point taken. I'll watch my mouth."

"You can watch your mouth, but not my ass." Sherri said, and laughed.

"Goddamn! Now you're going too far. If I can't look at your ass, I might as well go blind."

Sherri laughed. "Mazzetti, you're a dinosaur, but I love you."

"Do you love me enough to—"

"No!"

"Shit, Miller. You're no fun. Keep it up and I might turn you in for sexual harassment, talking to me that way."

"Oh, that'll be the day," Sherri said. "Mazzetti the Mouth turning me in. Snow would fall in July."

"Lieutenant Morreau walked in. "Mazzetti, you're up. Got another body about two blocks from the Met. A lot like Ramirez and Monfrer —rich, presumably gay, and hooked up with the charities."

"What? What the hell is going on down there?

"Probably haven't had three bodies in ten years down there, and now we've got three in the same week."

"And all high-profile cases," Sherri said. "We need to find the killers quickly."

~

CHIP FARMINGTON LAY face down in a pool of blood and sludge in the alley. His head had been bashed in, and there was a hole where it looked like a single GSW had entered by the nape of the neck.

"Looks like he never saw it coming," Sherri said.

"He didn't—unless he had eyes in the back of his head—literally, and from what I can see, he didn't. He's got a hole now," Lou said, "but no eyes."

"You're a sick son of a bitch," a uniformed cop at the scene said.

"I know that. Now tell me who found the body?"

"A passerby," the cop said. "Called it in about an hour ago."

"We got any idea what…" Lou looked at his notes. "Mr. Farmington was doing down here?"

The uni shook his head. "None. And his wallet is intact, plus he's wearing a watch that's probably worth a year's salary."

"Looks like another dump job," Sherri said. "There's definitely not enough blood for him to have been shot here."

"More than likely the same killer with the same motive as our other victim. So as soon as we figure out what that motive is, the better. Better yet, once we figure out who the *killer* is the better."

"Damn, you're sharp, Mazzetti. It's no wonder you've got a gold shield. And to think people say you just got it because you're old."

"Screw you, Miller. When you get a better suggestion, speak up. Oh, and when you make second grade, shout, though I doubt they'll ever be that desperate.

"By the way, we spoke to Farmington's wife and friends. His wife wasn't much nicer than Ramirez's, but she hid it better. His friends were a different story, and each one was eager to bury him.

"He liked boys," one friend told us. "Though whether you called them 'boys' or 'young men' was a matter of taste — and, I guess, a matter of law. Most of them fell into the sixteen to twenty range, usually Anglican, and always street boys."

"And what about his wife?" Sherri asked. "From what I can tell from talking to people, Sharon, his wife, knew of his preferences. And I don't think she cared. As long as good old Chip paid the bills — and there were plenty of them — she was happy. Well, maybe not happy, but satisfied."

"And who was keeping her satisfied?" Lou asked. "Anybody special on her end? If so, we need to find that out."

"None that I know of, or at least no one is saying. Seems like Mrs. Farmington was more interested in clothes and jewelry, and the Mister gave her plenty of both. Friends said he needed someone to hold his arm when he attended events. She was more than willing to do that. She just wanted to look good doing it."

"Any 'special' boys Chip was fond of?" Lou asked.

"I don't know about 'special,' but he was frequently seen with Paul Raymond, according to Mrs. Nightshaw. Paul is a good-looking young man, about nineteen or twenty. Lives over in Chelsea and hangs out with the well-to-do crowd."

"Does Paul play for both teams or is he strictly with the guys?"

"Not only is he strictly with the guys, but the word is, he is only a 'catcher,' if you get my drift."

"Did you get an address on Raymond?"

"I know where he hangs out, but no address," Sherri said. "I thought we'd cruise on by."

"Whatever you got, helps," Lou said, and took out his notepad. "I better write this down so it looks like I was doing something."

"If someone sees you writing it might look suspicious," Sherri said, with a laugh.

WHERE PAUL HUNG out turned out to be a coffee shop next to a gay bar. To a knowledgeable observer, it looked as if it would be an ideal pick-up spot for young hustlers, and the word on the street confirmed it.

Lou found Paul chatting up a meticulously dressed middle-aged gentleman. He walked up to Paul and showed his badge. "I need a minute for a few questions," Lou said.

Paul nodded and followed him outside. "What do you need?"

"Do you know Jacques Monfrer or Manual Ramirez?"

"I know them, but you're tossing around some big names, Detective. Why? What did they do?"

"Got themselves killed," Lou said. "Now, try answering the questions. You can do it here, or at the station."

"What?" Raymond seemed genuinely shocked. "I hadn't heard, but if they're dead, someone was probably blackmailing them. In my opinion, both men were great people. Kind. Generous and giving. Never mean to anyone. Somebody went after them because they were gay. I'd bet money on it."

"Any suspects?"

Paul thought for a moment. "They frequented a gallery run by Ricky Santiago—a straight guy. He pretended to like them so they'd spend money, but he talked behind their back. And he said some nasty things."

"What kind of nasty things?" Sherri asked as she stepped closer.

Paul turned to look at her, then continued. "One night, at a gathering, he said 'When Monfrer and Ramirez pulled their dicks out of each other, they weren't fudge brown but Franklin green.' Ricky always had comments like that, trying to draw a laugh from the straight crowd."

"Franklin green I know. Fudge brown, I'm pretty sure about but explain," Sherri said.

"Franklin, as in Ben Franklin. His image is on the $100 bill, indicating wealth." Lou coughed. "I won't say what the fudge brown refers to. I'll leave that up to him."

"Don't worry, Lou. I know what it refers to, and it's disgusting," Sherri said. "I only asked to get confirmation."

"Do you know of anybody who laughed extra hard at those jokes?" Lou asked.

"Not really," Paul said. "But you have to understand there weren't many straights in the crowd Ricky was talking to. He might have thought so—he might even have wished so—but he was wrong."

"Besides Ricky, is there anyone else we should look at?" Sherri asked.

Paul shook his head. "Not that I can think of."

"What about Foster Wentworth?" Lou asked.

"I don't know. They seemed like good pals to me. Good business pals, too, from what I heard. Both guys spent a lot of money there, more than they spent at Santiago's."

Lou thanked him for his time, then walked to the car. As he and Sherri got in, he said, "That's something we might look into, the money angle."

"No doubt," Sherri said. "I'll get on it right away."

By morning, Sherri received confirmation that the men had spent a tidy sum with Ramirez; in fact, between them, they had spent almost three million.

"That's a lot of money," Lou said. "We need to find out who else dished out those kind of bucks."

BUGS AND THE CANVASS

Frankie made a few stops, but eventually he picked up Alex from Nicky's house and took him home.

"Did you have a good time?" he asked.

"Yeah," Alex said. "We had meatball sandwiches for lunch. Can't be much wrong with a day that includes meatball sandwiches, especially if the day starts that way. You taught me that."

"You've got a point. I would find a hard time complaining about any day that starts out with Angela's or Rosa's meatball sandwiches for lunch."

Alex became more animated. "Yeah, and I like the way they make them too. Rosa puts the rolls under the broiler just long enough to melt the cheese onto the bread, *then* she puts on the meatballs and sauce, *then* melts more cheese on top. That way the rolls don't get soggy, because the sauce doesn't soak into the bread."

"Hot damn," Frankie said. "I might have to keep you here longer to learn some cooking lessons."

"Won't find me complaining," Alex said. "I had some leftover lasagna before you picked me up. Let me tell you, your shit don't compare. I don't know how I'm gonna eat that crap you make now."

"You little turd. It was good enough for you before; it will have to be good enough for you now."

Frankie drove a few more blocks, parked, then shooed Alex to his room. "Go dream about hot women and cool cars," Frankie said. "And it better be in that order because I'm sure the women will come before the cars do."

Alex ran up the steps, but hollered back, "I think I'll stick to meatballs and lasagna."

Frankie laughed, then went upstairs to work on the folder. The first thing he did was pull out the initial canvass and then he started reading.

Detective Fred Carnahan had gone up and down Franklin Street the morning after the abduction, or alleged abduction. He went door-to-door asking questions. Three people had agreed on one fact—they had seen a blue car or possibly a black one, around 10 p.m. It had driven slowly down the street and might have even stopped for a moment before taking off again. One person mentioned that the car was big, perhaps an SUV.

The phone rang while Frankie was studying the files. Mrozinski's caller ID showed on the screen. "What's up?" he asked.

"Remember I told you that the McDermott kid wasn't out of the woods?"

"Yeah."

"I've got four phone calls between Smiles and McDermott. One—if it was short—could be explained any number of ways, including a wrong number. Hell, one of my aunts once talked thirty minutes to a wrong number, but they didn't stay friends; she didn't keep calling. And McDermott had four calls over two weeks. Too many to be anything but business, and we know what kind of business Smiles deals in."

"Fuck me twice," Frankie said. "I don't like the sound of that."

"I didn't think you would," Mrozinski said. "But what are you gonna do about it? I know you've got some connection to McDermott. You want me to question him, or do you want a shot first?"

Frankie lit up. "I'll talk to him and see what I can find out. Thanks, Mrozinski."

"Call me after you talk," Mrozinski said. "I need to hear his explanation."

"You'll be the first to know. By the way, you got anything else?"

"Not *yet*. And I hope you picked up on the emphasis of *yet*. I plan on proceeding with this. As I'm sure you know. With this new information, it doesn't look the best for McDermott, but it looks a whole lot better for the Campisis."

"I hear you," Frankie said. "Just let me know if you find anything."

FRANKIE THOUGHT about what he knew. A dark-blue or black car—or SUV—had been spotted at the potential crime scenes. McDermott owned a dark-blue SUV but so did the Campisis.

On the negative side, there was also a record of phone calls between Patti's brother and Johnny Smiles, a known distributor of porn. And so far, no connection had been made between Smiles and the Campisis, not as far as hard evidence goes. That didn't necessarily prove anything, but it didn't help the case against them either.

Frankie picked up the phone and called Patti. She answered right away. "Patti, this is Frankie Donovan. I'm doing some work with the

Wilmington Police Department and I had a few questions for Raff. You think you guys could meet for lunch and chat?"

"Sure, Frankie. Where do you want to meet?"

"Nothing formal. How about Casapulla's? When you live as far away as I do, Casapulla's is always a consideration, especially for lunch."

Patti laughed. "Sounds great," she said. "Let's do it around 11:30? We'll try to beat the lunch crowd. It will be good to see you again, Frankie; besides, I'm always up for subs."

"You've got a deal," Frankie said. "As far as eats, what do you say to a few large Italian subs? I'll have 'em ready when you get there, with peppers on the side—sweet and hot."

"Sounds great," Patti said. "Chips and water, too, if you don't mind."

Frankie felt guilty about being so excited to see her. Despite that, he couldn't deny that he *did* feel that way. It reminded him of being sixteen again.

~

FRANKIE ARRIVED at 11:25 and got the subs. A few minutes later, Patti and Raff showed, and they sat on a bench across from the store, Raff on one side and Patti alongside of Frankie—which aroused him more than it should have—on the other.

"So what's up, Donovan?" Raff asked. "You said you had a few questions. What do you need to know?"

Frankie leaned over the table. "Did you hear about the missing girls a few weeks ago? There were seven of them."

Raff shook his head. "I haven't heard anything."

Frankie heard what he said, but he noticed Raff looked to the side when answering—not at him. That bothered Frankie. He'd have rather Raff stare him in the eyes and say "Yeah, I heard about them. Everybody has." He'd rather have had Raff say that, but he didn't.

If Raff *had* said that, it would have been closer to the truth, because as far as Frankie could tell, almost everyone *had* heard about them. It was the gossip of the town. *So why did Raff said he hadn't heard?*

"Regardless," Frankie said. "At the scene of the kidnappings, they saw a car that looks like yours—big, dark blue."

"A lot of cars look like mine," Raff said. "I don't think that means anything."

"Not by itself it doesn't," Frankie said. "But we also have phone calls between you and Johnny Smiles."

He kept his eyes glued to Raff, judging his reaction. "And you know about Smiles. He doesn't have the best reputation."

Raff took a bite of his sub, then smiled. "I know about Smiles. And I called him *because* he doesn't have the best reputation. I needed some advice on distributing movies and music, and it was not the kind of advice you get at Wharton—this is a tough business. It's not the same as it was back in the day, but it's still tough.

"I also know Smiles does porn, but he knows who to talk to regarding *any* type of movie, not just porn. That's what I called him about. Besides, I didn't think it was illegal to call someone."

Frankie nodded. "I got it. You talked about innocent shit. Who-do-I-need-to-talk-to type stuff."

Patti grabbed Frankie's hand and squeezed. At the same time she spread her legs a little. It didn't go unnoticed by Frankie. "You've got it right," she said. "Raff didn't do anything wrong. If he did, there'd be some kind of record. An invoice or sales receipt. But there wasn't, was there? I'm sure there wasn't." She looked across the table. "Tell him, Raff."

Raff was being quiet, and Frankie didn't like that. At the same time, his sister was doing such a good job of protecting Raff that Frankie didn't know if he blamed him. "Is that right, Raff? What Patti says."

He smiled. "Yeah. Everybody I talked to was stonewalling me, so I called Smiles. I was told he had the connections—you know, he knew the right people—and, sure as shit, I needed them, but I didn't do any business with him directly."

Frankie nodded again. "Yeah. Smiles *does* have connections, and everyone knows it." He turned toward Patti, apparently placated. "So, Patti, what have you been doing with yourself? Are you married? Working?"

She flashed Frankie a sexy smile. "No and yes. I never did see the benefit of getting married. I sure as hell didn't want kids after damn near raising eight of them, and yes, I'm working my ass off in real estate, though sometimes I wonder why."

Patti sprinkled a few more peppers—hot ones—on her sub, then said,

"Although the market seems to be picking up. I just picked up a listing in Westover Hills that could fix me up good—it would constitute half of my income for the whole year."

Frankie smiled. "Does it look like the deal will close?"

"It's gonna close one way or another. I'll go to bed with him if I have to. And with the wife he's got, that should cinch the deal." Patti laughed. Frankie pretended to, but he was shocked to hear her talk that way. In another sense, he was kind of excited. *If she would go to bed with a guy just to close a deal on a house, she would surely do the same for a guy who helped her brother stay out of prison.*

AFTER LUNCH, Frankie drove to pick up Alex, then took him around to some of the historical sites. Alex hadn't visited any of the old stand-bys, and by this age he should have. If nothing else, it would be good for him to just be able to say he'd been there.

Frankie took him to see where the Battle of the Brandywine happened, then up to see Valley Forge and then the Liberty Bell, followed by a cheesesteak at Pat's Steaks. It was a toss-up between Pat's and Gino's, but Frankie opted for tradition and went to Pat's.

As Alex sat on the curb and ate his steak, he said, "Damn, I might never go home if you keep introducing me to food like this."

Frankie smiled, but he was thinking about his conversation with Raff. And with Patti.

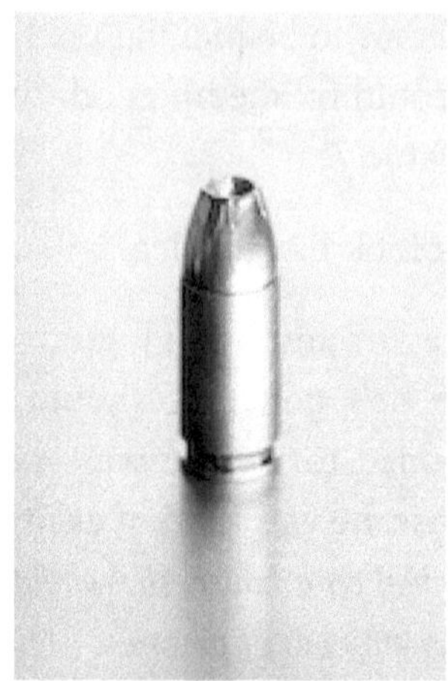

I was sitting poolside, relaxing, when the phone rang. I grabbed for it, worried that something might be wrong with Angela.

"Yeah, it's me," I said.

"It's just me," Bugs said. "I wanted to fill you in."

I breathed a sigh of relief. "Fill me in on what? Have you got something new?"

"Not really *new*, but interesting. Mrozinski said there were four phone calls between Smiles and Raff."

I waited for more, but nothing was coming. "Did you talk to McDermott?"

"I had lunch with Raff and his sister."

"Do you mean Patti 'Make my dick hard' McDermott?"

"I think you know who I mean, and I also think you know where you can go with comments like that."

"You brought it on yourself, saying you had lunch with Raff and his *sister*? You think that by saying 'his sister' you'd take the stink out of that statement? His sister just happens to be Patti, who you've had more than a strong crush on for twenty years.

"I know what you're doing," I said. "You're watching Patti's tight little butt wiggle in front of your face and you're thinking with your dick instead of your brain, what little is left. And you know what's worse? She *knows* it."

"Bullshit!" Frankie said.

"Bullshit, my ass. You've wanted to get into her pants since you were twelve. Hell, maybe earlier. If her brother's a suspect, you shouldn't even be talking to her—let Mrozinski do that—but I don't have to tell you that. What you need to do is lock his ass up and get to the bottom of this. And put a clothespin on your dick."

"Screw you," Frankie said.

"Yeah, just what I expected from a pussy-whipped mick."

"You…" Frankie started to say, then he laughed. "You prick. You knew you'd get me, didn't you? Pussy-whipped, my ass. If anyone is pussy-whipped, it's you. You can't take a piss without asking Angela first. You couldn't twenty years ago and you still can't now."

"At least I can *take* a piss," I said. "Your member is continuously hard from staring at Patti's back side."

"Screw you again."

"Oh, boy, you really know how to hurt a guy, don't you? Sister Thomas would be proud of your grammar, especially the vocabulary."

Frankie laughed again.

I said, "Look, Bugs, Patti McDermott never had a problem wiggling her ass to get what she wanted back in grade school, and she still doesn't. And why should she? It works."

"Speaking of knowing how to hurt a guy…I've been dreaming of her since before I can remember and now you're telling me she's taboo—to leave her alone."

"I'm not telling you what to do, but I will remind you of the consequences. That's what friends are for. So figure out a way to work without distractions and solve this case. Besides, Kate is a good woman. She doesn't deserve this."

"Shut up! What the hell do you know about Kate?"

"I know she puts up with you and Alex. And I saw the way she looked at you in the hospital, when she stood by your bed night-and-day. Not much else I need to know. She might not like me, but she *loves* you."

"What do you mean by that? Kate likes you."

"No need for bullshit," I said. "I could tell the first time I met her, but it doesn't bother me. She doesn't need to like me. Who she needs to like is you, and she does that in spades."

"All right. All right," Frankie said. "What do *you* think I should do?"

"Do what I said. Do what you do best. Find out who really took these girls and get them—no matter who they are."

"You know how to hurt a guy, don't you?"

"I only hurt guys who hurt themselves," I said.

BODY NUMBER THREE

*C*hip Farmington was the name in the third victim's wallet. The murder scene was similar to the others—GSW to the back of the head, no robbery, and what appeared to be a surprise attack. And not enough blood to support evidence of an at-the-scene shooting.

"It's wild speculation," Lou said. "But it looks like they must have known the attackers. Otherwise, with three people, you'd think *somebody* would have seen it coming, although every one of them was shot in the back."

The uniform at the scene brought over what appeared to be a tranny.

"Found her, or him, hanging out on the park bench across the street," the uniform said.

"He" reached out his hand. "Chester Arthur," he said. "I'm guessing you want to know what I've seen."

"There was a president named Chester Arthur," Lou said.

"Oh, my. Aren't we up-to-date on our political history? For your information, there was a stripper named Chesty Morgan. Did you know her, too? Or is your knowledge limited to politics?"

Lou grimaced, and Sherri laughed. "Got somebody who's giving it right back to you, huh, Lou?"

Lou didn't smile. He stared at Chester and said, "Why don't you tell me what happened."

"I was sitting on the bench, when—"

"Doing what?" Lou asked.

Chester leaned forward and got close to Lou's face. "Drinking a beer, if you must know. If the drinking a beer part had been important or relevant, I'd have told you."

"Go on."

"Do you need to know what brand of beer, Detective?"

"Keep talking, smart ass."

"Anyway, a red pick-up, fairly new Chevy, pulled to a stop and two people got out of the back—the bed I think they call it—and tossed something out. It looked suspicious, so I went over to check it out after they left.

The tranny put a finger to his pursed lips. "I wonder why they call that a 'bed.' Do you think it had anything to do with what those naughty teens did in it way back in the 60s?"

"Do you ever shut up?" Lou said.

"I don't suppose you got a plate?" Sherri said.

"Partially. It had a '9' on it. That's all I know. I definitely saw the number '9' but couldn't swear to anything else."

"What happened next?"

"Regarding the plate, or in the alley?"

"The goddamn alley," Lou said, then turned to Sherri. "I'm about ready to run this…thing…in."

Chester grinned. "I looked in the alley and saw the body. That's when I called the police."

"How many letters and how many numbers on the plate?" Lou asked.

"Oh, back to the plate, now. I have no idea. I know it was mixed, but all I can swear to is the number '9.' Nothing else."

"Think hard about what you saw," Sherri said. "If you remember anything else, let us know. It might be useful to you. We can be good friends to have."

When Chester couldn't think of anything new, Lou and Sherri left. Once out of earshot, Lou said, "There's a connection somewhere. What do you think it is?"

"Maybe the connection is that they all donated money to the same place, or they all bought paintings from the same artist. It must have been blackmail of some sort," Sherri said. "But I don't know why."

"But why was he killing them? Who cares where they donated money or which artist they bought from?" Lou scratched his quickly balding head. "I sure wish that goddamn Irishman were here. We could use somebody with stupid ideas to toss around."

"I'm gonna tell Frankie you said that."

"I'll tell him myself when I talk to him," Lou said. "Matter of fact, I might call him tonight. Stupid, fuckin' mick is probably eating potatoes and drinking beer anyway. He needs an intelligent conversation."

LOU TALKED to Frankie that night and told him what he had. "We've got three bodies, Donovan, and no good reason for them to be dead. These guys were throwing money all over town, and everybody agrees they were nice people. Why the hell would somebody kill them?"

Frankie thought for a minute. "There's a reason, Lou. You just haven't found it yet. Underneath all that clean living and money-spending, something else is going on. When you find that, you'll find who did it."

"So dig deeper is all you've got for me?"

"That's all I've got."

"I could have prayed to that fuckin' saint of yours—that guy who played with snakes—he would have given me more than that."

Lou waited for a response, but when none came, he said, "At least the French had a lady who led an army into battle, and the Italians had St. Francis. He was friends with all of the animals, a regular Dr. Doolittle type. And what did the Irish have? A snake chaser. Goddamn!"

"Lou, if you could have prayed to him, then that's what you should have done, because I've got nothing else for you."

"You're a prick, Donovan. You know that?"

"Yeah, I know, Mazzetti. I love you, too. By the way, do Joan of Arc and Saint Francis have holidays?" Frankie hung up quickly before Lou's barrage began.

ALLISON DOES THEM ALL

*M*rozinski had been busy all morning, checking with VICAP—violent criminal apprehension program— looking for similar crimes, then checking the details against his, to compare similarities. It had been hours and he had nothing. Not one new clue.

He rode to Canby Park and staked out the Campisis. At this point, the Campisi brothers were his number one suspect—as well as numbers two, three, and four.

He had a possibility on Raff McDermott, but that didn't look good. Raff seemed to be a good kid, despite some suspicion based on the calls to Smiles. The Campisis, on the other hand, were into about every level of corruption you could name, including porn—albeit soft porn—and all three of the brothers had sheets.

The Campisis had been nothing but trouble all of their lives—all of them. The oldest one was killed by Nicky Fusco in a gang fight. Two years ago, Bobby, the second oldest, had died after stealing money from a drug dealer. And the last three were skating just outside the reach of the law, though, if Mrozinski had his way, it wouldn't be for long.

Mrozinski sucked hard on a dry cigarette; he had quit three years ago, but the habitual part nagged him. Every now and then he bought a pack to use dry. This one had lasted him six months. He didn't make the mistake of buying the brand he used to smoke though. That would be too tempting. He used menthols for his dry habit; they did the job, but they weren't tempting. He'd never smoke menthols.

Thoughts of the Campisis returned. If he could bust the whole Campisi family for jaywalking and send them to prison for life, he'd do it, and furthermore, he wouldn't feel the least bit guilty. They deserved it.

McDermott was another story. There had always been bad blood between the McDermotts and Campisis. Tommy McDermott had been killed by a Campisi in the same gang fight that took the older Campisi, and the Campisis blamed Jack McDermott on Bobby's death. Mrozinski wouldn't put it past them to be staging a frame up, no matter how elaborate.

He watched the front door for any signs of life, while keeping his eye on the SUV that belonged to Paul. It was parked on the street, and had been for days. Mrozinski was looking for any reason to be able to take it in for a DNA sweep. It would probably yield nothing, but he'd like to try it nonetheless.

The middle-aged Campisi brother—Mrozinski forgot his name— came out and got in the car. He drove off, and Mrozinski followed at a discrete distance. He tailed him for a few miles, and his patience finally paid off when Campisi ran a stop sign.

Mrozinski turned on his lights and pulled Campisi over. "In a hurry?"

Campisi rolled the window down. "What'd I do?"

"Didn't come to a complete stop back there," Mrozinski said. He stuck his head in the back window. "What's that smell? Smells like dope."

"You're full of shit," Campisi said. "No dope in here. If you smell dope, it's in your own nose, or was earlier."

"I better have a look," Mrozinski said, and opened the back door. He searched around under the seat, came up with something in his hand and said, "What's this?"

"What's what?" Campisi said. "It's goddamn dirt."

"Step out of the car," Mrozinski said. "I'm impounding the vehicle for further testing."

"What the hell are you talking about? There's nothing in this car. What is this, some kind of set up?"

"No, this is a routine traffic violation stop where drugs were suspected. As to whether there are drugs or not, we'll see about that."

Mrozinski called it in, and a tow truck showed up in half an hour. Campisi was still cursing in the back seat of Mrozinski's car.

"This is bullshit," he said. "There are no goddamn drugs, and I didn't do shit."

"Where you want it?" the driver asked.

Take it to the lab. I want it tested front to back. Dust everything. Test everything. And don't forget to tell them that I saw hair in the back seat. I want that run, too. I don't care if it's canine, feline, equine, ovine, or bovine, tell them to test it and get the results to me as soon as they have them. And I mean *all* of the results."

"Yes, sir," the man said, and he started hooking the car up.

Mrozinski walked back to the tow-truck driver and tapped him on the shoulder. "Tell them I'm looking mostly for signs of young females —teenagers—and they might be black, Asian, or any nationality. Don't forget to tell them."

"I won't, sir. I promise, but you know that's not my job."

"I don't give a shit what your job is. Do it," Mrozinski said. He drove Campisi home, then headed back to the station.

Mr. Parker, Allison's father, was waiting on the steps at the entrance to the police station. He held something in his hand.

When Mrozinski arrived, Parker intercepted him. He shoved a DVD into Mrozinski's hand. "You see this? This is what somebody's done to my little girl. What the hell are you gonna do about it?" Tears formed in Parker's eyes. "Tell me. What're you gonna do? I want 'em dead. I want these sons of bitches dead. If you ain't gonna do it, I am."

Mrozinski risked a glance down at the DVD. It was packaged in a plastic case with pictures of nude women on the outside. One of them was shown performing fellatio on a man to the side. The title of the film was *Ally Does Them All*, and a nude picture of Allison lying on a bed surrounded by naked men was front and center. It was the same DVD that Donovan had given him, but he didn't want to tell Parker that. Not now anyway.

"Go on, take it and look at it. Gape and gawk. Maybe it'll make you find them. Find the sons of bitches who took my little girl." He handed Mrozinski the tape and said, "I'll wait here."

Mrozinski took the DVD into his office and put it in the TV. He watched the film, cringing the whole time, and embarrassed, afraid someone might walk in on him. Even though it was work, he would have been ashamed to have been caught watching it. It was that bad. Only perverts would watch this stuff, and he had no idea how even they put up with it. At least he confirmed one thing—it was the same DVD as the one Donovan had given him. Without a doubt.

He wondered—and not for the first time—how Parker lived with this nightmare. And he wondered—also not for the first time—what he'd do if it were his kid.

Mrozinski had two kids of his own—not as old as Allison, but still, he could empathize with the man. Nobody, *nobody* wanted to see their daughter like that. He never finished the film; he'd seen enough. He ejected it and put it back in the case, then he walked back into the hall.

"Mr. Parker, we'd like to keep this for evidence if you don't mind. I promise you no one will see it who doesn't have to. And I'll make one more promise, Mr. Parker."

Mrozinski put his arms around Parker and held him. Tears formed in his eyes. "We'll get 'em, Mr. Parker. I promise, we'll get the pricks who did this. We'll get Allison back, too. I won't rest until I get her back."

Then he thought about the case his ex-partner, Borelli, had worked, and Mrozinski recalled what he knew about it.

And I might just give 'em to Nicky Fusco for justice. It would only be fair.

THE INVESTIGATION CONTINUES

Frankie dug into the files, or the copy of the files, that Mrozinski had given him. Any word of this getting out and somebody would have Mrozinski's ass—and Frankie knew it, which is one reason why he didn't even tell Nicky.

Nicky had forced him to be honest with himself, and now that he was trying to do that, he had to admit that he hadn't liked the responses he'd gotten from Raff. On top of that, Patti seemed to be in cover-up mode. Flashing too much thigh to him, maybe in return for overlooking things in the case.

So where does that leave me?

As much as he didn't want to, Frankie figured he'd better go see the Campisis—if nothing else to get a gut feel for what they did or didn't know. No matter what they said, he'd be able to tell if they were guilty by *how* they said it. After having their brother for an in-law for so many years, he knew them well enough for that.

IN THE MORNING, he took Alex to get a sausage-and-egg sandwich, one of his all-time favorites, and then dropped him at Angela's house. Rosa and Angela were great with Alex, and he loved it there.

Unfortunately, Frankie's family had been less than warm about accepting Alex, prejudiced pricks that they were. His sister Donna spoke to him nicely, but you could hear her reservations underneath. His other two sisters barely made eye contact, and his mother was, well…his mother. She didn't like anybody, including her kids. When it came down to it, she wasn't much better than Alex's mother—a no-good bitch who happened to have kids. One of the only differences was that his mother wasn't a junkie.

Angela was a different story. She and Rosa didn't care a lick about a person's background or what color they were and it showed. They played with Alex, got him to cook, and most importantly, repri-manded him if he did something wrong. That made him feel at home. It felt genuine. Frankie thought about it more and realized that if someone was going to take the time and trouble to correct you, it showed they cared.

Frankie dropped Alex off, and headed to Canby Park, where the Campisis still lived. They'd been there for thirty-five years occupying the same row house that they started in. If nothing happened to change the situation, Frankie imagined they'd be there for another thirty-five years.

It didn't take Frankie long to find their house; he'd been there plenty of times when his sister had been married to Bobby, and even though his memory for details was fading, he got it right.

He climbed the steps leading up from the street—all five of them—walked up the concrete sidewalk, then up the three porch steps, and knocked on the door. In a few seconds, Ralph answered. Ralph was about three years younger than Frankie but already going bald. He also dressed like a slob, something Frankie never learned to tolerate.

To Ralph, a Philly T-shirt was wedding attire, and a clean one was good enough to be married in.

"What do you want, Donovan? I thought we got rid of you when Bobby died."

Frankie grinned. The greeting was no more than he expected, and although there was nothing he wanted more than to smack Ralph, he grinned anyway. "If only it were so," Frankie said. "I'm here on business. I need to ask you and your brothers a few questions."

"Business?" Fred came bounding down the steps. Being the youngest, he was also the loudest. Maybe he thought he needed to be louder to make up for the age. Either way, it proved to be obnoxious. From the third step, he hollered. "What kind of business can a New York cop have down here?"

"Nothing official," Frankie said. "I'm just helping a friend. If you prefer, I'll have Detective Mrozinski drop by. He's local, and I'm sure you're familiar with him."

The mention of Mrozinski took them off guard. Ralph backed up a step, but Fred, the younger one, stayed put. "What do you want?"

Frankie stepped inside. "I need to know about the porn you boys are into."

"Porn? Is that what they're calling it?" Fred moved closer. "The stuff we deal in is no more porn, than HBO. Hell, HBO has regular shows that are worse, let alone movies."

Ralph held up his hand. "Maybe technically…"

"Bullshit," Fred said. "It's only called porn because the people who produce it want it called porn so that it sells more. You can see worse stuff on cable, like I said." Fred walked over to the dining room table and grabbed a DVD. "Take a look yourself. It's harmless. A couple of tits, a bare ass now and then. In the wildest ones you get a peek at a little snatch, but none of the movies feature sex."

"Can you account for your whereabouts on the nights of the abductions?" Frankie asked. "Witnesses saw your car at the crime scenes and more than one witness." He took out his notes. "Franklin Street, the Printz, Market…"

"If somebody's saying that, they're full of shit," Ralph said. "That's my older brother Paul's car, and he almost never drives it. I drive more in a week than he does in a year. And no, we can't account for our whereabouts or whatever shit you're asking. Do you know where you were two weeks ago?"

"Yeah, Ralph's right," Fred said. "Check out the odometer. He had the car serviced a few weeks ago. I bet he ain't put twenty miles on it since."

Frankie, eager for anything to go on, walked outside and looked at the sticker inside the door, then at the odometer—thirty-two miles difference. "That doesn't mean shit," Frankie said. "You could have backed it up."

"Yeah, we *could* have, but we didn't," Fred said. "And anyway, what's all this shit about? Mrozinski grabbed us up yesterday wanting to check the car. And what did he find? Nothin', that's what. Because there ain't nothin' to find."

Ralph stepped up. "Yeah, Fred's right. We *could* have switched the odometer, and the pope could have had an affair with Sister Margaret, but he didn't. And you know it." He spit to the side. "Go find a real suspect, Donovan, and leave us alone."

"You're disgusting," Frankie said. "You don't talk like that about the pope or a nun."

"And you don't tell me how to talk," Ralph said.

Fred got in Frankie's face. "If you ain't gonna arrest us, get the fuck outta here ,or I'll kick your Irish ass all the way down the street."

Pissed as he was—and as tempted as he was to take Fred up on the challenge—Frankie got in his car and left. He had nothing on them and no reason to drag them to see Mrozinski. He wished he did, but he didn't. And as much as he hated to admit it, he believed them. He didn't think there was any way they did it. He still wanted to kick Fred's ass, but he'd wanted to do that for a long time.

If the Campisis were eliminated, that left a stranger or Raff as suspects. Frankie hoped it was a stranger, because it would ruin any chances he had with Patti if it turned out to be Raff. It's the way she was.

Thinking these thoughts brought up another question. What about Kate? She was a good woman, and Frankie loved her—he thought. So if he loved her, what was he doing craving Patti? He had to think about that some more. He'd already ruined one marriage and it had taken forever to find another stable relationship. He didn't want to ruin this, too. Not if it could work.

HE PICKED up Alex and went home. Dinner that night consisted of fried zucchini, tomato and cucumber salad, and spaghetti—no meatballs, although it was a meat sauce.

Frankie's sisters were there, but hardly anyone spoke to Alex—they talked *over* him—and Frankie could tell Alex was bothered by it. After dinner, they went for a walk.

"I thought it would be different," Alex said. "Down here, I didn't think people would care what color I was."

Frankie put his hand on Alex's shoulder. "It's not everybody. My family is that way, and some others are too, but not everybody. Angela and Rosa and Nicky aren't that way. I think you've seen that."

Alex smiled. "Yeah, they're pretty nice. Rosa treats me the same as everybody else, and Angela said she never judges a person by what anybody says about them or even by what that person says, especially in a fit of anger. She judges a person by what he *does*. She said actions are what matter."

"And she's right," Frankie said. "I know the person who taught her that. We called her Mama Rosa, and she taught us all—Nicky too."

"The Rat, too? If she taught him, how'd he turn out so bad?"

Frankie tousled Alex's hair. "Nicky isn't bad. He might have done some bad things, but they were for good reason. That's the other thing Mama Rosa taught us: always look at intent. Always ask, *why* did a person do that?"

Alex shook his head. "You've got some weird friends, F.D."

Frankie stood and walked alongside Alex, his hand resting on his shoulder. "I guess I do," he said.

ANOTHER PHONE CALL

*L*ou picked up on the third ring. "What's up, Frankie?"

"Not a damn thing. I was hoping you'd tell me."

"I've been on a diet," Lou said. "Lost fifteen pounds since you've been gone. Other than that, nothing since we talked last time, and you gave me such wonderful advice."

"Goddamn!" Frankie said. "That's fantastic about the weight. What are you down to?"

"One eighty-two. I've only got twelve pounds to go."

"Shit, that's great, Lou. I remember when we first met, you were almost three hundred."

"Thanks for the memories, prick. That was the worst time in my life. Next time, let's talk about the day my father died. We can both have a laugh."

Frankie laughed. "You'll get over it."

"Fuck you," Lou said. "You're nothin' but an Irish Catholic prick."

"And you're not Catholic?"

Yeah, but I'm Italian Catholic. There's a big difference."

"What's the difference? And yes, I know that question just sets you up for one of your ethnic rants, but go ahead. I don't think I've heard this one."

"Italian Catholics are allowed to gamble and smoke, drink and curse. The church even holds 'bazaars' where that shit is legal. Hell, we can even fuck. Irish Catholics have to go to sleep with a picture of an angel on their bureau and a rubber band around their dick. And besides, at least one girl in each family must be named Mary."

"If they can't fuck, how do the Irish have such big families?"

Lou laughed. "Because they're fucking Italians, making a goddamn country full of half-breeds. Look at you."

Lou's remark hit home, and now Frankie wished he hadn't started this conversation. He was a half-breed—maybe—but he was pretty convinced his mother had screwed around. It was complicated and he no longer wanted to discuss the subject.

"You're hopeless," Frankie said.

"I may be hopeless," Lou said, "but at least I'm now skinny hopeless."

"I wouldn't call you skinny."

"Okay. Maybe not skinny, but not fat. I'll settle for that."

"Anyway, enough of the skinny/fat talk. What's going on? Got anything?"

"What we've got are a bunch of people—otherwise known as males— being killed. Oh, yeah, and they're all filthy rich."

"That's my buddy Lou. Politically correct at all times."

"What the hell!" Lou said. "I can't call them what they really are or somebody will write my ass up. Remember, I've only got a little while till I retire."

"And I'm sure a dozen or more people are eagerly awaiting the day."

"Fuck you, Donovan. I've got a case to solve. I'm not on vacation in some village outside of Philadelphia."

"I know. I know. Now listen, Lou. As far as your case, forget what you think you know about the victims. Forget that they're gay and focus on them being rich. I'd bet my last dollar that the rich angle is the key."

"Well, I've got news for you, Donovan. When you've got a key, all the parts have to fit to open the lock. Since these guys are rich *and* gay, I'm betting both angles make the key. Trust me, gay plays a part, and that's not me being biased. That's just logical."

Frankie thought for a minute, then nodded, even though Lou couldn't see through the phone. Maybe the nod was instinctive, a result of new technology like Facetime that came with the iPhone. "You might be right, Mazzetti. I hadn't thought of that, but it's probably true. Regardless, follow up both angles and you're bound to hit a motive."

Frankie thought for another moment, then said, "Scratch what I said. Even if the gay angle is valid, I'd go after the money. I'd still bet that's where you'll find the answers."

"How the hell am I going to find the answers. I don't have anything."

"You've got the money," Frankie said. "Didn't you say that all of the victims bought expensive paintings from one gallery?"

"Yeah, but they all checked out. According to their spouses—if you want to call them that—the guys—if you want to call them that—were satisfied with the purchases. An insurance appraiser had validated them, and the paintings are occupying a prominent spot in their collections or former collections."

"You're missing something, Lou. That's a hell of a lot of money to spend on a painting and suddenly be killed. There's a tie-in somewhere."

"Yeah, well maybe if you got your Irish ass back to work, instead of playing around with a bunch of dago killers, we could solve this."

"I miss you, too, Lou. But I'm confident that you and Miller can solve this on your own. Do what I suggested. Follow the money, and if you don't find anything, follow it further. Pirates bury their treasure deep."

"What the fuck!" Lou said. "I ain't looking for Long John Silver or some nutbag waving a skull and crossbones flag. I'm trying to catch some maniac who's taking out the elite of New York Society. Don't talk to me about buried treasure."

Frankie laughed so hard he thought he'd spit. "Lou, do what you need to. I'll be home soon."

THE MOVIEMAKERS HAVE A FEW QUESTIONS

Mike Servillo, the COO of Mezzanotte Productions, walked into the conference room. Despite being ten minutes early, three of the board members were already there.

"Hey, Pete," Mike said. "What's the special meeting for?"

"We heard from one of our contacts on the East Coast who said we might have visitors."

Mike raised his eyebrows. "Visitors? Who? And what for?"

"The inquisitive type. Looking for some missing girls. I'm assuming it's resulting from the latest acquisition, but that's only an assumption."

"Shut 'em down, like all the rest. We know nothing."

"I realize that, but apparently this is not a trivial matter. Supposedly, these guys mean business."

"Then have the sheriff handle it. We can't waste too much time on this; besides, that's what we pay him for, isn't it?"

Pete took a long sip of hot tea. "You won't consider it a waste of time if certain information gets in the wrong hands because of these intruders. Besides, I hear Calvin has a prospective deal."

"You're right about the potential information leak. We can't be too careful regarding which reporters know what information."

"Hell no," Pete said. "If the right papers get hold of what we're doing, you'll be living under the pier in Santa Monica. And you won't have good company."

The door opened and Calvin—Mezzanotte's CEO— walked in at the tail end of the conversation. He plopped all three hundred pounds down in an overstuffed chair at the end of the table. "As long as Mike has a young Asian girl to keep him warm, he won't mind."

"You're disgusting," Mike said.

"Disgusting or not, it's true," Pete said. "Strip the clothes off someone like that girl—what was her name—Mae Ling? Anyway, get her naked in front of Mike and he'd do anything—including dance." Pete laughed. "You've heard the old hippie term—mellow yellow—well, Mike has his own version—excitable yellow, and it applies to any shade of yellow skin."

Mike mumbled something, then said, "You're one to talk. You have your own perversions."

"I didn't say I didn't, but at least mine are restricted to adults—white adults."

"That's a farce! Then what are you doing producing child pornography?"

"Making money from sick fucks like you and your friends."

"All right. All right. Enough bickering," Calvin said. "Let's get to the business at hand. From what I've heard, we've received word that someone will be paying us a visit. If it's coming from Smiles, this is a credible threat that needs to be taken seriously. Even if it wasn't

Smiles, it needs to be taken seriously." Calvin cast glances around the table. "Any suggestions? Who got the tip?"

Joshua looked at a few notes he'd made in his book. He stood to address the board. "The tip came from a friend of Merk's down in San Bernardino, but his friend didn't know the source, and Merk's dead now. Murdered. Yet another reason to give credence to this warning."

"I said it before, let the sheriff take care of it," Pete said. "He's done a good job for us in the past, and we've never had trouble. Besides, he's on the payroll already, so it won't cost us any money other than what we already pay him."

"Good point," Mike said. "We pay the son of a bitch enough money. Let's make use of him. No matter who these visitors are, he'll make sure they disappear quietly. He always has."

"I agree," Marvin said. "I hate to put good talent to waste."

"How do we legally get them locked up?" Calvin asked.

"Let them come onto the property, then have the sheriff arrest them for trespassing and anything else he can think of. It shouldn't be too difficult. One time should be enough to scare them off. What we don't want is a big stink in case they're knowledgeable in legal affairs. That's all we need."

"I agree," Pete said. "We don't want any lawyers involved."

"I don't know," Joshua said. "Word is that the guys coming out are persistent. Not to be taken lightly. All of this came through our contact in San Bernardino, so I'm assuming it got to him via Merk, as has already been stated, although it could have been Smiles."

"I'd give it to Marcus," Mike said. "It'll cost us, but it will be worth it."

"Sure, it'll cost, but not as much as the bad press will if word of what we're doing leaks," Pete said. He leaned forward in his chair, then said, "Hey, weren't there a couple of trespassers caught a few days ago? You think it could have been them that he was talking about?"

"No way," Mike said. "They gave us no trouble, especially after the sheriff got hold of them. They probably pissed their pants in the jail cell."

Calvin added his cigarette butt to an ashtray already overflowing. "I say, fuck Johnny Smiles. Fuck Marcus. And fuck the sheriff. If we find anyone, we kill them. Who's going to know? Take the bodies about five miles out and dump them. Besides, I have a *real* customer who wants some movies made and it's right up our alley. I say we move the discussion in that direction."

The suggestion was met with silence. After a minute, Pete spoke. "Calvin's got a point, but if these guys are as good as we've heard, we might have trouble."

"Increase the guard. If we use enough men, we won't have any trouble. Five or six should do."

"I'm with that. Increase the guard, and get rid of anybody who gives us trouble."

"We'll take a vote," Calvin said. "Raise your hand if you want to give the sheriff a try. Continue playing with yourself if not."

After the laughter subsided, six men raised their hands, leaving Calvin and two others as the dissenters. It looked as if the sheriff would be used.

Calvin—a chain smoker—crushed another butt in the ashtray, then shoved it aside.

"Those smokes are going to kill you, you know?" Mike said. "You were supposed to quit years ago."

"We've all got to die sometime," Calvin said. "Besides, I'd wager those twelve-year-old Asian girls will kill you first."

"Sheriff or not," Leon said. "I suggest we stop farming the East Coast. It might be too hot, at least for a while. Getting people who are good at acquiring talent is not easy. I say we get a few more loads before we stop. Maybe some Latinas and a few more Asians."

"Agreed," Pete said. "And we should get a few more blacks, then stop Portland and Kansas City, too. There are plenty of other places to go, like Houston. Houston has about every nationality you could ask for. No sense in arousing suspicion. We'll just have to find more brokers."

"The guy who wants these movies made is ready to go now," Calvin said, stopping to light another smoke. "He can have a twenty-five percent down payment to us this week. And I've already checked him out, he's rich—and I mean really rich. And he's shady. I don't think we'll have any problem with the law. He shot a man right in front of me."

"What?" Mike asked. "Shot a man?"

"Yeah. Pulled a pistol and shot him in the head with no hesitation."

Calvin crushed out his cigarette and lit yet another smoke, gave a few drags on it, then crushed it out also. "Speaking of fucking," he said, panting. "I'm going home."

"Tell George hello" Mike said, and laughed.

"Fuck you," Calvin said.

"Not me," said Mike. "This tunnel is closed to all traffic. You can keep that habit for your own stable."

"Think about what I said. This guy is serious, and he wants three films." Calvin grabbed an extra pack of smokes and stuffed them into his briefcase. He smiled at Leon's scowl. "No sense in being caught short. "See you tomorrow," he said, and made a hasty exit.

Five minutes later, he was being chauffeured home while he worked from his briefcase in the back seat.

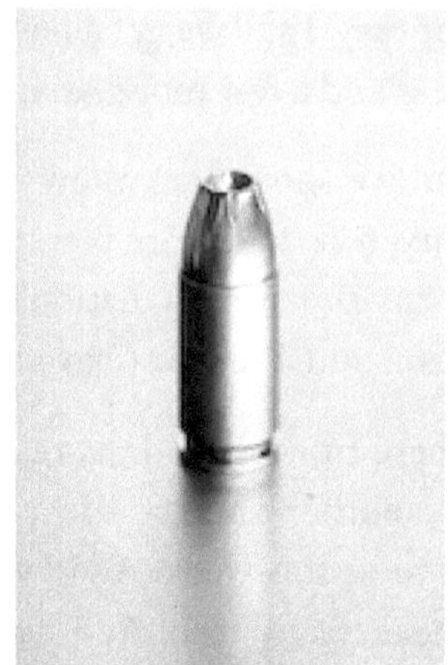

I crouched low in the back seat. DuPree was in the driver's side. "That's him," I said. "You know what to do."

"Good thing you mentioned that," DuPree said. "I might have taken offense if you'd given me directions."

Monroe laughed. "And what would you have done?"

"Fuck you," DuPree said.

"All right," Monroe said, "but I'll wait till we get back to the hotel. I never did like back seats."

DuPree laughed. "You're an asshole. You know that?"

Twenty minutes later, Calvin's car pulled into a long winding driveway that made a steep ascension up the side of a small mountain.

"What do we do now?" DuPree asked. "Can't follow him up there."

"Pull into that parking lot up the street, and put the car in any space that's open and next to another car."

"Why next to another car?" DuPree asked.

"Because if it's by itself, it may attract attention, but if it's next to other cars, it's just one of the crowd. The same theory as a person walking down a crowded street. If you're by yourself, you're noticed—in a crowd, you're not."

DuPree nodded. "Got it," he said, and parked next to a Ford Ranger. "What do we do now?"

I opened the car door and got out as if nothing were going on. "We find out where the girls are," I said.

"And what if he won't tell?" DuPree asked.

Monroe laughed, and I said, "Don't worry. He'll tell."

Monroe opened the trunk and removed a small canvas bag loaded with tools we had purchased at a local hardware store—one with no cameras. Inside was a two-pound mall, a screwdriver, a carpenter's awl, and a hand-cranked drill with a ¼" bit. "As Nicky said, *'he'll tell.'*"

Calvin answered the door after the second knock. "May I help you?" he asked, politely, but inquisitively.

"I'm sure you can," I said. "We came to pick up a few girls."

"I'm afraid I don't know what you're talking about," Calvin said, but then he seemed to recognize us as the men from dinner at Farouk's house.

"I'm afraid you do know," I said. "And if you don't produce them right away, we'll tell the papers everything Mezzanotte Productions is involved with and, who is responsible."

Calvin started to close the door. "I'm calling the police."

Monroe forced the door open and grabbed Calvin's collar, and I shoved a gun in his side. "You're calling nobody. Now sit and talk. I had hoped to do this with civility, but that seems out of the question."

"I don't think you know who I am," Calvin said, or what I've seen your boss do."

"I know *exactly* who you are," I said. "That's why we're here. As to what you *think* you've seen, let me introduce our friend."

DuPree stepped out of the shadows and smiled at Calvin. "Look, no bullets," he said, grinning widely.

Calvin was surprised, but he kept his cool. He was good. "I'm sure I don't know what you're talking about."

"And I'm sure that about the time this drill buries half an inch into your knee, you'll suddenly remember. Of course, by that time, you'll have already experienced broken fingers and toes, and maybe some other parts, so the drill might not seem so bad." I bent down, got within inches of his face, stared into his eyes, and whispered, "Of course, it *will* hurt, and I mean hurt like hell."

"You're insane!"

"People have been saying that all of my life, but I ignore them."

"I'm expecting company. They'll be here at any minute."

"That would be unfortunate for them," I said. "I don't want to have to kill them, but if they interrupt…"

I looked at DuPree. "Take his shoes off."

"What are you doing?" Calvin said.

"I want to see how far your conviction goes. But just so you know, if you withstand this, there's plenty more to come, so keep that in mind while I *hammer* away, so to speak."

Calvin's stocking feet were flat on the ground. I took hold of the mall and swung as hard as I could, smashing his toes.

His screams coincided with the crunching of bones, even though the screams drowned them out. I let him rest for a few minutes, then lifted his chin. "If you're ready to talk, do it. If not, I start on the other foot."

Calvin had regained some of his composure. His breath was controlled. "You're crazy. I'm not going to be blackmailed for anything."

"You're right," I said. "I'm here to elicit information, not to blackmail. So you either tell me what I want to know, or I smash one toe at a time. Then, and only then, will I start in on your instep. After that, your knees, hands, and then your dick."

The last one really registered. His eyes went wide. "You're insane!"

"You've already mentioned that," I said. "And as *I* said, I've been told that before, but I ignore it." I looked him in the eyes. "Now which will it be? Do you talk or do you scream?"

"I'm a businessman. I didn't do anything."

I grimaced. "When it comes to doing what you do to little girls, there is no punishment too severe. So prepare for the worst you can imagine, and then imagine again."

"What are you talking about?"

"You're about to find out," I said.

Calvin tried lifting his foot from the ground. I turned to DuPree. "Hold his foot down."

As soon as DuPree had it stable, I swung the hammer, then swung it again and again. Bones cracked and crunched, but the sound could barely be heard over Calvin's screams and pleading.

"Okay. Okay," he said. "I'll tell you what you want. Just don't hit me anymore."

"Good decision," I said, "because I wasn't going to stop hitting you, and you weren't going to last anyway."

"The girls are in the third building on the right. They're in the basement."

"How many guards?" Monroe asked.

"Six," Calvin said. "And they're armed at all times."

"When will the girls be there?" I asked.

"After 7:00 at night."

"How many?" I said.

"I think there are twelve." Calvin thought for a moment, then said, "No, there are thirteen."

"Anything else we should know?" I asked.

"No. Nothing."

"You sure? Because if there is, when I come back here…"

"I swear," Calvin said. "Nothing."

"Okay. I believe you," I said, then I pulled out a gun and shot him twice in the eye.

"What the fuck!" DuPree yelled. "What the hell did you do that for? He told you what you needed."

"Yeah, and he would have told his partners too. Besides, anyone who did what he did to girls deserves to die."

"Fuckin' right," Monroe said.

"When he shows up dead, they're gonna be suspicious," DuPree said.

"Yeah," I said, "but they're greedy also, and the lure of Farouk's money will be too much. The first day, they'll assume he's just taking a day off. We'll have time. If not, it's going to be a bloodbath."

"What about this mess? His body, and the blood. What are we gonna do?"

"We're gonna clean it up," I said. "Starting right now. Get some bleach and a bucket. Then get some gasoline or anything flammable. We don't want to leave any traces."

I know I probably sounded cool and collected, but I despised doing what I did. What I *had* to do. Killing people took its toll on a person, made them insensitive to the little things in life. I didn't want that; I had a good life with Angie and Rosa. I had too much to live for.

MROZINSKI

Frankie picked up the phone on the third ring. "Hello?"

"Donovan, I thought I told you to stay out of this, and to keep your friend out of it?"

"And I did," Frankie said. "Why?"

"Smiles is dead. Murdered."

"Shit. Well, I can tell you I had nothing to do with it, and Nicky isn't even in town." Frankie didn't want to say Nicky had nothing to do with it, because he might have, despite not being in town.

"It's a hell of a coincidence that Smiles turns up dead after we talk about him. And you know what I think of coincidences."

Mrozinski hollered for a refill on his coffee. "Get me some more. Black is fine."

"If you recall, Mrozinski, it was me who told you about Smiles. If I had wanted him dead, I wouldn't have given you the lead." Frankie let the silence sit. "And Nicky's the one who told *me* about him. If he planned on killing Smiles, he wouldn't have told me." Frankie said that, but he wasn't so sure. *Nicky, or Monroe, either one could have easily had Smiles killed.*

Mrozinski sighed. "Okay. Okay. But no matter who did it, we've still got a body. What are we gonna do about it?"

Frankie laughed. "Are you putting me on the payroll now? I don't work cheaply."

"Screw you, Donovan. I'm having somebody look into this hard. You and your buddy better come up clean."

"You've got nothing to worry about regarding us coming up clean," Frankie said. "I don't know when Smiles was killed, but I'm sure I've got an alibi, because I've been busy as shit."

"I'm sure you have been," Mrozinski said. "Anyway, what do we do next with the kidnappings? Time is running out for these girls."

"I can only imagine what they're going through, and I don't want to imagine. I'll get back on it tonight. I'm going through all of the files again. We must have missed something. I don't know what, but something."

TWO HOURS LATER, as Frankie was going through the case files, his phone rang.

"Forget the files, Donovan. We've just caught a break. I mean a big break."

"What kind of break?"

"Murphy's been out re-canvassing, and he got a partial plate from witnesses that he says are reliable."

"What? You're shitting me?"

"No. We've got a partial beginning combined with the last two digits.

When you add in the make and color of the car, we should be able to get a match."

"Do we *have* a make? I didn't think we had a make."

"No, but we've got a type. SUV. Either dark blue or black. So, a dark-blue or black SUV, with the license plate xxxxxx should produce a hit."

"Gonna be a lot of cars," Frankie said.

"Donovan, this isn't New York. The whole state's less than ten percent of New York's population. Trust me. It's *not* gonna be too many cars, especially just for Wilmington."

"Okay," Frankie said. "Let me know when you have something."

Despite what Mrozinski said, Frankie was going through the case files again. He didn't want to miss anything.

Four hours later, when his phone rang, he was still going through them. "Yeah?"

"Donovan, it's Mrozinski. We've got the reports, and guess who is on the list."

Frankie's heart sank, but he guessed with his gut. "McDermott?"

"No. Paul Campisi."

"No way?"

"We're headed over to Canby Park to pick him up now. Want to ride along?"

Frankie thought for a moment and then said, "Nah. Go ahead. I'll meet you at the station afterward. Forty minutes sound good?"

"Better make it an hour," Mrozinski said. "I'm going to get another detective and a couple of uniforms to accompany me.

"And don't tell anyone. I don't need any press on this. And 'don't tell anyone' includes McDermott. He's not off the hook yet."

"Don't worry," Frankie said.

Frankie was at the station in forty-five minutes, and he didn't have long to wait. Mrozinski pulled up a few minutes later with Campisi in the car. He was followed by Campisi's two brothers.

They got out of the car, screaming at Frankie. "I shoulda known," Ralph said. "I shoulda known a chicken-shit bastard like you would be behind this."

Fred stood to the side, being restrained by a few uniforms. "What's the matter, Donovan. Run out of real suspects? You fuckin' whore."

Frankie followed Mrozinski to the interrogation room, and watched from the other side of the window. Paul Campisi swore that he was innocent and demanded a lie-detector test to prove it.

Of course, a lie-detector test wasn't valid in a court of law, but it could go a long way during an investigation. The mere fact that he asked for one meant a lot to Frankie. He didn't view Paul Campisi as the type who thought that he could beat a lie-detector test.

Mrozinski refused to administer the test, but peppered him with questions. "Where were you the night of Allison's kidnapping? What were you doing? What time did you get home? Was anyone with you?"

Campisi said he had taken Fred's girl home, to Newark, then went home himself and watched TV. He didn't remember what, but he challenged Mrozinski to recall what he watched two to three weeks ago. Frankie thought for a moment, then nodded. He could barely remember what he watched three nights ago, let alone three weeks ago.

After two hours of grilling by two detectives, Campisi had given them nothing. Mrozinski wasn't convinced, but Frankie was—in his mind, there was no way Campisi did this. His story hadn't changed one iota, and it seemed solid. And he insisted on them verifying it with the girl. "She'll tell you I drove her home. She's gotta remember because she talked all the way."

Frankie waited for Mrozinski to exit the room, then approached. "Why didn't you let him take the test?"

"What good would it do?" Mrozinski said. "If he passed, we'd know either he was innocent or he beat the test. I'd go with, 'he beat the test.' And if he failed, we'd think he did it, which I already think. As you might be able to tell, I don't put much faith in lie detectors."

"So in other words, you'd think he did it, no matter the results?"

"Exactly, Donovan. No wonder you're a hero in Brooklyn. You're a genius."

Frankie left the station and walked past the lobby, where the Campisi brothers stood. His head was hung low. *If Paul didn't do it, and he now felt sure he didn't, then who did?*

But the bigger question remained. *If Campisi didn't do it, then how did witnesses have his plate number? It's hard as hell to get a plate number if it wasn't there. And how did they 'all of a sudden' remember the plate? This was going to take some looking into.*

ARE THE CAMPISIS DIRTY?

Frankie didn't necessarily want the Campisis to be dirty, but he wanted McDermott *not* to be dirty. He didn't really care *who* the guilty party was. The trouble now, was Mrozinski thought Paul Campisi was guilty and Frankie didn't.

Frankie had despised Bobby Campisi. He was sorry he was dead—sort of—but that didn't have anything to do with his feelings. Nor did it have anything to do with the fact that he didn't think any more of the rest of the Campisis than he had of Bobby. As far as Frankie was concerned, they were all filth.

But regardless of what he felt about his sister's former in-laws, he couldn't stand by and let innocent people suffer. He intended to get to the bottom of this no matter what it took.

After dinner, he called Angela to see if he could leave Alex with her and Rosa. No matter what they did for entertainment, it would be better than sitting at home with Frankie's sisters and mother. Sharing a night with them couldn't be considered entertainment by anyone.

Frankie walked Alex to Angela's door, then drove down to Patti's house and parked about one block away with the lights off and the windows down. It might be a long wait, but he intended to find out what was going on.

For the first two hours, Frankie played Angry Birds, doing his best to figure out which bird he should use to blow up the pigs' forts, or whatever the hell they were. Alex could do it, so why couldn't he?

While he was launching a boomerang bird, he noticed a car's headlights approaching perpendicularly about halfway down the block. It wasn't the first one to come by, but he paid attention to all of them, and this one was driving exceptionally slow.

An older guy got out and walked to a house a few doors down from Patti's. Frankie sighed, and went back to his game, but before fifteen minutes were up, another car pulled up quickly and parked. A younger guy opened the car door, got out, and walked to Patti's house and went inside without knocking.

Frankie waited for almost an hour, paying close attention to what was going on and playing his game. All the while he pondered his life.

He had almost been killed six months ago. Now he had a chance to start a new life with a wonderful woman and a great kid. And he was risking throwing it all away for some slut who was willing to screw a man in order to sell a house. *What the hell is wrong with me? Kate would never do such a thing. Hell, she wouldn't even think of such a thing.*

An image of Alex came unwanted to him and he smiled. That boy adored him. That thought made Frankie realize that he needed to be a role model in more ways than one. Role models didn't run around with trampy women. Role models didn't cheat on the women they loved.

The front door opened and brought Frankie to a state of alertness. The guy came back out, got in his car, and left.

Frankie followed him, being careful not to be spotted. He followed him almost all the way to Hockessin, then watched as the man exited the car and went into a house. Frankie wrote the address in his notepad, then called Nicky to get him to check on it. He knew Nicky had connections, and Frankie didn't trust Mrozinski at this time; besides, Nicky was probably faster, ridiculous as that sounded.

"Yo, Bugs. What's up?" Nicky said.

"I need an address checked out. Don't ask me why or any other questions. Just get me the address."

"Text me the details," Nicky said.

Twenty minutes later, Nicky called back. "I hope this is something important. That address belongs to a Detective Murphy."

"What? Son of a bitch!"

"What's going on?" Nicky asked. "Does that help?"

"It explains a lot on one end, but opens up more questions on the other," Frankie said. "But yeah, it helps. Thanks."

Frankie thought while he drove to pick up Alex. What the hell was Murphy doing at McDermott's house?

The more he thought about it, the more he realized it couldn't be good. This case had turned around on the vehicle ID—found conveniently by Murphy. If that ID wasn't rock solid, then Campisi was innocent, as Frankie suspected.

The question was, why was Murphy falsifying evidence? Frankie could say that now—at least to himself—because that's what he believed. He had no proof to that effect, but he had a strong gut feel, and Murphy visiting McDermott's house tonight solidified that feel.

Frankie picked up Alex, thanked Angela, then drove the few blocks to his house. When he got in, he called Nicky and filled him in on what was going on.

"Let me do some checking," Nicky said. "I know people who could help."

"I don't want any trouble," Frankie said. "And by the way, did you have anything to do with Smiles being killed? I told Mrozinski you didn't."

Nicky laughed. "I've been in California, Bugs. For Christ's sake, I can't teleport, and I'm not a ghost."

"You didn't answer my question," Frankie said. "Being in California and having something to do with the murder are separate issues. So, did you?"

"I didn't do anything, so don't worry," Nicky said. "Now, let me find out about Murphy, and I'll call you back."

An hour later, Frankie's phone rang. "Hello?"

"He's McDermott's cousin," Nicky said. "That's the connection. The fix must have been set up from the beginning."

"Son of a bitch!" Frankie said.

"You know what this means, Bugs?"

"Son of a bitch."

"Hey, Bugs. If you're done cursing, hear me out."

Nicky waited for a lull. "This means the Campisis probably had nothing to do with it. It means it was likely Raff all along, and Murphy stepped in to cover up for him."

"Looks that way," Frankie said. "By the way, how did you find out Murphy was McDermott's cousin?"

I called Doggs, who asked Jimmy the Gem. Jimmy knows everybody who came out of Forty Acres, and he said Murphy's mother and McDermott's mother were first cousins."

"Son of a bitch!" said Frankie. "Murphy never mentioned it, which means he was in on it."

"Now you've got to prove it," Nicky said. "Don't let that scum-sucking son of a bitch get away with it."

"Now, it's my turn to say, 'Don't worry.' I'll get him."

Before Frankie hung up, he saw a call coming in from Mrozinski. "Gotta go," he said and answered the incoming call.

"Donovan."

"You promised me you'd stay out of it," Mrozinski said. "I already told you that Smiles is dead. Now, I've connected him to an earlier murder of a guy named Merck. I gotta ask, Donovan. Is this Nicky's work?"

"I am staying out of it," Frankie said. "I didn't even know where Smiles lived, other than 10th Street, and I don't know this guy Merck at all. And I never heard Nicky even mention his name. I'm telling you, Mrozinski. You're barking up the wrong tree. Nicky's been out of town."

"Okay, assuming I buy your story, now I've got to ask about your alibis and your involvement."

"What are you talking about? I already told you I had nothing to do with this."

"I know what you said, Frankie, but I checked the phone records again, and there were two calls to Smiles from pay phones—one on Maryland Avenue by Clayton Road—not far from McDermott's house —and one by where Maryland Avenue intersects with Broom Street—

also not far from Raff's house." Mrozinski waited for a response, but Frankie stayed silent.

"Raff could have made either one of those calls," Mrozinski said. "And you know what? They were made the same night you had lunch with him and his sister. So even if I grant you that you had nothing personal to do with it, the question remains, did you say anything inappropriate to Raff? Tip him off in any way?"

"Damn," Frankie said.

"Damn is right," Mrozinski said. "It was probably Raff delivering a message to Smiles that we were onto them. You should have kept your mouth shut, Donovan. You know better."

FOLLOW THE MONEY

"It has to be the money," Lou said to Sherri. "They all had money and too much of it."

"But they were all gay," Sherri said. "Maybe that has something to do with it."

Lou raised his eyebrows and turned to Sherri. "I didn't know you were so prejudiced, Miller. I expected more out of you."

Sherri laughed. "Mazzetti, you're incorrigible. Despite your enlightened views, I still think gay has something to do with it."

"Maybe," Lou said. "But I'd be willing to bet ten dollars to a doughnut that money is the main reason. Gay may be secondary, but money is the driver. That's what Donovan thinks, and he convinced me."

Sherri thought for a moment. "Okay. I'll go with that. Who am I to argue with two wise old men?" She smiled when she said it. "So what do you suggest?"

"We already know where they were spending their money—Ricky Santiago's and Foster Wentworth's galleries. And from what little we know now, most of the money went to Wentworth. Now we have to figure out why he'd want them dead. What would the benefit be to Wentworth? Why would he kill big clients?"

Sherri nodded. "That's the key. He's not gonna kill somebody who spends millions of dollars at his studio. You don't kill the goose that lays the golden eggs."

"Not unless the goose is reaching sterility," Lou said.

"What the hell does that mean?"

"I don't know," Lou said. "But we'll find out. I'll have forensic accounting go through all of their books with a fine-toothed comb. They'll find something. They usually do."

THE INVESTIGATION SHOWED that WOW sold expensive paintings to each of the dead men. Manual Ramirez bought one for about 1.4 million. It was a picture of a vineyard set in the rolling hills of Tuscany with a newly restored villa as the backdrop.

Monfrer bought one for 800,000, a beautiful landscape of Lake Champlain when the leaves were turning color, and Farmington purchased a stunning picture of the Brooklyn Bridge while it was under construction, and during a fierce snowstorm. That set him back more than 1.1 million.

A deeper investigation also turned up the fact that Manual Ramirez had sold his painting to an acquaintance—Sam Defibaugh—for the paltry sum of 1.75 million, a handsome profit of 345,000 dollars though further checking showed no such deposit into Manual's account.

"Something's wrong here," Lou said. "We need to talk to this Defibaugh guy. You don't sell something for 1.75 million then *not* deposit the check."

The bigger question," Sherri said, "is why would you pay a million dollars plus for a painting then turn around and sell it? Even if it was for profit, Ramirez didn't need the money."

"Let's see if Mr. Defibaugh can shed some light on the subject," Lou said.

Lou and Sherri drove to Defibaugh's house, a brownstone ideally situated near Williamsburg. "That's gotta be about four million," Sherri said.

"A drop in the bucket for these guys," Lou said. "If you can afford to spend almost two million on a goddamn painting, then four million for a house ain't shit."

Sherri shrugged. "I guess so, but I'd kill to be able to afford either one. Makes my apartment and my Thomas Kinkades seem unimportant at best."

An older gentleman answered the knock at the door. "Mr. Defibaugh?" Sherri asked.

"No. I'll get him, though. Come inside and wait."

Sherri and Lou stepped inside. The entry was a huge, with a staircase that appeared to go "to heaven." Lou shook his head. "Maybe this was the inspiration for that old song."

After a few moments, a middle-aged man made his appearance. "May I help you?"

Sherri displayed her badge and hoped Mazzetti would be civil.

"We're here about Manual Ramirez," she said. "In case you haven't heard, Mr. Ramirez was murdered. Routine investigation into his financial affairs turned up a transaction with you—a rather large one. We need background data on that."

Defibaugh smiled. "Ah, the 'Grapes of Wrath,'" he said. "That's what the painting was called. It was an homage to the wonderful Mr. Steinbeck, but positioned in a much more beautiful setting."

"Our records show you paid 1.75 million for it, but we show no deposit into Mr. Ramirez's account."

Defibaugh turned and walked into a sitting room to the side. "Please, come in," he said. "Sit."

"I was visiting Manual and saw the painting. I admired it and asked if it was for sale. Manual said no, that he had recently purchased it."

Sam took a sip of a drink that had been served. "I pleaded with him to sell it. I admit, I was relentless. Finally, Manual agreed. I insisted he make a profit on it, and when he told me what he had paid, I offered 1.75 million."

"Pretty generous," Sherri said.

Defibaugh brushed his hand in the air, as if it were nothing. "A few weeks later, I was hosting a party, and I had the painting on display. One of my guests was Jeanine Mischa, the famed art critic. I asked her if she would appraise the picture for the insurance company (something she does), but when she examined the picture, she told me, 'It's worthless, trash. Garbage. No better than an Etch-a-Sketch drawing.'"

"At first, I was shocked, appalled by her statement, but then I had her opinion confirmed by another appraiser. Subsequent to that, I informed Manual, and the next week he confronted Foster, who was supposed to have had it inspected prior to the sale. Foster even provided a report—fake, I presume."

Defibaugh cocked his head and raised his eyebrows. "I don't know if *all* of what Jeanine said is true, but according to her, it definitely wasn't worth 1.75 million or anything close to that. Whoever painted it had talent. It fooled me, and obviously fooled Manual, but it couldn't fool Jeanine. Neither did it fool the other art critic."

"How could it have fooled an official insurance appraiser?" Lou asked.

"From what Jeanine said, it wouldn't have. Something is fishy with Foster's *appraisal* process."

Sherri made some notes in her book to follow up on the appraisal, then asked, "What did you do about the money?"

"I called Manual and confronted him. I told him what Jeanine had said and demanded that he provide an explanation. When he didn't have one, I asked for my money back."

"Did he put up a fight?" Miller asked.

"Of course not. Not over that." Defibaugh spoke as if he were referring to a Hamilton or even a Grant. "Manual seemed shocked, but immediately told me to cancel the check as he hadn't even deposited it yet.

"I thought it odd that he hadn't deposited it, but I was glad to see the transaction had been an honest mistake and not something else. I had put Manual on a much higher level than that."

"Who painted the picture?" Lou said.

"Supposedly some exotic siren from the Philippines or someplace like that. If you hold on a moment, I'll get you the name. I wrote it down when I purchased it from Manual."

Defibaugh left the room, but returned in a moment with a slip of paper. "Speranza Desdaemona—or something like that. You should talk to Foster Wentworth. He knows her. I'm shocked he didn't pick up on the quality, or, according to Jeanine, the lack of quality.

"Nonetheless, Foster knows her, and he obviously knows her work, as he is the one who brokered the deal."

As Lou and Sherri exited the house, Lou turned to Miller. "Things don't look so good for Foster Wentworth."

Miller shook her head. "He better have a damn good excuse, and I mean damn good."

"And a good alibi, too," Lou said. "I'm liking him more and more for this."

When they got back to the office, Lou ran Speranza Desdaemona's name through the database, but nothing came up. He tried the DMV, social security, and even the IRS. Nobody had a listing for Speranza Desdaemona.

"Try spelling it differently," Sherri said. "She's gotta be there somewhere."

"Unless she ain't," Lou said.

"What do you mean?"

"I mean, suppose it's some kind of scam and there is no Speranza, and Wentworth is taking it all himself. Or paying some talented kid a few bucks to paint garbage, then selling it as gold. If he had an appraiser in his pocket, or who was in on it with him, that would be all he'd need."

"That would explain a lot," Sherri said. "But why haven't we heard until now? How did the scam go undetected all this time?"

"I don't think it did," Lou said. "I think it sprung a leak when Ramirez wanted to sell to Defibaugh. Which would explain why the killings started when they did. If the scam was exposed to Ramirez, he would have likely told Farmington and Monfrer. Then Wentworth would have to silence them all."

"What do we do?" Sherri asked. "How do we prove anything?"

"We cheat," Lou said, and picked up the phone. After a few rings,

Frankie answered. "This better be good, Mazzetti. I didn't go on vacation to talk to you every day and listen to ethic rants about…everything."

"Who do you know that can get me a wiretap *without* a judge's approval?"

"Ah, shit. What have you got yourself into?"

"Never mind that, just give me a name. I know you have one."

"Try Lucky Samuello. He lives in an apartment above the shoe store by Canal Street. And use my name or he won't do it; in fact, he probably won't even talk to you. Remind him he owes me one."

Lou jotted down the address, then hung up the phone.

"What the hell was that?" Sherri asked.

"Nothin' you want to know about," Lou said.

"Lou, if that's what I think it is, you know we can't use it."

"True, but it may give us information that will lead us to other information that we *can* use."

Sherri threw her hands up in the air. "Jesus Christ, Mazzetti. Is this how things were done in the old days?"

"Hell no," Lou said. "In the old days, Donovan would have just had his dago buddies shoot the son of a bitch. It was a lot cleaner that way."

"And how are his dago buddies different from yours?" Sherri asked.

"His buddies are gangsters. I hung out with the good crowd."

TIME TO RE-CANVASS

Frankie got up and went downstairs to have his coffee, but not before he went through the case files again.

A lady named Sally Conker had provided the first few numbers of the plate—according to Murphy—and another witness, Phil Sugar had seen the last two numbers—supposedly. Frankie looked at the addresses and then at the map. If they were looking out the front windows, they would have surely been in position to identify the car —the question was, *did* they identify the car, or were they spoon-fed the information? Frankie gathered the files and went downstairs.

And why had it taken them so long to come forward? Or did they come forward?

Alex was already at the table, and Frankie's mother was in the kitchen, but no conversation was going on. Frankie's mother had long ago perfected the art of "talking" without speaking. She could say volumes with a look of the eye or a twist of the lips. From what Frankie could tell, Alex was getting a crash course in learning this new "language."

"Hey, F.D.," Alex said, eyes lighting up. "About time you got out of bed. I was getting bored."

"I'll bet you were," Frankie said, and shot an accusing look at his mother. He had picked up a trick or two of his own during his time at home.

Fifteen minutes later, Frankie walked out the door. He decided to take Alex with him, figuring Alex would have a more enjoyable time with Angela and Rosa than he if he stayed with Frankie's mother.

Hell, he'd have a better time with a nest of vipers.

Frankie dropped Alex off, then headed to see Mrozinski. He walked in while Mrozinski was gulping the last of what was sure to have been a bad cup of coffee. He was sitting at a makeshift desk in a temporary office off the lobby.

"Still drinking coffee?" Frankie asked.

"This is my third cup," Mrozinski said. "I'm sure you were still deep in a dream when I poured my first one."

"And a good dream it was," Frankie said.

Mrozinski lowered his head and looked at some papers. "What's up, Donovan? Anything new?"

Frankie turned his head back and forth, looking for listeners. "A lot," he said. "But we might want to discuss it privately." He gestured toward Mrozinski's private office and headed that way.

Mrozinski followed Frankie, a curious look on his face. When the door closed, he said, "What's going on, Donovan? Not like you to be so secretive."

"I figured you'd want it that way," Frankie said. "What I've got to tell you isn't for everyone's ears."

"Spit it out."

"Murphy's plates are bullshit." Frankie held up his hand. "And before you say anything else, know that Murphy is McDermott's cousin. I just found this out."

"What the fuck?"

"Yeah, and before you go off on some crazy defense of your detective, know that last night Murphy visited Raff for almost an hour. I know this because I followed him and staked him out, then I followed him home."

Frankie was braced for a raft of shit. He had prepped himself for it, even to the point of putting together logical arguments. What he wasn't ready for was Mrozinski's reaction.

"Don't tell anybody," Mrozinski said, and wagged his finger at Frankie. "We need to get ahead of this and now."

He turned to the wall, then back to Frankie. "Donovan, can you do me a solid and re-canvass the neighborhood? Talk to all the people that Murphy did and press them hard. See what the real story is. Let's get to the bottom of this. And make sure to talk to the ones who supposedly gave us the plate numbers."

Frankie took a seat and wiped his forehead with a napkin. "I wasn't expecting that. I thought you'd be pissed."

"I *am* pissed," Mrozinski said. "But I'm pissed at Murphy. We've got seven girls—that we know of—out there being subjected to God knows what, and he's in here lying his ass off to protect his fuckin' cousin. Fuck him. Fuck him twice. And fuck his cousin three times. If I find out it was McDermott, then Murphy's gonna be crucified."

Mrozinski grabbed Frankie by the arm. "I sat here and promised that girl's father we'd find the men who did this, and I intend to keep that promise. If one of my detectives gets in the way, shame on him."

Frankie smiled, but it didn't reach his eyes. "For what it's worth, Mrozinski. I'm with you. The focus has to be on the girls." Frankie started out the door. "I'm heading to Franklin Street now."

≈

IT TOOK all day and a couple of visits, but finally Frankie got a response at Sally's house. It was shortly after 1:00 o'clock.

"I'm Detective Frankie Donovan," he said, and held out his hand.

"I already spoke to the police," she said. "Talked to them twice, and told them everything I know."

"Twice?" Frankie said. He looked at his notes. "I don't see where you spoke to anyone twice. I see one time to a Detective Murphy. That's all."

Sally shrugged. "That's probably because the first time I didn't know anything."

"Didn't know anything? Do you mean you didn't remember seeing the car?"

"That's what I said." Sally raised her voice when she answered.

"So how did you go from not remembering anything to remembering the first few numbers of the license plate? And being willing to swear to it?"

"Because he asked me," she said.

Frankie jotted something down. "Who asked you what?" He was going to press her with Murphy's name, but he figured he'd try this by the book first.

"The other detective," she said. "He asked me if I saw a big blue car, and I told him I didn't think so."

"So, he asked if you saw a big blue car? Then what?"

"Then he asked if I was sure, because my neighbor Mr. Sugar had seen it, and so had the others. After I thought about it, I realized I may have seen it."

"And then what?" Frankie asked.

"Then he asked if I remembered the license plate. I said no. So then he asked if I maybe saw any of the numbers. He asked if the first few were 'w' and '7.'"

"Were they?"

"How do I know? Now, I don't even know if I saw the damn car. Wish I had never said anything."

"Why did you say anything?" Frankie asked. "If you weren't sure, you should have said so."

"I did say so, but he kept insisting I must have seen something, so I said I did."

"But you really didn't?"

Sally frowned. "I guess not. Not like he said I did, anyway."

"Okay. Thanks," Frankie said. "You've been a big help."

"Am I still gonna get the reward?" Sally asked.

"Reward?" Frankie was intrigued now, his curiosity piqued.

"Yeah. The hundred dollar reward the cop mentioned for helping out. He said if I remembered the plate numbers that I would get it."

"I'll ask my captain, ma'am. I'm sure we can manage something."

Frankie left the house smiling, but only on the outside. He really wanted to scowl. How could this prick do this? How could he falsify a report like this? He silently cursed while walking to Sugar's house, where a car now sat parked in front.

Phil Sugar was more open about things. He said he didn't give two shits about the supposed reward, which he brought up with Frankie right away, but he did wonder why the cop seemed to be pushing him in one direction. "I kept telling him the last number was a '9' and he insisted it was a 'q.' After a while, I agreed with him because he said three other people had seen the 'q' and I must have been mistaken." He shook his head. "I don't mean to brag none, but my eyesight is still pretty good and what I saw was a '9' not any damn 'q.' I know the difference. I got a 'q' on my own damn license plate. I know what a 'q' looks like."

"Would you be willing to testify to that in court?" Frankie asked.

"I'll testify to that any damn place you want me to," he said. "It was a goddamn '9.' I know that. And I want the people who did this to those girls caught. I've got a granddaughter who just turned eleven. God forbid something like this ever happened to her."

"Okay. Thanks," Frankie said. "Mr. Sugar, we're going to get this son of a bitch. You can bet on that."

Back in his car, Frankie dialed the phone while he drove. "Mrozinski, the lady—a Sally Conker—said she doesn't know shit, and the guy said Murphy all but forced him to say what he did. In fact, he swears the last number on the plate was a '9,' not a 'q,' and he said he's willing to go to court on that."

"Son of a bitch," Mrozinski said. "That changes things up a little."

"More than a little," Frankie said. "Sally said Murphy told her there would be a reward of a hundred bucks. Same thing with Sugar, but Sugar didn't seem interested."

"Okay, thanks, Donovan. I'll get back to you."

Before Frankie had gotten two miles, the phone rang.

"Guess whose plate ends in '9?'" Mrozinski asked.

"Since you're asking, I'm going to take a wild stab and say Raff McDermott's."

"You'd win the stuffed animal," Mrozinski said. "The big giraffe. Or the elephant if you want it."

"Now we've got to figure out what to do," Frankie said. "One number on a license plate isn't going to make the case."

"No, but it's gonna bust Murphy's ass, and that'll give me some pleasure, so the day's not a total waste."

"Maybe he'll talk," Frankie said. "I doubt it, but maybe."

"No way. He won't say a thing," Mrozinski said. "Not even when I shove his gold badge up his ass."

"Okay. Keep your hat on," Frankie said. "Let me talk to Raff and his sister. I'll see if I can kick anything loose."

"Go for it," Mrozinski said. "Anything you get will be more than what we have,"

FRANKIE CALLED Angela to ask if Alex could stay a while longer. "If you don't mind watching him, Angela. I've got to talk to a few more people."

"No problem, Frankie. He's no trouble, and Rosa loves spending time with him. You know she loves to teach. She's been playing school with him, teaching geography and history."

"Are you sure?"

"I'm positive. He's been talking Rosa's ear off and wearing out Dante. They've been playing with Legos and playing catch with the neighbor's dog. He's been wonderful."

"Okay, great. See you in a little while. And thanks so much. It means a lot to me."

Frankie drove to Patti's house and parked out front. She answered the door in a tube top that was too tight—in a good way—and jeans that should have been outlawed for someone with her figure.

He realized as he stepped inside he shouldn't be thinking like this, and tried to clear his mind.

Think of Kate. Think of Alex. Think of anything, but her.

Patti brought a cold beer from the kitchen, and Raff showed up twenty minutes later. Frankie wondered if the delay was by design, to give Patti a chance to work her magic—or not. Under normal circumstances twenty minutes may have been enough time, but Nicky had embarrassed him into behaving, so he was behaving—or at least he was trying. The glimpses of Patti's bare skin underneath the tube top and the crack of her ass peeking out from those jeans were almost too much, but Frankie held out.

Raff entered with a noticeable spring in his step—thank God he appeared when he did—and Patti excused herself at the same time. *It must have been a cue.*

"Detective Frankie Donovan," Raff said. "I remember when you were…well, not a detective."

Frankie laughed. "And I remember when you were…well, not what you are now. But that was a long time ago for both of us," Frankie said, and patted the seat next to him on the sofa. "Anyway, sit, Raff. I've got a few questions."

"What, a New York detective is working a case this far south? Has something changed since you were last here?"

"Mrozinski asked me to help," Frankie said. "I can hardly refuse a polite request from a fellow officer, especially since I'm originally from the area."

"I guess not," Raff said, and he leaned against the back of the sofa. "What can I do for you?"

Frankie decided the best tactic was to get right into it. "To start with, I guess you can tell me what you were doing at 6th and Franklin on the night Allison Parker was kidnapped."

"What the hell are you talking about?" Raff leaned forward as he spoke.

"I'm talking about the fact that we have three witnesses that ID'd your car, with your plates. And not only on Franklin but on the Printz as well." The last part Frankie threw in for effect. No one had seen Raff's car on the Printz.

"You're full of shit, Donovan. You know how I know that? Because I wasn't there. I haven't been on the Printz in years."

"Really? You *know* you weren't there, and yet you haven't even asked me which night it was or what time it was."

"I don't have to ask, because I wasn't up there. As I said, I haven't been on the Printz in years. I may have been on Franklin Street, but not in the last month, and I'm not asking for a specific night because I have no idea where I was on any given night, and I don't think it matters."

"In the past month you haven't been to Franklin Street? I find that hard to believe."

"Tough shit, Donovan. I said I wasn't there—that I can remember—now, move on. Next question." Raff's tone had gotten combative.

"Next question is we'd like to do some DNA testing on your car. Is that all right?"

"Bust your balls, Donovan. Look all you want. I might say that I recently had it cleaned, but who knows? Maybe I missed something, or at least you can hope that."

Patti came down the stairs and walked back into the room. She had changed into shorts, very short shorts, and the cheeks of her ass were hanging out.

Frankie instinctively wanted to lick his lips. It was going to be difficult to concentrate on business with her looking like that, but then again, that's probably what she was counting on. He gritted his teeth and moved on, doing his best not to stare at her or even look at her.

"We'll take our chances on the cleaning, Raff. You never know what those guys may find. Expect us to pick it up tomorrow."

"Good. It'll be even cleaner by tomorrow. I'll make sure of that tonight."

"In that case, I'll take it with me," Frankie said.

"I don't think so, Detective. Not unless you have a warrant, which I'm sure you don't."

Frankie smiled. Raff's last bit of attitude had made up his mind. "You think you're a smart-ass, don't you, Raff. Let me tell you something— you better hope that Mrozinski busts you, because if he doesn't, you'll be answering to Nicky Fusco and Monroe."

Raff got a frightened look in his eye.

"That's right, Raff. You messed up. One of the girls you took was Monroe's cousin. And Monroe is good friends with the Rat. So good luck. I kind of hope Mrozinski *doesn't* catch you, because the Rat doesn't need hard evidence. He doesn't need DNA or fingerprints. All he needs is suspicion. And I'll give him plenty of that."

Frankie got up to leave. Patti leaned forward, letting her top show. "No need to rush, Frankie. Have another beer."

"No thanks," Frankie said. "I've had about all the hospitality I can stand."

As he walked out the door, he said, "See ya around, Raff. Or maybe I won't."

THE FILMS, PLEASE?

I drank my morning espresso and shot the shit with Monroe. He was already drinking a beer, which would kill my stomach, but it didn't seem to bother him.

"Time is of the essence," I said. "I figured this would only require six days in L.A. We're gonna be half again that if we're lucky."

"What do you want to do?" Monroe asked.

"We've got to get Farouk to pressure them. Make them act. We've got to get in there with those girls."

"I'll have him make a call," Monroe said.

The board got together first thing in the morning. Calvin had been killed, and despite the fire damage, the initial report was that it appeared to have been murder.

"You think it was those guys we were warned about?" Mike Servillo asked.

"Who knows?" Pete said. "I tried getting hold of Smiles to see if he knew them, but I couldn't reach him. And as we already know, Merk is dead. I don't like the sound of it."

"First Merk is killed, then Calvin is killed, and now Smiles disappears," Mike said.

"We don't know that anything has happened to Smiles," Pete said. "He might be at the mall shopping for all we know. And Calvin could have fallen victim to anyone. After all, he led a risqué lifestyle. Between George and his friends, anything could have happened. Think about it, has anyone seen or heard from George?"

"That's true," Mike said. "I hadn't thought about his lifestyle in general, or about George in particular. I'll echo Pete's question: anyone hear from George?"

Leon chimed in. "I haven't heard from George, but I did hear from Calvin's potential customer—that guy Farouk. He called this morning and wanted to know when we'd be shooting? He apparently wants to start soon."

"Do we know anything about him?" Mike asked. "Is he reliable? Safe to deal with?"

"Calvin seemed to have thought so. He gave it the thumbs up, and remember, Calvin was tougher than all of us as far as approval goes. This guy spent time in prison for statutory rape. And did I mention he has a hell of a lot of money? He could buy the whole damn company, let alone a few films."

"You may be right," Pete said. "It probably would not be prudent to ignore him. When does this guy want to start?"

"Friday," Leon said. "And he wants two of his men to supervise."

"Bullshit," Pete said.

"We may want to listen," Leon said. "The guy said if we don't agree to his terms, he'll find someone else. He said there were plenty of people willing to make films in Southern California, and if we didn't want to work with him, he was sure someone else would."

"What's his hurry?"

"He said he is expecting 'guests' from the Middle East, and he wants the films prior to their arrival. We've all hosted big events. I can see why he'd want things done on time."

"Screw him," Pete said.

"Not so quick," Leon said. "If he's so cocky that he's willing to take business elsewhere, maybe we shouldn't be so hasty. Look at the reports; he's rich as hell. He could buy all of us and not bat an eyelash."

"Study it hard. I don't see any harm in it," Leon said. "He's putting more than a million down. I doubt he'd risk that for nothing. A million bucks buys a lot of pussy."

"What are the terms?" Mike asked.

"Pretty plain," Leon said. "We finish in twelve weeks or we refund the money. The second film must be delivered in eighteen weeks, and the third in twenty-two. Hell, we could do them all in twelve weeks if we wanted. All they consist of is a few girls getting screwed."

Mike laughed. "If he wants to start Friday, let's do it. We could use the money."

～

LEON GOT Farouk's check on Friday, verified funds, then called to tell him they were ready to start shooting. He gave Farouk the address where his men could go to supervise. Afterward, they discussed the financial terms again, then Leon hung up.

Farouk immediately called the bank to cancel his check. Since it was Friday, Mezzanotte Productions would not be notified until Monday at the earliest. When he finished, he hung up and turned to Nicky. "We're all set to go. They're expecting you at Mezzanotte Productions. You're listed as Spencer Dancer and Mike Randolph." Farouk dropped his smile and stared. "Those were the names you gave me, right?"

Monroe smiled. "You did good, my man."

I went over the details with DuPree one more time before leaving. "You know what to do, right? Be there on time, or we'll be left out in the cold.

"Don't worry, Nicky. I got it."

"You better have it," Monroe said. "If you don't, your ass is mine."

MONROE and I arrived at the gate to Mezzanotte Productions just as the afternoon shift was starting. We waited a few minutes, as we didn't want to run into the guard who had let us in the first time.

I said, "They're expecting us," then flashed my fake ID—Spencer Dancer. Monroe did the same with his—Mike Randolph. Within minutes we were being escorted to building number three—the building where Calvin said the girls were being kept.

We were dropped off at the front door, where another set of guards greeted us, or should I say "screened us," asking for identification again. We showed our licenses, then we were frisked one more time before being allowed entry. Fortunately for us, they were amateurs, and didn't think to look under my hat. We had planned on them frisking us. It would have been disastrous otherwise.

We walked down a long hallway to a room in the back. This was tighter security than I had expected. Maybe Calvin's death put them on high alert.

Shooting for the "film" had already started, and two Asian girls were lying on the bed—naked—surrounded by four large men of varying nationalities. One man was Latino, one was black, and the other two appeared to be of mixed nationality. They were naked also.

First they took turns doing the girls, then they ganged up and double-teamed them, then they made the girls do each other. I was only glad that we had insisted on the Asians first, not because I didn't like Asians, but because I didn't want this to be Allison. I don't think I could have stood by and let this happen to someone I knew, even if not well. It was only because I kept reminding myself that I had to stick to the plan that I was able to stand by and do nothing.

After witnessing hours of more despicable acts that made me feel as if my skin was crawling and my blood boiling, we called it a day.

The film crew was wrapping up, while two guards came to escort the girls back to their "quarters" for the night. The guards waited for the girls to dress, frisked them, a little too friendly of a frisk, then walked them down the hall, with the girls three steps in front of them.

I took note of the process, while we slowly exited the building, but I wondered what kind of room the girls were kept in. *Would we need to take the guards alive?* There was bound to be a lock on the door. *If it were a key lock, no problem. But if it were a combination lock, we'd need the guards alive and coherent. I'd have to see if I could find that out.*

Monroe and I said goodbye to the crew, said we'd rejoin them on Monday, then began our walk to the front gate. About halfway there, I turned to the boss and asked if we could pick up shooting on Sunday, as my boss was in a big hurry.

"It would mean a lot to him," I said. "Enough that he'd more than likely feel especially generous—in a financial way—if the picture came in ahead of schedule. Generous to the whole crew," I added.

After a *very* slight hesitation, he nodded. "Be here at 5:00 p.m. on Saturday. It would be better to shoot then. We'll get more of the guys to work that shift, because it's tough to convince guys to work on Sundays. And make sure to mention our "cooperation" to your boss."

"You got it," I said, then Monroe and I continued our walk. Within ten minutes, we exited the building, but before we got thirty feet, a uniformed guard showed up driving a golf-cart-type vehicle and offered us a ride. Insisted on a ride is more like it. We accepted his "hospitality," rode the cart to the front gate, then said goodnight and walked across the street to where DuPree waited.

WE DISCUSSED the plan as we drove back.

"Not gonna be easy," Monroe said.

"It'll be easy enough," I said. "With the silencers Farouk got us, and the bombs if we need them, we'll be fine."

"What about DuPree?"

"If we plan it right, he'll be here just in time."

"Those bombs make a lot of noise," Monroe said.

"I know. I haven't figured out how to handle that yet. Who knows? We may not even need them."

~

"Farouk, we need to know where the top brass lives. The ones who make the decisions," I said. "How long will it take you to find out?"

"Probably by tomorrow morning," he said. "Maybe Sunday."

"Make it tomorrow morning," I said.

The first one was Mike Servillo. He lived in another mountain-top retreat at the end of a quarter-mile driveway. We parked on the side, by the garage door, and walked to the front. DuPree rang the bell while Monroe and I stood to the side.

Servillo answered in less than a minute. "Can I help you?" he said.

I stepped in front of him, and said, "Probably. But that depends on you."

"What do you mean? What are you talking about?" Mike said.

I gestured to a chair visible from the entry. "Take a seat. We have a lot to discuss."

Mike began to object, then must have thought better of it and took a seat. "What do you want?" he asked.

"I want to know where the girls are, and who is guarding them?"

Since we already knew the answers to this, the question served as more of a lie detector—establishing a base line.

"I don't know what you're talking about."

"Don't try it," I said. "Calvin held out for a while, but it cost him undue pain. I don't think you want to suffer the same way."

"Calvin? Suffer? What are you talking about? I don't know anything about any girls."

"If you keep up that line, you will be screaming in about five minutes as I break every bone in your foot. Think hard before you answer this time. Where are the girls? And who is guarding them?"

"I don't—"

I shook my head. "Don't do it. If you say 'I don't know,' I'll find out what you really know, and I don't think you want me to do that."

Servillo must have been thinking. Finally, he said, "The girls are in building three. There are six guards. Two at the front door, two at the intersection of hallways, and two guarding the girls."

Mike thought for a moment more, then said, "And the guards are all armed with instructions to shoot intruders."

"Good," I said. "That's good, Mike. That coincides with what Calvin told us, so I'm inclined to believe you."

"Now, another question. Are the locks securing the girls combination locks or keyed? And remember, we're going to find out the truth, so if you lie, you'll suffer. "

"Key locks. The guards at the rooms have the keys. I know this because they joked about letting themselves in for a little nightly pleasure."

"Good. That's what I needed to know. So far you're doing great. Your story is coinciding with Calvin's."

A puzzled look came to Mike's eyes. "If Calvin told you what you wanted, why is he dead?"

I pulled out my gun and held it to his temple. "Because he was in the same business as you," I said, and pulled the trigger—twice.

"Looks like we're done," DuPree said. "We got what we need."

"We're far from done," Monroe said. "All of these pricks are involved, so they're all gonna pay."

I nodded. "I'm afraid so, DuPree."

We continued with our work, going to visit Leon, Pete, and the rest of them, one by one. Each one gave us identical information, which led me to believe that they were telling the truth, and in all but Pete's case we got the information without resorting to the hammer.

"Why'd you have to do this shit?" DuPree asked. "They gave up what they knew."

I shook my head, disappointed in DuPree. "They only gave up what they knew because they were afraid of being hurt. If they thought for a minute that they could save their ass any other way, they'd have done it. Besides, they deserved what they got. *They* chose their life, not me."

"You didn't have to kill them."

"Did you see the DVD? Did you see what they did to those girls? It will be with them forever. For that, these people deserved to die and a lot more." I turned and looked at DuPree. "You can't do that shit to people and expect to live. Somebody's gonna catch up with you."

We cleaned up and began our exit. "Don't forget to tell Farouk we'll need that van tomorrow."

"He already knows," Monroe said. "It's ready."

MEZZANOTTE AGAIN

e rolled out at about 4:00 p.m., which worked perfectly. This way, we didn't have to wait for the second guard shift to take effect. Monroe drove the car and DuPree the van. I rode with Monroe. This would be a good test for Johnny Muck's "invisibility" theory, as a lot of people were going to see us. It remained to be seen if they'd remember us.

Monroe drove up to the gate, and I presented my license for Spencer Dancer, which got us through and onto the property where we proceeded to building three. Monroe and I were supposed to be part of the shooting, and even though they didn't normally work on weekends, they had made an exception in anticipation of financial rewards.

"What about if they frisk us again?" Monroe asked.

"They won't. We're part of the crew now. We promised them money. Nothing buys trust like money, or the promise of money. Besides, if they ignored the hat yesterday, I'm sure they will today."

Monroe shook his head. "You better hope so or our ass is in jail. Or dead."

We got through the gate and into the building with nothing more than a few smiles. "Told you," I whispered to Monroe as we got near building three.

"We ain't in yet," he said, but moments later we were in, and as I predicted, without being frisked.

The production crew was already working when we arrived, and the girls were "in action" on the bed. I wanted to shoot everybody except the girls right then, but I held back. Killing them this early wasn't part of the plan.

After enduring numerous hours of disgusting material, the crew stopped shooting. It was about 11:00 p.m. Two guards appeared a few minutes later and took the girls away. Monroe and I pretended to head down the long hallway toward the exit, but took a right turn toward the girls' rooms, following them.

Monroe talked loudly, and we made a point of clicking our heels on the hard flooring so that we made plenty of noise. We didn't want it to seem as if we were sneaking, just lost.

As we neared the next intersection, a guard appeared, gun drawn. "Hold up," he said.

"Whoa!" I said. "What the hell are you doing?"

"What are you doing down here?" he asked.

"Down where? We just came from shooting," I said. "Ask Ted. He's been with us all day."

"The mention of Ted, the production manager, put him at ease. "Well, you're in the wrong place." He pointed the opposite way. "That's the way out of here."

"Shit, we must have made a wrong turn," Monroe said. He grabbed my arm. "Let's go."

Relaxed now, the guard started putting his gun away. As he did, I drew mine and shoved it in his face. "One wrong move and I'll blow your head off," I said.

"Holler to the other guard that everything's all right," I said. "Do it right and you may live. Do it wrong, and…"

He nodded, then leaned down the hall. "Got it, Bud."

"Wait a moment, then call him down here. Don't make it seem like anything's wrong. And the girls' rooms—are they locked with key locks or combinations?"

"Keys," he said, gesturing to his belt. "I've got them right here. If you let me move, I'll get them."

So, Mike was telling the truth. It is key locks. This was working out better than expected. "Go ahead," I said. "But no wrong moves."

He handed me a set of keys, then said, "Shall I call him now?" His voice was cracking.

"Take time to get your breath, then do it."

The guard waited a moment, then leaned to the side, and said, "Hey, Bud, give me a hand, will ya?"

A moment later, Bud wandered down the hall. At the corner, where it intersected the next hall, Monroe hit him in the head with the butt of his gun, knocking him out. Simultaneously, I hit the first guard, knocking him out also.

We taped them up and gagged them in case they came to. Monroe grabbed the other guard's keys in the event the ones we had weren't the right ones. Once we had what we wanted, we ran down the hall to where the girls were being kept and set them loose.

I hadn't seen such happiness or heard such squealing since Rosa had her thirteenth birthday party, but it sounded great. All of the noise was mixed with tears, but they were happy tears. "Shh. Shh," Monroe said. Keep it quiet or the other guards will hear."

That settled the girls down. They continued with their smiles but restrained the noise. One of them, a Middle Eastern girl from the looks of her, walked over to the guards on the floor and kicked the taller one—the first guard—in the face.

"What's that for?" I asked.

"That son of a bitch raped us every night. He'd come into our cells in the middle of the night and do his thing with whoever was the unlucky one. Sometimes, he brought other men with him."

I quietly walked over to the guard, pulled out my gun—with silencer attached—and plugged him in the head. He wouldn't be raping anyone else. Not ever.

"What about him?" I asked, pointing to the other.

She shook her head. "Not him. At least not with us."

"Us neither," an Asian girl said. "He was always pretty nice. Considering."

"Okay," I said. "We're getting you out of here, but you need to listen closely. Don't make any noise. No talking. No loud walking. Do what I say, and you'll be home in a few days. If you don't listen, you'll probably be back where you were. Your choice."

"Oh my God, just get us out of here," one of the girls said.

She was a short, thin Asian girl, and I now felt bad about having told Farouk to ask them for Asians first. Another one of them grabbed me and kissed me. A third did the same to Monroe. He smiled, then he realized it was Allison. "We got you now, girl. You're safe."

"I told them you'd get us, Monroe. I told them."

"Yeah," he said. "Well do me a favor and keep it to yourself. Don't tell anybody you know me."

She whispered, "Thanks," and kissed him again.

"Save that shit for when we get home," he said. "We've still got work to do."

We walked slowly back down the hall, careful not to make much noise. At the intersection before the main doors, I crept up, got on the floor, and peeked down the hall. Two men stood guard, and they appeared to be holding automatic rifles. They were too far away to pop with the silencers we had, and I didn't want to use the bombs—at least not yet..

I thought about what to do, then came up with a plan. I addressed the girls in a whisper. "Here's what I need," I said. "I want you to go back down the hall about fifty feet, then all together, start singing. I don't care what, just sing."

"What for?" one girl asked.

Another girl started crying. "They'll hear us. I'm not doing it. I want to get out of here."

"We will get out of here," I said. "And this will help. The female voices will throw them off. Or at least I hope they will. If the guards hear female voices, they won't expect much trouble. Monroe and I will wait at the corner and take them out when they come around."

Allison took charge, gathering the girls together, then she led them down the hall. After about fifty or sixty feet, she turned to me and shrugged. "Here?" she mouthed silently.

I nodded, not wanting to risk a male voice.

A moment later, the girls started singing.

"London Bridge is falling down, falling down, falling down. London..."

They continued singing, and before long the noise must have captured the attention of the guards in the front hall, as I heard their footsteps approaching. The steps sounded cautious at first, then more relaxed as the guards neared the corner.

Monroe and I crouched by the wall at the intersection. We listened to the guards' footsteps, judging how far they were by the sound. When it seemed as if they were at the corner, I jumped up and hit one with the butt of my gun. Monroe hit the other. Everything went smooth.

Monroe taped their mouths shut, taped their arms and legs, then hit them again for safe measure.

I pulled my gun, ready to shoot them, when Allison said, "They didn't do anything."

I looked to her with a doubtful glance, as if to say, are you sure?

She nodded, and said, "I'd tell you if they did. Believe me."

I put the gun away, turned to Monroe, and said, "Get the girls. Let's get the hell out of here."

When Monroe waved his arm, a signal for them to come, one of them shrieked, but soon stopped. When they caught up to us, I reminded them to be quiet, then we walked slowly—and quietly—down the hall. The problem was it wasn't quiet; their shoes were making noise.

I stopped and turned to the girls. "You need to take off your shoes," I said. "They're making too much noise and we don't want to risk alerting the guards next door."

The girls took off the shoes, then we continued. There were still two guards at the front door. And another building full of them next to us. The last thing we wanted was the building next to us alerted to our presence.

As we approached the steps leading outside, I said to Monroe, "It may be better if we go out by ourselves."

Monroe agreed. We told the girls of our plans, then climbed the steps. The guards turned with guns drawn. Monroe laughed. "Goddamn, don't go shootin' me before I view the final product."

Upon hearing that, one guard, a rotund bald man, joined Monroe in laughter. "Wouldn't do that, my man."

The other said, "Sorry, dude. Can't be too careful."

I pulled my gun and put it next to the rotund guy's face. "No, you can't be too careful. Now, put your guns down."

Monroe had his gun out too. "Do it now, or I pop you," he said. "I won't hesitate."

The guards—now with frowns on their faces—laid their guns on the sidewalk. Monroe took both of the guards inside and taped their mouths shut and then taped their arms to their sides. Afterward, he got the girls.

"We're going to get in that van," I said, pointing to the van DuPree was just pulling up in. "But I need you to walk, don't run. We don't want to attract attention."

The girls agreed, and we exited the building, and moved down the sidewalk at a quick pace. I could tell by the look on the girls' faces, they were doing everything they could not to run, but they were doing a good job of it. DuPree was waiting at the curb with the van. He was nervous. I could tell by the way he shifted his glance from building two to the gate and back again.

We opened the van's side door, and the girls couldn't control themselves. They piled in. It was a squeeze, but they fit, and we were on our way inside of five minutes.

DuPree stopped just short of the main gate. I got out, approached the younger guard and pulled my gun on him. I held him at bay while Monroe taped him. I asked where the hard drive that held the video of people coming and going was, and when he pointed to it, I smashed it, tossed one of the bombs next to it, dragged him out of harm's way, then we split.

"Where to?" DuPree asked.

"To get the other car, drive to the hotel to wash up, then the bus station," I said. "Let's get these girls home. We don't have extra time, because that bomb will make a lot of noise. The mess at the scene will delay them for a while but not forever."

A rousing cheer arose from the back. This time I didn't squelch it.

THE WIRETAP PAYS OFF

With the wiretap in place, it wasn't long before Lou got the name of the driver of the red pick-up. Now all he had to do was stake out Wentworth's place for a few days and wait for the truck to show up, then follow him and spring a trap.

For two days, Lou and Sherri parked about a block away, waiting for him to show. They were thinking they may have it wrong, when he appeared.

They sat in the car, playing trivia games and waited for him to leave. Once he pulled away, they followed him for a few miles. He eventually returned to Wentworth's. They watched him go into the gallery, waited while he talked to Foster, and then started the tail again when he left.

Lou let him go a few miles, but was careful not to be seen, then he pulled Roger over for a "routine" traffic stop, which was anything but routine.

After the perfunctory driver's license and registration statement, Lou mentioned that he had an "eye witness" to a crime that described a red pick-up like his. He said "eye" witness because it sounded better. But really, if you thought about it, what the hell else was it going to be?

It's just that people were so accustomed to hearing the words "eye witness" from TV shows and movies, that those words are what they expected. They sounded stronger than just a *witness*.

This was a lucky break for them, but it didn't hurt that Lou's illegal wiretap gave them the information on when Roger would be there, at least to within a few days.

Back at the station, they put Roger into one of the interview rooms. Lou had previously written his license plate number and truck description on a yellow pad, which they had in one of the desk drawers.

Once they had Roger seated, Lou started in. "We've got you dead to rights, boy. Got an eye witness that places you square at the scene of two murders."

Lou stopped to put a dry cigarette in his mouth. "Now, either you did the killing—which I don't think you did—or you know who committed the murders." He leaned in close, and yelled, "Which is it?"

Lou then nodded to Sherri and she yanked the yellow pad from the drawer. Lou shoved it in front of him. "Is this your plate? Is it?"

Roger didn't say anything, so Lou hollered again. "Think hard, boy. You've been with us the whole time. We didn't write that down, and the video over there will confirm it. That pad *is* your license plate number. It means you're guilty. The only thing left is to decide what you're guilty of—murder or just illegal disposal of a body. One will get you twenty-five years; the other may turn into a walk—if you cooperate."

After a little pressure—and seeing the evidence they had against him —Roger folded like a guy holding a busted flush. Before an hour was up, he was spilling information about Foster that they had no inkling about and wouldn't have gotten any other way. Any other legal way.

Roger explained that Foster paid him ten grand cash per dump. He also told the detectives that Foster had arranged for a "critic" to provide a formal appraisal of the paintings upon receipt. The critic got twenty grand per painting. Roger didn't know what Speranza's cut was, but he confirmed that she *was* the one doing the painting.

"Who pulled the trigger?" Lou asked.

"Foster did. He lured them to the back of the studio with some excuse, then shot them while Timothy—that's the critic's name—was talking to them. He always shot them in the back."

"So Timothy was there when the people were killed?"

"Every one of them," Roger said.

"I would wait outside in my truck most of the time, but one time I came inside to use the restroom. That's when I saw Foster shoot him. It was Mr. Monfrer."

"Then what happened?" Sherri asked.

"Then Timothy and Foster loaded the body into the bed of the truck and climbed in. Foster told me where to go, then when we got there, he got out with Timothy and dumped the body." Roger's eyes got wide. "I swear, I never did anything except drive the truck."

"You'll still face charges," Sherri said, "but if you testify against Foster, the DA will likely go easy on you."

"Count on it," Roger said. "I ain't doin' time for that prick."

"That sounds good," Lou said. "Now, let's go get the painter."

THEY SAT outside the coffee shop for forty-five minutes, watching dozens of people come and go. Finally, Speranza came out, walking alongside a tall gentleman with graying hair. Sherri approached and said, "I'm Detective Sherri Miller. Are you Speranza Desdaemona?"

"That depends."

"You're right," Sherri said. "Maybe your name doesn't depend on it, but a lot depends on whether you cooperate. If you do, you may not go to prison or only go for a short while. If you don't, you *will* go for a long time. You and Foster both."

Speranza tossed her coffee cup into the trash can next to her. The man she had been with was long gone. He disappeared when Sherri identified herself.

Speranza looked up at Sherri with a scowl. Her tone and attitude matched her expression. "What the hell are you talking about? I don't know anybody named Foster."

Sherri moved forward and brought Speranza's hands behind her back to cuff her, but just then Lou walked up so Sherri held off. "We've got you dead to rights. Pictures of you leaving Foster's shop. Records of payments made by Foster to you for the paintings. If you don't want to go down with an accessory to murder charge, you better convince me otherwise."

The girl backed up, holding her hands in front of her face. "Whoa! I wasn't part of killing anybody."

"You'll have to convince a judge of that, honey, but right now, the evidence points to you being a *big* part of it."

~

BACK AT THE STATION, Speranza sat quietly in the chair of interrogation room two. You can talk now, or you can talk later," Lou said, "but you *are* gonna talk."

"I've got nothing to say," she said.

"How much were you getting per painting? Fifty grand? You know how much Foster sold them for? More than a million."

A surprised look came over her face. "Bullshit."

"No bullshit," Lou said, then turned to Sherri. "Get that canceled check so we can show it to her."

A moment later, Sherri returned with a canceled check for 1.4 million made out to WOW—Wentworth of Williamsburg. "This is from Manual," Lou said, pushing it in front of her. "We have two more checks—one from Monfrer and one from Farmington. Farmington's check is for slightly less, but not much. I'm convinced the sale price was substantially more than your cut."

"Son of a bitch!"

"Yeah, son of a bitch is right. You did all the work and got what, maybe 150,000 total. Maybe not even that. Meanwhile, Wentorth gets about three million. Doesn't seem equitable to me. Certainly not the kind of guy I'd be willing to do time for."

"Son of a bitch," she said, then looked up at Lou. "What do I get if I cooperate? And what do I have to do?"

WRAPPED IN A BOW

*L*ou and Sherri arrived at the Wentworth Gallery at opening time. Foster was already inside, but it didn't look like any customers were there.

Lou walked into the gallery with Sherri hot on his heels. Unlike the visit to Ricky's, there were no Hermes scarves, but there were no Levi's jeans either; in fact, there wasn't anybody. The place was empty, save for Foster Wentworth.

Foster was standing behind the counter. "May I help you?"

"Where is everybody?" Lou asked. "Did you kill them all?"

Lou pulled his gun and pointed it at Wentworth. "Hands behind your back," he said. "My partner is gonna cuff you."

Wentworth risked a glance to a spot under the counter but must have thought better of it. "What's this about?"

Lou smiled. "I think you know, Wentworth, but in case you don't, you're under arrest for the murders of Manual Ramirez, Jacques Monfrer, and Chip Farmington, among other things."

"You're crazy. They were my customers and darn good ones."

As Sherri put the cuffs on Wentworth, Lou put his gun away and said, "Yeah, we know, and Speranza and Roger will tell everyone all about it, as I'm sure Timothy will when we find him."

"By the way," Sherri said, "you have the right to remain silent. Anything you say…" She finished the mandatory reading of his Miranda rights, then spun him around again.

"This is insane. I didn't do anything. And who are those people? I certainly don't know them."

"Really?" Lou said. "Is that what you're going with? Because if it is, you're in deep shit. We sat outside of your gallery and took pictures of Roger exiting—after a lengthy visit, I might add. And he's willing to testify to everything, including the money you paid him to dump the bodies—ten G's per. So you may want to rethink your position."

"And as far as killing those gentlemen, I would never…"

"Not even when they found out your paintings weren't worth the materials they were made from? Not even when you lured them into your backroom with Timothy, shot them, then had Roger drive you to dump them?"

Lou laughed. "Yeah, Foster. We know it all. And you're going to have a long time to think about what you did. Of course, your cellmates may not allow you those privileges, but that's up to you to work out."

Lou's phone rang. He thought about not answering it, then did anyway. "Mazzetti."

"It's Simpson. We found your guy. Where do you want him?"

Lou thought for a moment, then gave them the address of the gallery. "Bring him here," Lou said. "It should prove interesting."

Lou hung up, walked over and whispered to Sherri, who looked at Wentworth and smiled.

"You know who that was?" Lou said. "It was my people calling. They found Timothy and they're bringing him here."

Foster looked aside. "I don't know any Timothy."

"Sure you do. He's the one who joined you in the back room and stood by while you shot those people. He's also the one who did the so-called appraisals on the art work."

"I don't know where you're going with this, but—"

"I'm not going anywhere with it," Lou said. "But Timothy is coming here. After that, we'll determine where to go, but my bet is the station, then Rikers." Lou laughed. "And the stay at Rikers could be a long time, although they may decide to send you upstate."

Wentworth pretended to fiddle with some files, while shaking his head. "You're out of your mind. I'm not going anywhere."

"You're right about that," Lou said. "And Sherri and I are here to make sure of it. The only place you're going is prison."

"You don't have a thing on me."

"We've got you selling paintings to all three of the men—Ramirez, Monfrer, and Farmington. We've got a beyond-reproach gentleman who will testify that he purchased that same painting, and will further testify that his appraiser—another beyond-reproach witness—will swear it is worthless. Furthermore, this same gentleman will swear that Ramirez said he was going to confront you on the day he was killed."

"All circumstantial," Wentworth said.

"That's true," Lou said. "But circumstantial adds up. When we combine those sales with the testimony of the appraiser, Roger's statement that he witnessed the shooting of Jacques Monfrer, and that he dumped the other bodies, and Timothy's soon-to-be statement, added to Speranza's sworn testimony—when you put it all together and stir it gently with the right DA, you're toast. I'd estimate twenty-five-to-life toast."

Wentworth worked in silence for a few moments, then Simpson entered the gallery pushing Timothy ahead of him. "Meet Timothy Randolph," Simpson said. "He had three or four licenses on him, all in different names, but a fingerprint check revealed the right one."

Lou approached. "Well, Timothy, what's it going to be—murder or accomplice to murder?"

"What are you talking about? I was sitting at home, minding my own business when this…brute barged in."

Simpson laughed. "Ask him about the money in the bank accounts in his other name. Almost fifty-two grand. I had them run a check based on books we found at his house. It's verified."

"Well?" Lou said.

"I've got nothing to say."

"You better," Lou said. "Roger is testifying that you were present when all the murders were committed, and we've got the money, which I'm positive will connect you to Foster. There's not much left except to determine who pulled the trigger. I don't care who the jury thinks did it, you or Wentworth."

"It was him," Timothy said. "I did nothing other than appraise the art and help dispose of the bodies."

"You stupid fuck," Wentworth said. "You stupid—"

Lou walked behind Foster and took the cuffs off. "Foster Wentworth, you're still under arrest for the murders of Manual Ramirez, Jacques Monfrer, and Chip Farmington, but I'm gonna give you a couple of minutes to lock up your shop, because you're going to be gone for a long time. "

Wentworth locked up, then accompanied Lou and Sherri to the

station. Six hours later, after much cajoling, blackmailing, lying, and about everything else, he confessed. He took a plea bargain for three counts of murder in the second, though Lou recommended that the DA hold out for a first-degree charge. Lou felt confident he could get the evidence to make it stick. The district attorney was happy, though. Three counts of second-degree was not a puny sentence.

Lou and Sherri celebrated their success by going out for a beer and a roast beef sandwich. Lou had pickles on the side with his. Sherri ordered chips.

"Looks like we did it, Mazzetti

"It's a good way to go out," Lou said. "Now, I can retire in peace."

THE BUS STATION

$\mathcal{W}$e drove down the 405, then went east on I-10 until we got to the bus station. It didn't take long to get there, and—even at this time of night—it was crowded. Not with the best class of people but crowded nonetheless.

Old newspapers and empty bags from lunch and dinner littered the floors and one of seats was covered in spilled Coke, or at least I hoped it was Coke. To the side, a trio of hippie-looking teenagers huddled in the corner. They looked to be doing more than talking and appeared to be avoiding company as well.

Two black guys with dirty scarves on their heads were eyeing everyone who came in, and my bets were on them mugging someone before the night was through.

I gathered the girls together near the center of the room and asked, "Who's going where?"

"Portland," a few shouted.

"Provo," said another.

"Kansas City," said three or four at once.

If my calculations were correct, that left only the girls from Wilmington.

I walked to the ticket counter, followed by the girls, and purchased one-way tickets for two to Portland, one to Provo, and three to Kansas City. There was one more girl than I had thought, but that was better than one less. I must have counted wrong.

Miraculously, we were making it out of California with no casualties — at least none so far.

Before the buses left, I gathered the girls one last time. As soon as they were in front of me, I said, "Listen up, girls. It's going to be a long ride for all of you, but you'll make it. Just sit tight, stick together, and don't go *anywhere* with anyone."

I looked at the girl going to Provo, alone, and said, "Your best bet is to find an older woman, tell her you're traveling alone and ask if you can sit with her." I stood and addressed them all one final time. "And whatever else you do, forget my name."

"I don't even know your name," said the one from Provo.

"Good," I said. "Let's leave it that way. I had to do bad things to get you out of that place, and I don't want to attract attention for what was done. So no matter what happens, or who asks you, tell them you know nothing. You owe me that much."

"We'll do it," they all said in unison.

I hustled them on their way, and made sure each group got on the appropriate bus safely, then I joined Monroe and DuPree. The other seven girls would be riding home with us—to Wilmington.

There was no way we were going to fit in one car, and they weren't keen on a bus trip, so we were going to have to keep the van and use both cars until we got to Baltimore. I wouldn't turn the van in there, as it would be suspicious, having been rented in California—or could be viewed as suspicious—so I'd have to pay someone to drive it back to Los Angeles.

It shouldn't be a problem. Jobs like that were always easy to fill; in fact, I felt certain that Monroe would be able to find a suitable candidate or two.

Within two hours, the other three buses had left, and we were ready to go. "Get the van ready, DuPree. We're leaving in fifteen minutes. Don't forget, we're taking two cars."

"You know which way you're heading?" DuPree asked.

"Got it covered," I said. "We're taking I-15 up to I-40, then shooting down Highway 93 to I-10 at Phoenix. From there, we'll alternate so no one can predict what we're doing or which way we're going."

"What are we being so secretive about?" DuPree asked.

"Because somebody, at sometime—more than likely as soon as the shit hits the fan in Los Angeles—will think to look at cameras on the interstates heading east. We don't want them to *know* which route we're taking. Doing it this way, if they spot us on I-10 in Phoenix, and look for us on I-10 in Tucson, we won't be there. Or if they see us on I-40 in Flagstaff, we won't still be on 40 in Amarillo."

DuPree shook his head. "You're a suspicious mother, aren't you?"

"That's how you stay alive—and out of prison," I said. "Which reminds me. Call Dixon and make sure he has somebody lined up to drive this van back to Farouk. They'll need to take it from Wilmington to Los Angeles, and I want it delivered in less than six days. On second thought, I'd prefer to have two people. One to follow the van and be available to drive home."

"Got it," Monroe said. "Shouldn't be a problem." He must have thought about it and said, "*Won't* be a problem."

I had DuPree stop in St. Louis so we could buy a burner phone at a

Walmart. I used it to call the Los Angeles Times and I told them what Mezzanotte Productions was into.

With all the bodies they'd soon discover of Mezzanotte executives, I figured the Times would find it interesting; besides, when you had dirt like that on people, sympathy was difficult to generate. People would forget what was done to them a lot sooner.

It took us five days to drive home, and that included a detour over the Arkansas River so that we could get rid of the hammer—the mall as well. I cleaned them first—for the second time—then pulled over to the side of the road and had DuPree bury both of them, but in different spots. I made sure he buried them deep, and more than a few feet from the edge. That way, no one would be likely to find either one of them.

Four days was more than I had hoped, but considering the route I laid out, it was better than expected. We dropped the rental off in Baltimore and drove back to Wilmington in a crowded van and the car we originally used—seven girls and three of us. Fortunately, the trip from Baltimore to Wilmington wasn't long, so the discomfort was short-lived.

Monroe mapped out the shortest route for dropping the girls off, then we set out to do it. The girl who had been taken on the Governor Printz was first.

I reminded each one who I was—Spencer Dancer—and told them not to talk about it. I knew they would, but this way, the name of Spencer Dancer would stick in their head, not anything else. And by the time anyone got around to checking, Spencer Dancer would be long gone.

Allison was the last person to go home. We drove up Franklin Street and parked about half a block from her house. She got out of the van and did a controlled run/walk to the house.

Instead of walking in, she knocked on the door and stood, shaking with excitement. After a few seconds, her father opened the wooden door. His expression went from one of "What the hell do you want" to "Oh my God."

"My baby!" he screamed, and threw his arms around her. She cried and hugged him back.

"Lizzie! Lizzie!" Mr. Parker yelled. "Come here. Our baby is back."

Seconds later, Mrs. Parker emerged from the kitchen, tears in her eyes. She opened her arms to hug her. "Praise the Lord," she said. "Praise the Lord."

Monroe and I stood at the foot of the steps, smiling. Times like this made everything worthwhile, no matter what we'd done.

Mr. Parker turned to me and held his arms out. "I don't know what to say. You've saved my girl."

"It wasn't just me," I said. "Monroe did as much as I did. He deserves credit."

Parker wrapped his arms around Monroe and cried. "Willie! Willie boy. I don't know how to thank you."

"You just did," Monroe said, then he pointed to me. "But this guy is who you need to thank. He did most of the work and all of the planning. And in case you haven't noticed, he's white."

"I ain't never been indebted to a white man before, but I am now," Parker said.

He reached to hug me. I hugged him back, and I felt him sobbing, then I pushed away. "Mr. Parker, this is something I would have done for anyone. It just so happens my little girl and Allison are friends, and the best thing you can do for me is forget that.

Pretend you don't know me. Never saw me. Same goes for Monroe. We had to do some things that normal people may object to. It was necessary, but it wasn't what society would condone. It may cause us trouble if anyone finds out."

"I never heard of you," Parker said, "But I thank you. From the bottom of my heart, I thank you."

Allison ran over and hugged me. "Thanks, Mr. Fusco. I mean Mr. Dancer." She stepped back and smiled. "And don't worry, I'll forget I ever heard of Mr. Fusco."

"Thanks, Allison." I kissed her on the cheek and said, "And remember, none of this was your fault. It's no different than being mugged. You were the victim and they were the assholes." Then I leaned close to her ear and whispered, "And you're the one that's still alive."

She smiled. "That's what's important."

"You've got that right," I said. "See you later."

NOTHING IS RANDOM

*R*aff's car had come up clean, not surprising, but Frankie had hoped for *something. Anything.*

"What do we do now?" he asked Mrozinski.

Mrozinski plopped his feet up on the desk. "I don't know, Donovan. I wish I did."

"They're going to be coming for more girls," Frankie said.

"Why do you say that?"

"Because I have it on good authority that someone made sure of it. The other girls are freed."

"Jesus Christ! Don't tell me shit like that. Is that how you knew Nicky didn't kill Smiles, because he was in California killing other people?"

"I never mentioned Nicky's name, and I sure as hell didn't mention anything about killing. All I said is that I had it on good authority that the girls had been freed. Take what you will from that."

Mrozinski said, "All right. I'm not happy with what's going on, but I'm not going to be sad over shit like them biting the bullet." Mrozinski looked at Frankie. "Have you talked to Nicky? Did he say anything?"

Frankie half laughed, half scoffed. "If you think I'm telling you anything about what Nicky did, you're crazier than I thought."

"I don't mean about what he did. I mean anything that may help us."

Frankie thought for a moment. "He said there was about every nationality of girl imaginable there—black, white, Hispanic, Middle Eastern, Asian, you name it—and he said they were from a bunch of different cities."

As Frankie said it, something struck him as odd. "Hang on a minute," he said. "Wait." Frankie thought for a moment, then said, "That's it! That's the pattern."

"What's the pattern?" Mrozinski asked.

"There is no pattern," Frankie said. "The pattern is that there is no pattern. Think about it."

"I am thinking about it, but I don't see anything," Mrozinski said.

"When is random not random?" Frankie asked. "When they're *trying* to be random. When they are targeting different locations. When they are *not* targeting nationalities. What we have to look for is the opposite. Find the locations they *haven't* picked. Find the nationalities they *haven't* picked. In other words, the opposite."

"You mean who they haven't snatched yet?"

"Exactly," Frankie said. "They're going to need new girls since *someone* set the others free. What better place to go than somewhere you've been before? But I'd bet ten dollars to a doughnut that they won't target the same types. They'll go after the ones they never got."

"Like what?"

"I don't know. Let's look at the facts. Who did they get before? Asian, black, Middle Easterner, white. So what are they missing?"

"I have no idea," Mrozinski said.

Frankie explained his theory again and waited for an answer.

Mrozinski stared at Frankie. "Hispanics would be the logical choice. Or Indians, but we don't have a big population of Indians. And since you already said they got Asians, Arabs, blacks and whites, we'll ignore them for now."

"And if we did have a lot of Indians, they probably wouldn't be concentrated in any one area. Grabbing an Arab would be hit or miss, and they'd have no logical place to stake out for a black or a white—maybe Asian, but not black or white. On the other hand, Harrison Street would be ideal for Hispanics."

Mrozinski jumped up. "I think you may have something, Donovan. Goddamn, if I don't think so."

Mrozinski leaned forward and yelled into the intercom. "Get me Jones and Matuscek. And I mean now."

They didn't have long to wait for Matuscek. Jones followed a minute later.

"What's up? Matuscek asked.

"We need a stakeout team—four people—and ones that can keep their mouths shut," Mrozinski said. "If one word gets out, it will be some-body's ass, and I bet you can guess whose ass that would be."

"Yes, sir," both of them said.

After they departed, Frankie said, "I want in on this. I want this guy bad."

"I don't blame you," Mrozinski said. "You can pair up with me. I want his ass, too."

Mrozinski sent someone for more coffee and said, "As for how to handle this, let's post pairs for each night. We'll take the Friday-night watch, but we have to use your car. My wife's taking mine to the mall."

"I won't say what you are, but suffice it to say that the letter 'p' and the word 'whipped' are prominent in the description," Frankie said. "Regardless, we'll take my car."

❦

FRANKIE PARKED about fifty feet from the corner of Second and Harrison Streets. He and Mrozinski slumped into the seats and pretended to be asleep, but all the while they kept their eyes open and scanned the area.

It was a clear sky and the moon was almost full, so visibility was decent despite the street lights being non-functional. The street traffic had been mostly local toughs—male teens—not the target Frankie was looking for.

About nine o'clock Mrozinski asked, "See anything, Donovan?"

Frankie turned slightly. "Yeah, I see three girls getting molested and two people getting mugged." He shook his head and sneered. "What the hell do you think? I'd say something if I saw it."

"All right, you dick. I was just asking. Don't get worked up."

They sat through the next few hours talking about the Eagles, Phillies, and Flyers, then Donovan changed the subject. "How long you been doing this, Mrozinski?"

"Too long. Around fifteen years. How about you?"

"About the same," Frankie said. "A hair longer, but only a hair. I'm thinking of giving it up when I hit twenty."

"You'd be young," Mrozinski said. "But it would make for a pretty nice retirement. Got plans?"

"I've got a girl, who may possibly become a wife. She wants me to retire. I got stabbed last year and almost died, so that is the impetus for her nagging."

Mrozinski laughed. "Shit, you're lucky. My wife nags me about retiring and I've never gotten a scratch. If I'd have been hurt, that would have sealed it."

Frankie laughed. "That may be it for me, too. I haven't been back yet. Still officially recovering. She hasn't asked me to stay home, but I wouldn't be surprised if she hasn't been thinking of it."

"What would you do for money? Retirement wouldn't be enough, would it?"

Frankie rolled the window down and lit a cigarette. "She's an M.E., so she makes plenty of money. That part isn't a concern."

"Shit, you've got it made. Maybe you should set up a PI practice," Mrozinski said. "We don't have any decent ones down here, and you know the area."

Frankie leaned his head back. "Maybe I should. Nicky and I could—"

"Whoa! I never mentioned Nicky. You go in with him and I may change my friendly attitude."

"You don't know him," Frankie said. "He's a good guy. I've known him all my life."

"Don't get me started on Nicky Fusco. Good guys don't do the kind of things I've heard he's done. I don't know what you see as the benefit of staying friends with him."

"Good guys don't sit idle while bad things happen to good people, either," Frankie said. "He helped Borelli when his kid was taken, and last year he dropped everything to come to New York and help me—without being asked. Now, he's risking it all again to help a girl he doesn't even know. You don't get much better than that in my book." Frankie flipped his cigarette butt out the window. "You asked about the benefit of being friends with someone like Nicky—the benefits are too numerous to mention."

Between 9:30 and 10:00, a few Puerto Rican girls strutted up the side-walk, but there was no trouble. Frankie watched until they went inside their house.

Frankie and Mrozinski waited around until past midnight. By then the traffic was thin; there were no girls to speak of unless they were with a man. And Frankie didn't see anybody attempting a grab with a guy present.

"We should call it a night," Mrozinski said. "I've got two more guys on stakeout tomorrow. Let's see what happens then."

THE NEXT NIGHT, Matuscek and Jones were parked about halfway up Harrison Street, between 6th and 7th. Several Puerto Rican girls walked the street that night, but they were in pairs, not the ideal choice for kidnapping. Around 9:45, a blue SUV turned onto Harrison and slowly made its way down the street. If Matuscek wasn't mistaken, Raff McDermott was driving.

"Don't look," Matuscek said. "It's him. We don't want him to make us."

"Got it," Jones said and slumped in the seat.

When McDermott passed, Matuscek got on the radio and called Attanasio, who was parked between 2nd and 3rd. "Coming your way in a blue SUV."

McDermott cruised by Attanasio at a decent speed. If anything, it was a little fast. Five minutes later, he was heading back down Harrison at maybe ten miles per hour.

He came to a crawl when he passed Attanasio's car, all the while staring inside. Then he hit the gas and took off. He'd made him.

"He made me," Attanasio said into the radio. "I don't know how, but he did."

Matuscek punched the steering wheel. "Fuck!" he said. "Mrozinski is gonna have our asses."

~

"How the fuck did he make you? How do you blow a simple stakeout?"

"I don't know," Jones said, "but he made us for sure. One minute he's cruising the street at ten miles per hour and the next minute, he's gone. No other explanation for it."

"Now, what the hell are we gonna do?" Mrozinski said. "It's not like we have a lot of leads."

A WELL-DESERVED SUB

I met Frankie at Casapulla's just before lunch. After two weeks away, this was going to taste good. Bugs had already gotten the subs and was sitting on the bench across the street. Alex was next to him.

"Bugs!" I said.

He stood to greet me, then we both sat and I unwrapped my sandwich.

"I'm glad you're back," Frankie said. "How was the Coast?"

"No different than it was before I went."

"That's not what the papers say," he said. "The papers mention a little trouble."

"I may have heard of a little trouble," I said, "but I don't want to talk about it."

"But the girls got home safe?" he asked.

"From what I heard, they did."

"Hey, Rat," Alex said.

Frankie slapped the back of his head. "That's Mr. Fusco to you," he said. "I told you that before."

"It's whatever he wants it to be," I said. "'Rat' is fine. I told him that back in Brooklyn. Of course some people were out of it back then."

Frankie looked at Alex then at me. "I can't say what I want to say right now, but I think you know what it is."

I laughed. "I think I do.," I said. "So what have you got?"

Alex got up. "I may only be young squirt, but I recognize my cue to leave," he said while standing. "See ya, Mr. Fusco."

"Hey, it's Rat to you. None of this Mr. Fusco shit."

Alex laughed and headed toward the car.

I looked at Bugs. "You keep that Mr. Fusco shit up and I'll have Rosa call you Mr. Donovan."

"Okay, truce," he said, and he proceeded to fill me in on his end of things.

"Campisi is out of the picture. I originally thought it was Paul or one of his brothers, but it's not. I think it's Raff; in fact, I'm pretty damn sure of it."

"Pretty damn sure of it? Or *damn* sure of it?"

"Goddamn sure of it," Frankie said. "We just don't have enough to convict."

"What do we need?" I asked.

"I don't know," Frankie said. "We thought we had him, but we blew a stakeout. He was trying to grab some girls on Harrison Street."

I stared at Bugs, shocked. "When?"

"Just the other night," he said.

"Son of a bitch," I said. "Maybe he didn't hear of what happened in California, or maybe he has another client."

Frankie took a bite of sub, chewed, then said, "However, if the girls were able to identify Raff as the guy who snatched them, it would help big time with a conviction."

"Would it guarantee it?" I asked.

"I don't know about *guarantee*, because the lawyers would no doubt claim emotional distress, the probability of error in witness identification, etc., but it *will* help."

"So, in other words, the girls will be put through more shit and still have no assurance it will do any good?"

Frankie looked down at the table. "I hate to say it, but yeah. That's basically it. I think it will work but that's only me. It's up to a jury and how good a lawyer McDermott can get."

"Have you got a picture?" I asked.

"On my phone," Frankie said. "It's good enough to use for a photo array."

"Text me a copy," I said. "I'll check with Allison and the others and let you know."

"Okay," Frankie said, and got up to leave.

"Bugs, hang on."

"What?"

"What's going on with Kate?"

"What do you mean?"

"I mean you did everything but throw yourself at Patti while you were here. I know you always liked her, or at least always lusted for her, but she's not your style, Bugs. Kate is."

"It's none of your business," he said.

"I think it is. I've known you longer than anyone except your mother and sisters, and I think I feel safe saying I care at least as much, so when I see my best friend throwing his life away, I'm gonna say something. Like it or not."

Frankie sat on the bench again. "Okay, maybe you're right. Maybe I was hoping for something to happen to…I don't know, maybe to mess things up."

"Looking for an excuse to get out of commitments?"

"Maybe."

"Bugs, I know you had a tough first marriage and that things weren't right, but marriages are not all that way. I think Kate is the right one. I think she's good for you."

Frankie shrugged. "Maybe so," he said. "I'll think about it."

"Promise? Promise me you'll be honest with yourself? I think if you look at when you're happy, you'll see it's when you're with Kate."

"I promise," he said. "You're probably right."

"I *know* I'm right. I just have to convince my stubborn Irish friend I am."

Frankie laughed. "Okay. I'll work on it."

I WENT to Melissa's house, the girl who was abducted from Baynard Boulevard, and knocked on the door.

"Mr. Dancer," she said, surprised. "I never expected to see you."

"And you shouldn't have, but I need you to look at some photos. We caught the people in California, but we haven't caught their partner here. Not yet. I've got some pictures of men who *might* be one of the. If you could take a look?"

I pulled out a sheet of pictures—nine of them, including three pics of the Campisis—and showed them to her. It didn't take her long to point to Raff.

"It's him. Oh my God, it's him. He's the one."

"Are you sure?" I asked.

"Positive," she said. "I've never been more positive of anything in my life. That's the son of a bitch who took me. No doubt."

"Okay, thanks," I said.

"One thing I never asked," Melissa said. "You never told us how you got involved."

I thought about what I should say, then opted for, "One of the girls' families hired someone in New Jersey who hired me. Let's leave it at that."

Melissa blushed. "Okay. Sorry. And thanks again," she said.

By the time I was ready to leave, I was convinced she had identified him, so I walked to the car to head out. I had parked several blocks away so she wouldn't see the car. When I got there, I started the engine and drove off. The next stop was Market Street.

I went to Shaniqua's house on Market and had the same results, with the exception she wanted Raff's address so she and her brothers could carry out execution—according to her. I naturally refused that, but reminded her that she had never seen or heard of me and then departed.

I was now convinced that McDermott was the guy, but I wanted to make one last stop—I wasn't going to all the girls' houses, but I did want to ask Allison.

Allison was even more adamant than Melissa had been. She showed no hesitation when I set the photos down. I asked if it could have been the Campisis by pointing to their pictures, but she said no, that it was definitely McDermott.

"Is that the son of a bitch who took my daughter?" Parker asked. "I'll kill that son of a bitch. Who is it? Where does he live?"

He went on and on, telling me the things he was going to do to McDermott. Finally, I felt it was unproductive to remain, so I gathered up the pictures and left.

At least one thing had been decided. I now knew beyond the shadow of a doubt that McDermott had done it. All that remained was the punishment.

WELCOME HOME, RAFF

*R*aff McDermott parked his car in the usual spot, locked the door, and walked up the narrow sidewalk to his house. He opened the screened door, twisted the handle on the hardwood door, then went inside.

"Patti?"

No one answered. He was alone. He went through the living room and dining room, into the kitchen, grabbed a beer from the fridge and walked upstairs to change clothes.

It wasn't until he pushed through the bedroom door that he felt the presence of someone being in the room with him. Nicky Fusco sat in a chair in the corner of the room.

"Hey, Raff. Welcome home."

"What the hell are you doing here?" Raff asked. "What are you doing in my bedroom?"

Nicky stood. "I'll bet those girls you took had more questions than that."

"Girls? What are you talking about?"

"No sense in lying, Raff. Bugs told me all about it. And I asked Allison who it was who took her. She didn't know your name, but when I described you, she remembered. So did the others. Every one of them picked you out of a photo array."

"I...I didn't—"

"Yes, you did," Nicky said. "No matter what it is you're about to say, I don't believe you. That is, unless you say that you're a scum-sucking prick who would do nasty things to little girls."

Raff stepped backward a few paces, toward the door. "Nicky, I..."

Nicky pulled out a gun. "Raff, don't make me hurt you. For Tommy's sake I don't want to hurt you. He would not have been proud, you know. He'd have been ashamed. Tommy was a good kid."

"Fuck Tommy. This ain't about him."

"You're right, Raff. It's not. But don't make things worse by talking bad about Tommy. It's bad enough I have to kill you; I don't want to have to hurt you."

"Kill me? What are you talking about? I didn't do anything."

"Raff, try to be a man at the end. It's going to be the last thing you do, so try to do it right."

"Nicky, please?"

I STOPPED FOR A SECOND. He almost had me thinking about how I didn't want to hurt anyone. Then I thought about the girls, and what I'd recently witnessed. I raised the gun and put a bullet in his left eye and then another in his right.

I stepped over the body, careful not to put my foot in the blood. There wasn't much left of Raff's head, unless you count the brain matter splattered on the walls and the door jamb.

I hated to do that to Raff. I remembered him as a kid when I used to hang out with his brother, Tommy.

Raff was always a pain in the ass, but in a good way. Now, this. It's a shame what happens to some people.

Almost done, I thought. *I'll be glad to go home.*

GET RID OF THE GUN

$\mathscr{I}$ walked out the front door slowly, as if nothing had happened. I went to the car, got in, and drove off. Now, I had to get rid of the gun. I never liked keeping guns after a job—too much chance of getting caught. When I was in New York, I used to bury them in the Pine Barrens in New Jersey, where even I couldn't find them again. I thought about where to ditch this one, then it hit me.

I drove to Alban Park, but then changed my mind, opting for Browntown instead.

Browntown was a poor, old Polish neighborhood, which had decayed into just a poor neighborhood with a mix of everybody, though it was still predominantly Polish. I should have no trouble finding a willing participant. I headed down Maryland Avenue and turned right at the old Johnny's Supermarket.

Johnny's supermarket

It brought back plenty of memories—carrying groceries to earn money, buying comic books, and stealing cigarettes. All the things that fun-loving little kids did.

It didn't take long to locate a kid that fit the bill. He was about twelve, had a grimy face, and wore a strap T-shirt—which we always called a Philly T— with a wool cap and a pair of beat-up jeans.

I pulled up to him and rolled down the window. "Hey, kid. You want to make a few bucks?" A lot of people wouldn't have trusted kids to do this kind of work, but I did. A kid would keep your secret longer than an adult."

You want to make a few bucks? That was the best opening line you could use in a neighborhood like this. Despite what his parents may have told him about talking to strangers, he came over without hesitation.

"What do ya want?" he asked. There was suspicion in his voice, but not much. He'd done this kind of thing before, and he was in a stance that told me he was ready to run, if need be. That was good. He was exactly the kind of kid I wanted.

I looked him in the eyes. "What I want, and what I need are different things," I said. "I want a few million dollars, but *I need* someone to get rid of this piece." I showed him the gun, lying on the seat next to me.

"I can do that," he said with no hesitation, as if he'd done it before, and more than once, "but it'll cost you twenty-five."

"What's your name?" I asked.

"Chucky Sniadowski."

I reached into my pocket and pulled out a hundred-dollar bill. "Do it right, kid, and there will be a Franklin in it for you."

His eyes went wide, and he grabbed for the gun and the bill, probably in case I changed my mind.

I yanked my hand back inside the car window. "But you gotta do it right," I said. "You can't just toss it in the swamps. You've got to smash it first, then bury it. And I mean bury it deep."

"You got it," the kid said. "I'll go home and put my hip-boots on, and wade out there where I can dig down deep. Hell, I'd bury five of them for that much money."

I handed him the gun and the bill. "Good. Don't forget what I said about smashing it. Put the gun on the railroad tracks first, let a train run over it, then bury it. That's what I want. And keep quiet about this, too."

He had a smile on his face like Christmas morning. "You can count on it," he said, and slowly walked away.

By the marsh

I liked what the kid said. It made me think of the Spencer Dancer identification, and what I had to do with it. Dancer had to die. I hated to get rid of a valuable identification, but this one had been used up. Too many people knew about it and too many bad things had been done in Dancer's name.

I had several good IDs. I had one in Philly and one in Baltimore. About once a month or more, I drove to each city, usually on business, and used the cards at places with no cameras so they wouldn't have pics of me. I usually checked the surrounding area too, to make sure there weren't cameras on the neighboring businesses, like ATMs or things like that. In addition, when I visited the cities, I shopped online at Amazon or B&N or other places and had whatever I bought shipped to P.O. boxes in each of the cities.

If the cards were ever checked, they would show activity in those cities, as if somebody who lived there used them. I also had an arrangement with one of Knuckle's cousins to pay a mortgage and electric bill in Philly. The guy paid me back, minus a hundred bucks. I was working on getting one in Baltimore, but it wasn't solid yet.

Doing it this way, I had an established credit history and a place to hide out if need be. It was a good system, and one I didn't want to mess up, so Dancer had to die—figuratively.

Long ago, I had figured the cops were never going to catch me with circumstantial evidence. They couldn't catch me using DNA in Brooklyn, and they were never going to get me on prints. And I got rid of my guns all the time. I also destroyed my used IDs, as I was doing with this one. These were the kind of things that got most people. People seemed to have a fondness for guns and IDs. I didn't. I liked them. But I liked freedom more.

And though it was becoming more difficult to do, I avoided public cameras at all costs, even when I wasn't doing something wrong.

What did that mean?

I didn't walk in front of ATMs or buildings where I knew they'd have surveillance, like banks or fancy hotels, and I kept my head tucked into my chest—while wearing sunglasses—at places like airports or train stations.

That way, they had no pattern for me and would have a damn tough time predicting what I might do. They were either going to catch me in the act or they weren't catching me, and there was no way they were catching me in the act of anything. Angela couldn't even catch me sneaking meatballs; she knew some were missing; she knew it was probably me, but she couldn't prove it.

We joked about it all the time, and she swore that someday she'd get me, but she won't.

I reached in my pocket and got the Dancer license and credit card, then pulled half a block down the street. "Kid, I hollered. I've got something else for you to do."

Browntown

He turned and came back and his eyes lit. "What?"

I handed him the cards. "I want you to get rid of these too, but it's got to be far away from where you bury the piece, maybe half a mile away. Do it right and there will be another twenty in it for you."

Chucky smiled. "Mister, I'll bury it two miles away for a twenty."

I handed him two twenties, and said, "I don't need two miles, but make it a mile and you've got a deal, though the same rules apply. Dig the hole deep, and bury it far from the shore."

"You got it, Mister. Don't worry about a thing. You've seen the last of these items. Hell, everyone has seen the last of them."

I smiled. That's what I was waiting for.

"By the way," I said, "if you're thinking you can sell that gun and make more from it, I'll hear about it."

"Don't worry," the kid said. "I ain't greedy. Leastwise not *dumb and greedy.*"

I laughed. "That's what I like to hear." I handed the kid another twenty and said, "Here's for being smart, Chucky." Then I pushed on the gas pedal and drove off, confident that the gun would never be found.

I thought about it after I left. I wasn't asking much. The Christina River and accompanying swamps were right behind Browntown, so it wasn't much of a jaunt. He'd have to cross a few train tracks, which actually made it perfect. He could lay the gun on the track, have a slow-moving freight run over it, then take it and bury it in the swamp. Then, even if it were discovered, it would be next to impossible to get a ballistics match.

I felt good about my chances now. No one had seen me enter Raff's house, and no one had seen me leave. Besides, even if somebody was peeking through the blinds, an eyewitness from that far away was worth next to nothing. Even a next door neighbor was questionable.

And if the kid did his job, there'd be no way to trace the gun, and no way in hell to connect it to me. No, this would go down as somebody having a beef with McDermott and finally settling the score.

Now, there was only one thing left.

A TALK WITH FATHER TOM

It didn't take long to get from Browntown to St. Elizabeth's, no more than five minutes. I parked by the school and walked across the street to the church, praying that Father Tom was holding confession. According to his schedule, he should be.

Inside the church, I dipped my fingers in the holy water, blessed myself, genuflected, and took a seat in a pew in the back row. I needed a minute to compose myself.

About ten minutes later, Father Tom made his entrance, meaning confession was about to begin. There was no one in line, so I walked up, and I pushed the red curtains aside and knelt. "Bless me Father for I have sinned. It has been three weeks since my last confession."

"What have you got to report, Niccolo?"

I always hated it when the priests did that, acknowledged that they knew who you were.

"I've done some bad things, Father."

"Sometimes good people do bad things."

"These are really bad things, Father. *Really bad.*"

"Everything is relative, my son. Sister Thomas told me of your dilemma. Perhaps she shouldn't have shared your problems, but she was worried. She cares about you."

"I hurt people, Father. And worse."

"Did they deserve it?"

"I think so."

"And are you sorry you committed violence?"

"Yes and no, Father. I didn't like committing the violence, but I did like dishing out the punishment. These people did nasty things."

"In the Bible, God punished people severely for wrongdoings. Some think it was too severe. Others think it was just. No matter what you think, though, you cannot take the law into your own hands."

"What would have happened to these girls if I hadn't? Which sin is worse?"

"That's what we have police for."

"But sometimes the police can't act fast enough or they're not able to do the right thing because of the law."

"We have to trust the system. We must have faith that God will do what's right."

"I know if God were here, He would have done what's right. And what's right would have been to set those girls free. But God wasn't here, so I helped him out."

I sat through a moment of silence, then Father Tom said, "Many people think God doesn't take an active role anymore, and maybe He doesn't, but maybe, just maybe, He does, but He doesn't do it Himself."

"Yes, Father."

"For your penance, say three Hail Marys and an Act of Contrition. May God go with you."

As I got up to leave, Father Tom said, "You're a good person, Niccolo. Always remember that."

I said my penance, then exited the church, feeling much better than when I went in. Father Tom had made me feel good about myself, and more importantly, about my actions. Now I just needed forgiveness from Angela.

I WALKED up to the house and climbed the steps, afraid to face the only people that mattered to me.

Rosa and Angela were waiting. Rosa ran to me and threw her arms around my shoulders.

"Dad!" she said. "I'm so glad you're home."

Angie smiled and moved toward me. "Oh God, baby. I'm so happy to have you home."

"I'm happy to be home," I said. "It's been a long time."

"It's all over the news, Dad. The girls are back home and safe. I can't believe you did this. What happened? Tell me about it."

"There's too much to tell," I said. "And I don't know if I want to tell it. It's not something I'm proud of."

Angela hugged me, then kissed me on the lips. "You *should* be proud. Those girls are home safe. Families are reunited. What more can you want?"

I squeezed her and pulled her close, then whispered, "I had to do things…things I didn't want to do."

"I know," Angela said. "I read about it in the Philadelphia paper."

My eyes went wide. "What paper? Let me see."

"There's no need," Angela said. "Just get ready for dinner."

"Give me the paper, please?"

Angela handed me the paper and sat on the sofa. I unfolded it to read.

"Page two," Angela said.

I turned to page two.

"Bloody Massacre in Los Angeles Suburb Unveils Hidden Pornographic Empire"

'At least ten people were slaughtered last week by unknown assailants. During the investigation—which is still continuing—it was revealed that Mezzanotte Productions, where all of the victims were employed, was a front for a child pornography operation that seems to have been operating worldwide.

'Police are still searching for clues to who the killers were, and why they did what they did, though initial speculation is that it may have something to do with a sex slave operation.

'...In a related story, seven girls, said to have been kidnapped from the streets in Wilmington, Delaware, have been returned safely to their homes after a three-week absence. No connection has been made of yet, but investigators believe it may have something to do with the pornographic operation at Mezzanotte Productions.

'Detective Ed Mrozinski, who was heading up the investigation into the missing girls was quoted as saying he had no idea how the girls were freed or how they showed up, he's just glad they did.'

I sat in my chair, sipping on a glass of wine Rosa had brought me. "And you didn't think I should see this? Doesn't this bother you?"

"I'd be lying if I said it didn't bother me, but having those girls missing would bother me more. Now I feel good that they're home."

Angela leaned over and kissed me. "I'm proud of you. And so is Rosa."

"Rosa?" I turned my head to look for her. "Does she know?"

"She figured it out," Angela said. "At first, she found it difficult to believe, but then Sister Thomas spoke with her. She made Rosa understand."

"Sister Thomas?" I said.

"She talked to Rosa for a long time. I think she made her understand."

I shook my head. "How could Sister Thomas make her understand? She'll never look at me the same way."

From the stairs, Rosa's voice came through loud. "She made me understand because she said she told you to go. She said sometimes God gets people on earth to do things for Him. I believed her. I saw what those people did to Allison. If anyone ever deserved to die, it was them."

Rose was holding on to the bannister as she spoke. "But you're right, I won't look at you the same way again. Now I'll be even prouder." Rosa walked over and hugged me. "I love you, Dad. You're the best."

I started to tear up. "Thanks, Rosa. I love you too."

Detective Ed Mrozinski sat at his desk, waiting for the onslaught of reporters. He'd known it was coming, but it didn't make the realization any more pleasant.

Channel Six was the first one to shove a mic into his face. "Detective

Mrozinski, what can you tell us about a man named Spencer Dancer? We've heard that name associated with the kidnapped girls. Also with the events in California."

Mrozinski frowned. "I never like reporters doing the investigative work because things always slip through the cracks. From what I've learned, this...Dancer...was someone in California who helped the girls escape. Who he is or was or what he did or does, I have no idea, and I don't expect to ever find out."

Mrozinski moved his head to the side, away from the mic. "Anything else?" he asked.

MURPHY

etective Pete Murphy stopped at the corner store to get milk and a couple of candy bars for his wife and kids before going home.

He cursed as he thought about the evening. He had promised the boys —aged six and eight now—that he'd play catch with them, but he was tired. Maybe they wouldn't mind waiting until tomorrow. All he wanted to do was stretch out and crack the top on a cold beer.

He went home, pulled the car into the garage, and went inside, plopping into the La-Z Boy—never a more appropriately named piece of furniture. Fifteen minutes later, a knock sounded on the front door.

"I'll get it," he yelled.

Pete opened the door to see Detective Frankie Donovan standing before him. "Donovan. What do you want?"

"Just a minute to chat, if you don't mind."

"Hell no. Come on in."

Frankie lowered his voice and whispered. "I think it would be better down the road, Pete. You have some explaining to do and a couple of Grants may fix it, if you get my drift."

Murphy appeared confused at first, but then said, "Of course. Hang on a minute." He tilted his head sideways a little, then hollered, "I'm going to get a drink with somebody from work, honey. Be back in a few."

As Frankie backed out of the driveway, Murphy said, "What's this all about, Donovan? You weren't very clear."

"You'll see in a minute," Frankie said. "Be patient."

Frankie drove for about three miles, then took a left on a small side road. Woods surrounded them.

"Where the hell are we going?" Murphy asked.

"To pay a visit to someone. Don't worry. We're almost there."

Frankie took a right, heading down a narrow dark road, then pulled alongside a car on the side. "Get out, Murphy. This is your stop."

Murphy looked at Frankie. "What are you talking about? I'm not getting out here."

Frankie pulled out his gun and forced Murphy out of the car. As he drove off, Murphy heard a voice. "I think you should thank the Lord you're still breathing." The voice came from behind Murphy, and to the right. He turned to see Nicky Fusco standing, a Derringer in his hand.

"Don't get any ideas, Murphy. I know this is a small caliber gun, but two bullets in the eye will hurt. So don't try anything."

Murphy nodded. "What do you want?"

"I want to know why a decent man like you would work with a scumbag like Raff and do such things to little girls?"

Nicky shook his head. "You've got kids, right? Two boys?"

"Don't even—"

"Shut-up," Nicky said. "I'd never hurt a kid. I'm just trying to imagine what went through your mind to make you help McDermott. You *had* to know what he was doing. If not at first, then later. You were part of the investigation."

"You've got to promise that you won't mess with my family," Murphy said.

"Did you make that promise to the family of the seven girls Raff took?" Nicky grabbed his collar and shook him. "Did you?"

"Look, what Raff did was wrong. Hell, it was disgusting, but he's family. He's my cousin, for Christ's sake." Murphy raised his hands and shrugged. "What am I supposed to do? I can't sit by and watch him go to prison. Maybe he'll get off and maybe he won't, but I'm through helping him."

"But you could sit by and watch the Campisis go to prison for something they *didn't* do?"

Murphy brushed his right hand in the air. "Screw them. They would have deserved whatever they got. It would have been justified punishment for all of the crimes they did and didn't get caught for."

Nicky smiled. "I'm glad you mentioned justified, Murphy. I'm a big proponent for *justified* punishment.

"I would tell you to ask Raff about that, but he's dead."

Murphy's eyes opened wide. "What? Dead? How? Why?"

Nicky smiled. "I think you know why. He did despicable things to innocent people. For that, he had to pay a price. I decided what that price would be."

"You can't. That's for the courts to decide. You can't just—"

"I did. I saw what he did to those girls. I watched Allison's father cry. I can still feel the pain they'll all feel for years. And for what? So Raff could have a few extra bucks?" Nicky spit on the ground to the side. "He should have found a better way to make money."

Nicky shrugged. "There are things in this world that are worth killing for, and things that are not. I've decided that innocent kids are worth killing for."

Murphy looked afraid, as if fear was infusing his body. "*You've* decided? *You* can't decide. There's a law against that."

"Funny that you mentioned that," Nicky said. "I often think of that law. What is it for? Who made it and why? Did you ever ponder that? And speaking of laws, isn't there one against kidnapping young women? I think there is, but McDermott broke the law, and you covered up for him, or tried to cover up."

Murphy shook his head, and looked at Nicky. "I'm going to raise my hands. Okay? Don't get excited."

"Go ahead," Nicky said.

Murphy reached into his shirt pocket and pulled a cigarette from the pack. He put the smoke in his mouth, lit it, then took a long drag. "Nicky, I didn't like what he did to those women. I don't agree with it, either. I've got kids of my own, so I understand."

"Do you?" Nicky asked. "If you really understood then you wouldn't have gone along. You wouldn't have tried covering up what McDermott did. You messed up, Murphy."

"What are you going to do?"

"Luckily for you, you didn't actually hurt anyone. If those young girls had suffered one more day, or if the Campisis had gone to prison, I'd think differently, but as it is, your failed attempt to cover up was just that—failed. So I'm not going to kill you."

Murphy relaxed, shoulders slumping. "Shit, thanks. I didn't mean anything, it's just…"

"You're not off the hook," Nicky said. "You're going to have to explain to Mrozinski what you did and why. He already knows anyway, but you're going to have to be a man and fess up to it."

"I'll tell him on Monday," Murphy said.

"You'll tell him tomorrow," Nicky said. "Go to his house if you have to. And don't think of backing out of this. If you do, I'll come to your house and drag you out in front of your wife and kids. And if you run, I'll find you."

"You got it," Murphy said. "I'll see Mrozinski first thing in the morning."

Nicky put his gun away. "Okay, we're done. But don't fail again, or you'll end up dead, like Raff." Nicky began to walk away, then he came back. "And don't tell Mrozinski about our little talk. Besides, it will go better for you if you fake remorse and say you confessed on your own."

AN ADMISSION OF GUILT

Frankie sat on the edge of the bed and wondered what to do. He knew how he felt—like a scum—and he knew what he *should* do, but that was different than what he *wanted* to do.

What he wanted to do was to call Kate, lie about what he'd done on his vacation, and tell her he'd be home tomorrow. He thought about the possible scenarios and opted for the truth—that's what Nicky would do. Besides, anything different would be a bad example for Alex.

He finally mustered up the courage and dialed her number. He needed to do it before Alex came into the room.

Kate answered quickly. "Well, about time I heard from the little village to the south."

"Hey," Frankie said. "What have you been up to?"

"Dead bodies. What else? The city is teeming with them."

"Anything interesting?" Frankie asked.

A long pause followed. "You tell me. You're the one who's been secretive. I've called four times with no call backs, unless you're going to tell me that my iPhone isn't recording missed calls properly."

Frankie laughed. "You know I wouldn't try that. I'm too good a detective for that kind of lie."

"And I'm too good of one to know things are all right down in Smallville. So tell me what's going on. *Something* is."

Frankie gathered all of his courage and said, "I *almost* cheated on you."

"Tell me something I don't know, Donovan. I could detect that by the way you talked—or should I say *didn't* talk—to me."

"You knew?"

"No. Let's say, I guessed. Anyway, the bigger questions are, if you did, why? And if you didn't, why not?"

"I *didn't* because I didn't like the way it made me feel when I thought about it. I realized I missed you…And I realized I want to marry you."

An extreme silent pause greeted Frankie. He kept quiet, not wanting to interrupt. Finally, Kate spoke. "What? Is that a proposal from Frankie Donovan? And if it really is, why?"

"It is. And I'm not taking it back. And it has no expiration date, so take your time. And the why is because I finally *recognized* my feelings. I truly love you."

"In that case, I don't need any time, Mr. Donovan. My answer is, 'yes.'"

"What? Are you shitting me?"

"No, and you better not be shitting *me*," Kate said.

"I only have two stipulations," Frankie said. "As far as best man goes, I want it to be Nicky."

"I figured as much," Kate said. "And I don't care if you choose the Son of Sam, or even Lou. You're on. But *my* only stipulation is my maid of honor won't be Sherri Miller; her ass is too nice."

Frankie laughed. "You'll disappoint Lou with that decision."

"Then Lou will have to be disappointed. Now, what is the second requirement?" Kate asked. "Or should I ask? If it involves threesomes of any sort, the answer is no."

"No. It's a simple one, I hope. I just want to make sure you're okay with Alex. I love—"

"Don't insult me. Of course I'm okay with Alex. I love him, too. Say no more."

"Then we're set," Frankie said. "All we need is a date."

"Men!"

"What?"

"A date, *and* a priest, and a hall, and flowers, and a maid of honor, and bridesmaids, and a hundred other things."

"You'll figure it out," Frankie said. "All I need is the date."

FRANKIE AND ALEX were packing when his mother called up the stairs.

"Frankie, someone's here to see you."

He wondered who it was, because if it was Nicky, she'd have just sent him up. "Sit tight, Ace. I won't be long," Frankie said.

He walked quickly down the stairs, and was shocked to see Patti McDermott standing in his living room.

"Patti, what are you doing here?"

"I came by to see if you wanted to go for a drink," she said.

Frankie looked at his wrist, where his watch used to be—before iPhones. "It's a little early for a drink, isn't it?"

Patti said, "Not for me, Frankie." Tears rolled down her cheek. "Raff's dead. Jesus Christ, Frankie. He's dead."

At first, Frankie didn't know what to do, then he grabbed her by the shoulders and pulled her to him. "It'll be okay, Patti. Don't worry."

Through heavy sobs, she said, "He's dead, Frankie. I'm losing all of my brothers. What am I going to do?" She pulled back from Frankie and said, "I need you, Frankie. I need someone to talk to."

Frankie looked her in the eye. "Patti, the sad part is that there was a time when that would have meant something, when it would have excited me, but not anymore. Now, all I can think about are the young girls you and Raff took advantage of, and for what—money?"

Patti's eyes opened wide, and she started to say something, but Frankie interrupted.

"Yes, I know all about it, Patti. I didn't kill Raff, but I wasn't far from pulling the trigger. Besides, as much as you used to mean to me, I realize now that I have the woman I love. She's waiting for me."

"When did this happen? From what I could tell, you didn't love her when you arrived. Or at least you didn't act like it."

Frankie sneered. "Go home, Patti. Go home and look at what you've done to yourself. Before you came here, I felt sorry for Raff; now, I think I feel sorrier for you. You still have to live with yourself."

"Screw you, Donovan," she said. "I can have a dozen men like you."

"Then you better go get them," Frankie said, "because you can't have me. There was a time when you would have just had to bat your eyelashes, or wiggle your pretty little ass, but not anymore."

Patti gestured with her middle finger, then stomped down the sidewalk.

Frankie went back upstairs to help Alex pack.

~

IT ONLY TOOK another fifteen minutes to gather the clothes they had brought, and unfortunately, there were no family presents for Alex to take home. It was just as well. Fake presents were just that—fake.

Angela had said to stop by before they left, so Frankie made a short detour to say goodbye. She and Rosa had made some food for them to take home, including a meatball sandwich for Alex, which meant more to him than anything. From the look in his eye, Frankie wouldn't bet on that sandwich lasting until they got to New Jersey.

Frankie gave Rosa a peck on the cheek, gave Angela a hug and a kiss, pinched Dante's cheeks, then grabbed Alex by the arm and got into the car. An hour later, he was in the middle of the Pine Barrens, in New Jersey.

After fifteen or twenty minutes of quiet, Frankie said, "There was a time when Patti…"

"Still a time for me," Alex said. "She was hot enough for me."

Frankie reached over and smacked the back of his head. "Watch your mouth! You can't talk like that."

"I just did. And don't tell me I can't talk like that. I'm at that age, and sure enough she's a 'looker' as you used to say. You and a bunch of dead people."

"She's also an ass," Frankie said.

"How come you didn't know that before? Why'd it take so long to figure out?"

Frankie thought for a moment, then said, "I don't know. It shouldn't have taken me so long."

"Some detective you are," Alex said, and laughed.

They drove another fifteen miles in silence, until Alex said, "You tellin' Kate?"

Frankie said, "Tellin' her what?"

"Tellin' her you almost tripped over your tongue—and God knows what else—sayin' hi to that girl."

Frankie laughed. "You're waaaaay too smart for your age, boy. You know that?"

"Blame yourself, old man. I learned it from you."

Frankie drove for about forty miles without saying a word. Finally, he broke the silence. "What do you want out of life, Alex? I realized that I never asked you that?"

Alex quit playing whatever game had his attention. He stared at Frankie, seemed to think for a moment, then said, "I want someone to call Mom. I think it should be Kate? But if it ain't Kate, it better be somebody good, because I'm not going with nobody like my old mom."

He set his phone on the seat next to him. "I'm not trying to be an ass, but you gotta ask yourself that same question, Dad. And yeah, I called you Dad because on this trip you showed me how dads are supposed to be, and Rat's family showed me how families are supposed to be. I'd sure like to be part of a family like that."

"Maybe you will," Frankie said.

"You know, F.D., people like Patti can only make you happy for a couple of minutes. Kate can make you laugh all night. I've seen it. I peek out my door when you guys watch movies together. You both laugh like crazy."

Frankie felt like crying. "When did you get so smart?"

Tears formed in Alex's eyes. "When I realized what I was missing. Now I want it all—a mom, a dad—the whole family deal."

Frankie drove for another couple of miles, then said, "Suppose I told you that you *could* have it all?"

"What do you mean?"

"I asked Kate to marry me. To be your mom."

A smile so wide it damn near cracked Alex's cheek appeared. "Holy shit! You're kiddin' me?"

"No. I'm not kiddin' you, and she said yes. And she even agreed to take you, though I don't know why."

"F.D., you just made me the happiest kid in the world. Now, I think I'm gonna eat this meatball sandwich—all by myself."

Frankie laughed. "Then let's go home and surprise Kate. We'll take her to dinner someplace nice."

"I know where I'd take her to dinner," Alex said. "I'd take her down to Rat's house. Damn, that food was good."

"Someday we'll go back, but in the meantime, we're going to have fun," Alex. Lots of fun."

MROZINSKI COMES TO DINNER

I was sitting in my favorite chair, studying a set of blueprints for a new apartment complex, when I heard a knock at the door.

I got out of the chair and answered the door. Detective Ed Mrozinski stood on the top step.

"Hey, Fusco," he said. "You got a minute?"

I invited him in and offered him a seat on the sofa. I sat in the chair opposite him. Angela brought two glasses of wine.

"What's up, Mrozinski? I heard you closed the kidnapping case."

He smiled, but it appeared to be only for show. "It was more than a kidnapping case. It was more like a pornography ring, but I'm guessing you knew that."

I leaned back in the chair. "I heard rumors to that effect."

"Rumors? That's all?"

"That's what I said. Now, what are the questions about?"

Mrozinski sat up and placed his wine glass on a coaster. "McDermott's dead, and Murphy turned himself in this morning. Seems like he was doing his best to cover for McDermott."

"Sounds complicated," I said.

"What it sounds like is—"

Angela walked in and started to sit. I looked at her and said, "We're busy talking, babe. Why don't you give us a minute?"

Her eyebrows bunched up, and she looked at Mrozinski, then me, but then she said, "No problem," and left the room.

Mrozinski watched her leave, made sure she was gone before he spoke. "What it looks like is someone is settling scores. First McDermott is killed, then Murphy turns himself in—or is forced to turn himself in. Did you have anything to do with this?"

I took a sip of wine, considered his statement, then said, "You give me too much credit. I'm just an estimator."

Mrozinski chuckled. "Yeah, and Don Corleone was just an olive-oil salesman."

"Wasn't he?" I asked.

Another chuckle, then, "Anyway, I'm not here to bust your chops. I know—or at least suspect—what you did for Borelli, and I have heard tales of what happened in this case from a few of the girls."

Mrozinski took several sips of wine before he continued. "I can't say I condone what you do, or have done, but when it's for a cause like this, I can't say it bothers me much. Murphy's going to find that out. If the system works, he'll go away for at least a few years."

Mrozinski stood, prompting me to stand as well. "As for me," he said, "I may not agree with what you do, hell, I may not even like you, but I'm proud to know you." He held out his hand. "Thanks," he said. "And a bigger thanks from all of the girls, Mr. Dancer."

I smiled as I shook his hand. "You want to stay for dinner?"

"Thanks anyway, but I've got work to do. Some maniac killed a bunch of people in California, and they think he may be here, in Wilmington."

"Imagine that," I said, then walked the detective to the door.

As he walked down the sidewalk, I called out to him from the doorway. "Hey, Mrozinski. Don't let anyone tell you that you're a stupid damn Polack."

He laughed and waved. "I won't. And thanks again."

ACKNOWLEDGMENTS

Many thanks to all of my loyal readers, my family, and especially to the beta readers who have worked so hard to make this a better book. You know who you are but I'll mention you anyway: Jeanne Haskin, Rose Hutchison, Missy, Cynthia, Monica, and Josh.

My eternal gratitude.

Images attribution:

(c) Can Stock Photo / demerzel21 Brooklyn Bridge

(c) Can Stock Photo / LianeM Tuscany Vineyard

ABOUT THE AUTHOR

Giacomo and Slick

Giacomo Giammatteo is the author of gritty crime dramas about murder, mystery, and family. He also writes non-fiction books including the No Mistakes Careers series.

When Giacomo isn't writing, he's helping his wife take care of the animals on their sanctuary. At last count they had 45 animals—11 dogs, a horse, 6 cats, and 26 pigs.

Oh, and one crazy—and very large—wild boar, who takes walks with Giacomo every day and happens to also be his best buddy.

giacomogiammatteo.com
gg@giacomog.com

Promises Kept, the Story of Number Two

Other Books Coming Soon

Fiction

A Promise of Vengeance (Fantasy)

My first fantasy, and the first book in a four-book series—the Rules of
Vengeance. (Three are already written and the fourth is being outlined.)

Murder Is Invisible ### (going through editing)

Frankie and Nicky are back.

Premeditated, Redemption IV

A Hard Life, the Story of Tip Denton

Non-Fiction

No Mistakes Grammar, Volume III, More Misused Words. (being proofread)

Whiskers and Bear—Volume I of the Life on the Farm Series (sent to editor)

No Mistakes Publishing, How to Self-Publish a Book

No Mistakes Writing, How to Write a Bestseller

Children's Books

No Mistakes Grammar for Kids, Volume I—Much and Many (Sent to editor)

No Mistakes Grammar for Kids, Volume II—Lie and Lay (Sent to editor)

No Mistakes Grammar for Kids, Volume III—Then and Than (Sent to editor)

Shinobi Goes to School—Life on the Farm for kids. (working on illustrations)

Get on the mailing list and you'll be sure to be notified of release dates and sales.

<u>Mailing list</u>

And don't forget to leave a review!